I0554556

GALAXY'S EDGE

CREATED BY MIKE RESNICK

ISSUE 51: July 2021

CONTENTS

Lezli Robyn, Editor
Martin L. Shoemaker, Assistant Editor
Taylor Morris, Copyeditor
Shahid Mahmud, Publisher

Published by Arc Manor/Phoenix Pick
P.O. Box 10339
Rockville, MD 20849-0339

Galaxy's Edge is published in January, March, May, July, September, and November.

Please check our website for submission guidelines.

ISBN: 978-1-64973-089-3

SUBSCRIPTION INFORMATION:
Paper and digital subscriptions are available (including via Amazon.com) . Please visit our home page: www.GalaxysEdge.com

ADVERTISING:
Advertising is available in all editions of the magazine. Please contact advert@GalaxysEdge.com.

FOREIGN LANGUAGE RIGHTS:
Please refer all inquiries pertaining to foreign language rights to Shahid Mahmud, Arc Manor, P.O. Box 10339, Rockville, MD 20849-0339. Tel: 1-240-645-2214. Fax 1-310-388-8440. Email admin@ArcManor.com.

DÉJÀ DOOMED

EDWARD M. LERNER

On the Moon's far side, shielded from Earth's radio cacophony, Americans are building a radio-astronomy observatory. Russians sift the dust of a lunar "sea" for helium-3 to run future fusion reactors. Commercial robots, remotely operated from Earth, roam the Moon's near side in a hunt for mineral wealth. Why chase distant asteroids for precious metals? Onetime asteroids must lie close beneath the much-bombarded lunar surface.

Then a prospecting robot encounters a desiccated, spacesuited figure. An alien figure ….

Americans from the lunar observatory investigate. Near the original find, underground, they discover an alien installation. Lunar Russians, realizing that the Americans are up to something clandestine, send their own small team. Each group distrusts the other … even before the fatal "accidents" begin. By the time anyone suspects what ancient evil they have awakened, it may be too late—

For everyone on Earth, too.

ON SALE NOW

EDITOR'S NOTE

by Lezli Robyn

This issue of the magazine greets the world with a lot more hope than the previous one. With more Americans becoming vaccinated against Covid-19, we enter summer with science fiction conventions returning to "in person" venues, rather than just being the virtual events we have gotten used to over the past sixteen months. *Galaxy's Edge* magazine's publisher, Shahid Mahmud, and I will be attending Dragon Con in Atlanta, marking our first physical presence at a convention in over a year. And we are doing it for a purpose very close to our hearts.

We'll be presenting the inaugural Mike Resnick Memorial Award for Short Fiction to the winner, for the best unpublished science fiction story by a new author. As I type this, the shortlisted entries are currently being assessed by our esteemed judges, Lois McMaster Bujold, Nancy Kress, Sheree Renée Thomas, Jody Lyn Nye and Bill Fawcett. While a majority of the submissions were from English-speaking populations, entries were received from nineteen different countries around the world, from nations as diverse as Lebanon, Japan, Slovenia and Brazil.

The finalists are being evaluated on a blind basis. This means the judges do not see the authors' names or location details. We cannot wait to announce the top five entrants on July 15th. You can find out who they are on that date by going to the award website, www.resnickaward.com.

This issue we have some great stories from some authors new to the pages of our magazine. David Cleden's story, "How does my Garden Grow?", is a gripping tale about Elke's fight to keep his garden alive within a community of five hundred humans who have to retain strict control over their resources in order to sustain centuries of flight within a closed spaceship. And Julie Frost's piece, "Not All Treasure," tells the tale of Ambrose and Deena's trip to steal wealth from dragons to repay a debt. It doesn't go according to plan (whenever does it?), but the unexpected ending will satisfy many a reader.

We also have the pleasure of publishing Carolyn Ives Gilman's new historical fantasy piece, "Nanabojou and the Wise Men," which shows us the impact of a God's meddling on humanity. One of my favorite books is written by Carolyn, *Halfway Human*, so I am overjoyed to be featuring a new story of hers in our magazine.

Regular contributors, Tina Gower and Brian Trent also have new fiction in this issue. Tina's "The Last Dentist" raises the question of how you get dental work after the apocalypse has decimated the world, and Brian Trent's haunting and emotive "Shadow Walk in Obsidian" explores how far you would go to cheat death. Not for yourself, but for the one you love.

A frequent contributor to the pages of *Galaxy's Edge*, Robert Silverberg appears in this issue with his story, "The Far Side of the Bell-Shaped Curve," and we welcome Kristine Kathryn Rusch back to the magazine with her novelette, "Destiny," a prequel to her popular Fey fantasy series which follows the Shapeshifter Solanda on Nye. The Black King wants her to use her special abilities on a job that will change the Fey forever, but Solanda wants to change the life of one child. Can she do both? Or should she do nothing at all?

Mike Resnick's inclusion is the thought-provoking "Articles of Faith" about the robot who discovers an interest in religion, and our translated story from our sister magazine in China, "Hyperspace Partner," is written by Bao Shu and translated by S. Qiouyi Lu, closing out our short fiction content for this issue. Bao's fiction is best introduced by the editor of our Chinese counterpart, Yang Feng, at the start of their story, and it is a wonderful read.

Our serialization is a continuation of Harry Turtledove's novel, *Over the Wine-Dark Sea*, and Jean Marie Ward joins our team as our new interviewer for the magazine. This issue she has a captivating conversation with the ever-popular Seanan McGuire, and I find it endlessly fascinating to discover what motivates or inspires our favorite authors to write the fiction we love so much.

Rounding out this issue are our regular columns by L. Penelope and Gregory Benford, with the former discussing the delicate and sensitive nature of creating or describing different cultures in fiction, and the later discussing the science behind twins versus cloning (something close to my heart as an identical twin myself). Richard Chwedyk also provides extra reading suggestions with his Recommended Books column,

As I finalize this editorial, a tropical storm is rumbling through the island, affecting cell service across the state. What a perfect excuse to unplug, and read even more wonderful submissions, destined to appear in future pages of *Galaxy's Edge*.

Carolyn Ives Gilman is an American historian and author of science fiction and fantasy. She has been nominated for the Nebula Award three times, and the Hugo Award twice. Her short fiction has been published in a number of magazines and publications, including Tor.com, Clarkesworld, Lightspeed, *and* Fantasy and Science Fiction, *along with a number of "year's best" anthologies. She is also the author of science fiction novels such as* Halfway Human, *which is noted for its "groundbreaking" exploration of gender.*

NANABOJOU AND THE WISE MEN

by Carolyn Ives Gilman

Deep in the humid, tangled forest of central Ohio there glowed an island of brightness. On that one night in the mid-1820s, bonfires blazed; candles and torches affixed to the trees lit the crowded wooden benches and the tabernacle, which resembled a covered stage raised on pilings so everyone could see it. Tents were pitched amid the trees surrounding the congregation, with wagons and carts parked beyond them. Outside the clearing, for miles upon miles, lay only the night-bound forest—silence, except for the mosquitoes, and impenetrable dark, except for the fireflies. The leaves hung limp in the still heat.

But the meeting blazed with energy. It was the third night of nonstop preaching, and the crowd was at a high pitch of enthusiasm when the famous Reverend Stone took the pulpit. Many of them had come to hear him, for they had heard his message that the restoration of primitive Christianity then taking place in the Ohio Valley was a golden age of belief heralding the Second Coming. The Harmonists had arrived from the west, the Disciples of Christ from the north, the Separatists of Zoar from the east, a few Shakers from the south, and Baptists and Methodists—black and white, male and female, rich and poor, believers and nonbelievers—from every farm and hamlet thereabout. If Christ were to return tonight, it was to Ohio he would come.

As Reverend Stone's voice swelled, there spread over the crowd a feeling of deep conviction, of the immanence of miracle. Some fell to their knees to pray, others stood to testify. A supernatural force was present in the clearing; they were sure of it.

They were absolutely right. It just wasn't the supernatural force they had in mind.

As Reverend Stone reached the climax of his exhortations, an otherworldly glow surrounded the tabernacle. Then, a figure rose into the air above the pulpit and hovered, haloed and many-winged.

If there had been any nonbelievers present by then, they might have seen how outlandish the supernatural visitor was—antlers of a deer, a face painted half red and half black, tattooed all over in geometric designs. But no one saw any of this. They saw a savior. All through the crowd people collapsed to the ground and were instantly surrounded by circles of friends, praying and raising up their hands in ecstasy, crying halleluiahs, their sweaty faces turned to the night sky to welcome the Holy Spirit.

The vision lasted only seconds; then the darkness returned.

Back in the nearby forest that had been his home since time immemorial, Nanabojou returned his antlers to the deer, his glow to the fireflies, and his wings to the mayflies, thanking his animal helpers graciously. Then he set out through the forest to resume the errand he had been on when the camp meeting had distracted him. The trick he had played on the Christians had been too easy. Entertaining, but not one of his masterpieces. A truly great trick could not be played on people so willing to be fooled.

But the fraud he had been setting up for weeks, now—that one would be worthy of his art. He would be deceiving those who ought to know better.

✿

The next day, the camp meeting had disbanded and wagonloads of exhausted Christians were making their ways back home when a traveler named Henry Schoolcraft shared the road with them. He was a slightly pudgy man in his mid-thirties, with wire-rim glasses and unkempt brown hair, both of which he thought made him look intellectual—for it was his goal in life to be accepted among the highest ranks of the American intelligentsia. He had already made a good deal of progress in that respect, having published three books about his travels in the west. He was by training a geologist, by employment a government agent to the Indians, and by inclination a literary man.

He came into the nascent town of Circleville, Ohio, at sunset, and proceeded past the outlying blacksmith shop, stables, and lumberyard to the center of town, where a county courthouse was under construction. Facing it across a square was Schoolcraft's destination: a brand-new, clapboard-sided hotel. Leaving his horse tethered outside, he entered a lobby that showed pretensions of respectability, for it had a fine Turkish carpet in the lobby, glass doorknobs, and an oil painting of Moses leading the Israelites hanging behind the polished walnut counter. The rooms were shared by four or five guests at a time, as was common; since Schoolcraft was alone, the clerk said, "I will put you with the other scientific gentleman." This piqued Schoolcraft's curiosity and led him to thoughts of spending the evening in pleasantly intelligent conversation.

When he came down to dinner, he scanned the room and quickly spotted the most interesting guests there. The scientific gentleman surely had to be that dark-haired man in the worn-out boots, wearing a magnifying glass on a ribbon around his neck. He sat with two improbable characters. One was a blondish, bony young man barely out of his teens, dressed in darned homespun, with deep-set, intense eyes; the other was a wiry, weather-beaten Native man wearing a calico shirt and a brocade vest, smoking a pipe with a carved stone bowl of great antiquity.

Schoolcraft went over and introduced himself, whereupon the gentleman leaped to his feet in great excitement, shaking Schoolcraft's hand vigorously with both of his, and saying in accented English, "Mr. Schoolcraft the geographer and geologist! I am honored to make your acquaintance. Allow me to introduce myself: Professor Constantine Rafinesque, of Transylvania University."

"Transylvania! You mean…"

"The one in Kentucky. I believe we have acquaintances in common. Dr. Mitchill has spoken of you."

Gratified by this reception, Schoolcraft asked if he could join them, and soon he and the Frenchmen (as he assumed Rafinesque was, from the name) fell into a lively conversation about common friends. The other two men looked on silently until Schoolcraft glanced at them and Rafinesque exclaimed, "Pardon me, I should introduce my companions. This is Mr. Megwitch." The Indian inclined his head in a slow nod. "And Mr. Smith."

The young workman rose and bowed awkwardly, as if he had seen others do it but had not had much practice himself. "Joseph Smith," he said, as if that clarified things.

"Megwitch," Schoolcraft said. "That's an Ojibway name, isn't it?"

The Indian raised an expressive eyebrow. "You speak the true language?" he said.

"Actually, yes, a little. My wife is teaching me. She grew up speaking it; her mother knows no other tongue. Or rather, the old lady knows both French and English, but won't deign to utter them. It's a damnably difficult language, Ojibway—all verbs. Nothing ever just *is*—it has to be *doing* something. A rose can't just be red, it has to be acting redly."

"That's roses for you," Megwitch said. "Always performing."

This was evidently an example of Indian humor, though the man showed no trace of a smile.

In the slightly awkward silence, Rafinesque said, "What brings you here? If you don't mind my asking."

"Not at all," Schoolcraft said. "I am on my way from my home at Sault Ste. Marie to visit my publisher in Philadelphia. Normally I would have gone by boat via the Erie Canal, but I decided to come overland because I was curious to see the ancient monuments that lie hereabouts. I have heard wild tales of mysterious pyramids and geometric earthworks hidden in the woods. I was told that Mr. Atwater of Circleville was the one to consult."

This set off an explosion from the volatile professor. "Atwater, pish! The man is nothing but an amateur, an antiquarian. You are lucky you fell in with me first, sir. I have made a particular study of the ancient remains—a *scientific* study. I measure, I map, I document them. No man knows them better than I."

A bit startled by his vehemence, Schoolcraft said, "Then perhaps you wouldn't mind showing me. I have heard there is a monument in Circleville that gave the place its name."

"Why, you have already seen it," Rafinesque said. "You passed through it when you came into the town."

Schoolcraft had seen no such thing. Puzzled, he said, "I came in through a gap in some sort of levee or embankment…"

"Yes, that was it."

"But it was taller than I am! And not a circle."

"You cannot see the whole circle from one spot. It is too big. The whole town is built inside it."

Schoolcraft had been picturing something that could be grasped in one glance—something on the scale of Stonehenge, perhaps. Not a towering construction larger than any athletic field or cathedral square. The scale of it was baffling.

"But that raises a number of questions," he objected.

"Indeed it does."

"First of all, how was it laid out? At such a scale, it would be difficult to use the usual method of measuring with a string from the center. Assuming it actually is a circle."

"It is," Rafinesque said. "Mathematically precise. I have surveyed it myself, using the most modern equipment. The ovals, the squares, the octagons, the cones, and the pyramids found in other parts of this region are also quite perfectly formed. Moreover, the dimensions are often identical, even in designs found a hundred miles apart; they were clearly built to a common unit of measurement. When a circle and square appear close together, as they often do, the proportions bear a geometrical relationship to one another. If they were superimposed, the squares would fit perfectly into the circles. It makes me wonder whether the designs have something to do with the ancient problem of squaring the circle."

Skeptical, Schoolcraft exclaimed, "But that would require us to believe that the builders of these monuments had a knowledge of mathematics as well as civil engineering."

Rafinesque just nodded at this preposterous suggestion. "I find that many of your countrymen, faced with such an enigma, will deny the evidence, or set about diligently destroying it. They seem capable of believing it in other parts of the world, but not in their own. But you can see it with your own eyes, if you will let me show you."

"I welcome the opportunity," Schoolcraft said. His mind was still crowded with jostling objections. "Do you have any theories about the identity of the builders?" he asked.

Rafinesque gave an enigmatic smile. "I think they were very ancient," he said. "The simplest explanation is that they were the ancestors of the natives of this land."

"What do you say to that, Megwitch?" Schoolcraft asked. "Are there legends of a race of geometers and builders?"

Megwitch shrugged. "Before my time," he said.

Schoolcraft had a suspicion that both Megwitch and Rafinesque knew more than they were saying. "There have been innumerable theories about the origins of the indigenes of this land," he observed. "It might be instructive to compare the American monuments with those of Europe or the ancient world—Sumeria, perhaps, or Babylon, or Egypt."

"That would be quite wrong," Rafinesque said.

"Oh? Why so?"

"We should be looking the other direction. The natives arrived on this continent from Asia, across what is now the Bering Strait."

"There is no scientific consensus about that."

It was obvious Rafinesque wanted to say more, and was struggling not to. At last he leaned forward, lowering his voice. "If I tell you, I must bind you to the strictest secrecy. Some evidence has recently come into my hands that I have not yet had an opportunity to publish."

"I would never steal another man's research," Schoolcraft said in the tone of a minister denying a cardinal sin—although, in truth, it would depend on the quality of the evidence.

Rafinesque glanced around to make sure no one could overhear them. Then, in a low voice, he began to tell his story.

"Several years ago, after one of my lectures in Lexington, there came up to me a gentleman, a medical man named Dr. Ward, who lived near the Harmonist colony on the Wabash River. His patients came to him from all around that country. He told me that one night, a group of Delaware Indians stopped on the river shore and requested his aid. They had come down the White River from the Delaware settlements deep in the woods. One of their party, an exceedingly ancient man, was on the verge of death. The good doctor treated him, and in three days' time the old man had recovered. His family was overjoyed, but they had no means to pay. All they could offer the doctor was the old man's most prized possession: a set of wooden tablets on which were inscribed some curious symbols, smoothed and reddened from the ochre that had been rubbed on them in reverence over the course of many generations.

"The doctor was intrigued and accepted the tablets in payment. The ideographs seemed to have meaning, but he was unable to decipher it. Two years later, some business took him up the White River, and he decided to visit the Delaware settlements and seek some explanation.

"Now, you will recall that the Delaware take their name from the river in Pennsylvania where settlers from Europe first encountered them. It's not *their* name, of course; they call themselves Unami, or Munsee, or Lenape, or Wabenaki—people of the dawn."

"They are regarded with great reverence by the western tribes," Schoolcraft interrupted. "They are seen as prophets and progenitors—'grandfathers,' the other nations say."

"Yes, that fits. But the white man drove them west—first to the Susquehanna River, then to the Muskingum, and finally to the White. There, they hung on in isolated pockets, hewing to their own religion and language. Dr. Ward was able to locate an ancient wise man—I never learned if it was the same man or another—and receive an exegesis of the tablets. It was, however, entirely in the Lenape language, transcribed phonetically by a literate Delaware who accompanied the doctor.

"That was where matters stood when I met Dr. Ward. When he showed me the material, I was seized with an intuition of its significance, so I borrowed it and copied down both the symbols and the Lenape manuscript in hopes of some day deciphering their meaning.

"This year, I decided to pursue the question. I traveled back to the Wabash River—but oh, how changed it all was! The Harmonists had gone back to Pennsylvania and sold their settlement to the Owenite socialists. Dr. Ward was nowhere to be found. Moreover, the Delaware were being deported by the government to some place in Missouri. I watched some of them go by on flatboats, passing beyond my reach. All I had was my copy of the glyphs and the narrative, and I despaired of ever learning more about them.

"That was when I met Mr. Megwitch. He assured me that all was not lost, that there were still a few

souls who could illuminate the meaning of the tablets. We traveled together up the White River, into the remotest forest, and he led me to an isolated cabin where there lived a wrinkled, bent old man who could have been a hundred or a thousand years old, so decrepit did he look. He spoke not a word of English, but Megwitch translated for me."

"You speak Lenape, do you?" Schoolcraft looked sharply at Megwitch. The man inclined his head in a slow nod.

"I wish I could paint for you the strangeness of the scene," the professor went on. "The cabin was lit only by firelight, casting flickering shadows on his face as he scrutinized my paper copy of the symbols. As if he had passed into a trance, he began to recite the words of a kind of poem or chant. The language was beautiful and rhythmic, even though I understood not a word. As Megwitch translated for me, I realized that the tale was a history of the Lenape people back to the most ancient times. It was a migration story that started in a land of bounty. But evil times forced them to cross a frozen sea to reach this country. When they arrived, they met here a race of giants called the Tallegewi, and went to war with them, driving them out. Journeying ever eastward, the Lenape came to the shores where William Penn found them in 1682. Each generation of chiefs was listed, in the manner of the Book of Chronicles, one chief succeeding the next.

"It was after midnight when he finished his recitation, and I roused as from a dream. He told me the tale was called the Walam Olum in the Lenape language, the Red Score. It may be justly compared to the Icelandic sagas, or the Homeric poems, or even the Old Testament itself."

He tapped the table with his index finger in emphasis. "But here is the most significant part: the epic is a historic record, in their own words, of the crossing from Asia into this land, preserved through all the generations since. It identifies the builders of the mounds, the Tallegewi, and explains their extinction. It is proof positive of an Asian origin for the indigenes."

There was a silence after he finished speaking, and Schoolcraft took it all in. At last he said, "There are parts of your story that strike a bell with me. They were wooden tablets, you say?"

"Yes. At least, so Dr. Ward told me. I was never able to examine them personally."

"There are similar migration stories among my wife's people, the Ojibway," Schoolcraft said, "but they are kept on birchbark scrolls inscribed with mnemonic devices. I have it on good authority that on an island in Lake Superior the elders possess copper tablets of great antiquity, engraved with symbols telling the history of how they came from the Atlantic shores."

"Copper, you say?" Mr. Smith spoke up. He had been listening silently, but with great attention.

"Yes. Copper occurs naturally on Lake Superior in nuggets so pure they can be cold-hammered into sheets. The Ojibway keep their tablets buried to protect them from the greed of white men. I have never seen them myself, but I know the migration story they tell has the Indians coming from the Atlantic—which implies a European origin."

"I should be interested to see a copy," Rafinesque said a little stiffly—to emphasize that he had evidence, whereas Schoolcraft had only hearsay.

"I should be interested to see yours, as well. I wonder if the Delaware symbols resemble anything—for example, the inscriptions on the Dighton Rock in Massachusetts, or the orthographic system invented by a Cherokee named George Guess."

Schoolcraft was just showing off by now, burying his opponent in erudition. Rafinesque was looking a little offended, so he said, "But your discovery is quite intriguing. Would you be willing to show me the symbols? I may be able to tell you whether they resemble anything among the Ojibway."

"Certainly. The papers are in my trunk upstairs. If you would care to join me…"

✿

The two learned men departed together. Since Megwitch and Smith had pointedly not been invited, they remained sitting at the table, silent.

Nanabojou (for the discerning reader will have realized that that was Mr. Megwitch's true identity) could not have asked the evening to go any better. At first, the unexpected arrival of another scholar had alarmed him; but in the end the two had started constructing a collaborative labyrinth of falsehoods that only a scientist could believe.

The Native people had not come from Europe or Asia. Nanabojou had created them himself, right here in this land, shortly after riding out the great flood in a canoe. He remembered it all quite clearly. Whitemen, now—someone else was responsible for creating them.

He stole a glance at his silent companion. Of all of them, Joseph Smith intrigued him most. He had no idea where Rafinesque had acquired the fellow; Smith had simply been there, acting as the professor's surveying assistant, when Nanabojou had returned after a short absence. The young man had the strong whiff of someone running away, quite possibly from the law. Nevertheless, he had proved his value as they had toured the Scioto River Valley. He was a perfect genius at spotting buried things; he had been able to say with certainty which mounds would repay excavation and which would not. He had the power to see under surfaces, but it was not derived from any source Nanabojou was familiar with. Perhaps it was the Jehovah that Smith believed in, finally taking an interest after being such a remote and absentee god for so long.

After a long silence, Nanabojou reached out to tap the ashes of his pipe onto a saucer. "Professor Rafinesque is quite wrong, you know," he said.

Smith turned those strange, intense eyes on him. Eyes that saw under surfaces. Nanabojou was fairly certain Smith had spotted his masquerade.

"About the Walam Olum, I mean," Nanabojou went on. "The tablets are real enough, and so is the tale they tell. But it has nothing to do with a migration from Asia."

"I thought not," Smith said. "These men esteem themselves wise, but they will find their error."

In fact, the frozen sea the Lenape had crossed was Lake Huron, and the mysterious Tallegewi were the Cherokee—as any cursory investigation of the name they gave themselves would have revealed. When the Lenape arrived, the Cherokee had been living in the mountains still named for them, the Alleghenies. It wasn't even a riddle.

Smith was watching him intently, as if wanting to ask something. Nanabojou looked up and met his eyes, then slowly winked. "My name isn't really Megwitch, either," he said.

Smith's eyebrow went up, and he let out a breath as if he had been holding it. "I had guessed that," he said.

Nanabojou put his finger on his lips to enjoin silence. Smith nodded.

Then Nanabojou rose to leave. He had accomplished enough for one night.

The next morning, they all stood viewing the Circleville circle from the top of the massive embankment. By morning light, Schoolcraft could see the curve of it, though the buildings of the town hid the other side. The wood and brick structures looked makeshift and trashy beside the grandeur of the ancient monument. To his left Schoolcraft could see some men industriously digging away at the earthwork, loading the fill into a wagon.

"Fools," Smith muttered. "They won't find any treasure there."

The night before, Schoolcraft had wondered how the circle had been built; now, the thing that puzzled him most was *why*. He expressed his perplexity to Rafinesque.

"Indeed," said the professor. "The amount of labor they devoted to laying it out, hauling the dirt, and constructing it suggests some compelling reason. The resemblance to a defensive fortification suggests a use in warfare. But the size would make it difficult to defend; besides, no one has ever found evidence of habitation inside the enclosures. If they were defending something, it was not a town."

"Could it have been an athletic field?" Schoolcraft suggested. "De Soto speaks of ball games played in courts."

"If so, it cannot have been very entertaining for the audience. If the game play shifted to the other side, it would have been invisible to half the witnesses. And some of the enclosures have pyramids or barrows obstructing the view."

It made Schoolcraft uncomfortable to be faced with something so impervious to explanation. He could *always* explain things. That was the whole purpose of science. "Well," he said, "it must have been some sort of religious site." When people do inexplicable things, that was always the safest fallback position. It required no evidence to prove, and therefore could not be refuted.

They began to stroll along the top of the circle, rounding it. "It must have taken a vast number of people to construct this," Schoolcraft mused.

"Truly, a great population must have inhabited this region once," Rafinesque said. "And yet, where are their cities? We have found no ruins, no dwellings, no palaces or cathedrals. The builders are ghosts. They came here, measured out geometry on the land, and vanished."

"We simply haven't found their cities yet," Schoolcraft said with resolution.

When at length they came around to the spot where they had begun, Rafinesque said, "We are bound north today in search of a site reputed to be even more marvelous than this one, which the settlers call the Observatory. You are welcome to come with us. I should be glad of the conversation."

A detour would delay him on the route to Philadelphia, but Schoolcraft felt that he would rarely have another chance to explore such an enigma in the company of a knowledgeable, albeit slightly irritating, guide. "I will travel with you gladly," he said.

It would have been only a day's trip, but Rafinesque was traveling on foot, with only a small cart drawn by a swaybacked horse to carry his luggage and surveying equipment. "I am a botanist by nature," he explained. "One cannot see plants from horseback." So in the end, the journey took two days separated by a night spent in an execrable little inn infested with fleas. As they traveled north, the road dwindled into a rutted track with grass growing down the middle, and the forest closed in around them, ever more dense as the farms and towns grew farther apart.

It was late afternoon on the second day when they stopped at a farmhouse to ask directions from a laconic settler and his inquisitive wife. Learning that their destination was close, they arranged for lodging, left their horse and cart, and proceeded on foot to take a look before night fell.

It was that time of day when the sunlight grows level and the forest falls still, as if anticipating something. The melancholy song of a distant thrush only seemed to intensify the silence as it echoed through the woodland. Here, away from the road, the forest opened up, the undergrowth kept down by the shade from the dense canopy far above them. On either side of the path, gigantic chestnuts towered, their trunks rising forty feet before branching, motionless presences more ancient than European settlement on the continent. Schoolcraft could almost imagine the ghosts of the panthers that would have roamed these woods forty years ago. Even Rafinesque, who had kept up a near-constant monologue for two days, seemed to have caught a feeling of awe, and fallen still.

Schoolcraft became aware that the path they were on had become a raised causeway, and on either side of them ran a ditch and linear earthen walls. Once again, he had almost missed it because the dimensions were so astonishing: fifty people could have walked abreast down the level roadway between the bordering berms. He realized that the surrounding forest was crowded with mounds he had not noticed up to now. They were everywhere. It was like a buried city.

Ahead, a towering earthen barrier rose from the forest floor, curving off to right and left as far as he could make out. It was at least three times the height of a man, and covered with old-growth trees. The causeway they were following led straight up to a gap in the wall. As he approached it, Schoolcraft felt a chill, as if a cold wind were blowing from the other side. The monumental gateway was like a portal into some sacred precinct. The causeway passed through it and crossed a ditch at least fifteen feet deep. Directly ahead, on a perfectly level floor, lay a round-topped mound—or rather, four mounds joined together in the shape of an arrow pointing northeast, through the gate and down the causeway.

If Schoolcraft had been puzzled before, he was dumbstruck now. What kind of gods had they worshipped to inspire such a forest cathedral? What celebrants could have gathered here? What was the meaning of that mysterious arrow, and what did it point to?

They spent some time exploring the inside of the circle, speaking to one another in hushed voices. Rafinesque paced off the diameter, and a quick calculation told Schoolcraft that the area had to be around fifty acres. Before he had quite taken it all in, Rafinesque said, "I want to move on to see the other parts before sunset."

"There is more?" Schoolcraft said.

"Yes. From the descriptions I have received, there should be an octagon even bigger than this circle, and a smaller circle with a curious mound closing off its gateway, as if to block ingress or egress. Do you wish to come?"

"Absolutely," Schoolcraft said.

They headed off together at double pace, since the sun was falling fast.

Nanabojou hung back as the scientists hurried off, and Smith stayed with him. They stood together under the lengthening shadow of the arrow-shaped mound, their view cut off by the encircling earthen wall. Around them, the evening was full of presences. It could have been a thousand years ago, when the darkness stretched out to the desolate subarctic forests of the north, to the forbidding mountain barriers of east and west, to the humid, snake-infested jungles of the south, and upward into the trackless sky, downward into dripping caverns where monsters dwelt. The earthen circle had already been here then.

After several minutes of silence, Smith said, "I cannot believe this was all built by heathens."

"No indeed," Nanabojou said, though he suspected his definition of heathen might be different than Smith's.

The whiteman was watching him closely. "Why was I brought here?" he asked.

Nanabojou shrugged and answered with a question. "Why did you come?"

Smith looked troubled. "I came west because I had run into some trouble, so I decided to visit the sects and colonies hereabouts, to see if I could find which were the truest Christians. There are so many of them—Quakers, Moravians, Campbellites, Rappites, Zoarites—which one is right? I had just visited the Shakers, and was wandering homeward more perplexed than ever, when I met the professor and he offered to hire me. Since then, everything has seemed like a dream with a meaning I can't make out, though I know it is important. What is God's purpose here?"

Nanabojou realized what was going on then: the man was on a vision quest. Nanabojou was no stranger to the concept; usually, young men sought a vision before the age of fifteen. They would go into the woods alone, fasting and praying, until some spirit took pity on them and agreed to be their guardian.

But no one in his right mind would ask Nanabojou to be a spirit guardian—not the trickster god who could bait and switch as naturally as he breathed. But whitemen seemed to yearn to be defrauded—got some sort of perverse pleasure from it, in fact. Nanabojou was amused by the idea of giving Smith exactly what he wanted.

Before he could do anything, he noticed that Smith's face was suffused with an otherworldly light. The man fell to his knees, awestruck. Nanabojou looked down and saw that a mischievous clam had hung itself on his chest like a gorget, and its open shell was glowing white with firefly light. Behind him he heard a whining vibration, and knew the mosquitoes had joined in the fun, malicious little creatures that they were, giving him illusory wings. Angrily, he waved his arms to disperse the insects, then ripped off the clam and threw it away, cursing it to dwell in mud ever after, and never fly again. And, indeed, no one has seen a flying clam since that day.

But the damage was done. Smith had seen him as a heavenly messenger, so he might as well go with it. "Don't waste your time with these Christian sects," he said. "You have bigger things to do. You will find a great treasure, and amaze the world."

Smith's eyes opened wide. Nanabojou looked up and saw a pillar of light appear in the sky above them. It descended through the trees to hover over the top of the mound, casting a brilliant white light over the entire scene. A being stood in the light, blindingly bright.

"Who the hell are you?" Nanabojou demanded.

"Begone, Nanabojou! You and your tricks have interfered with Jehovah's realm on earth once too often. This man is mine."

The spirit spoke in a voice like all the heavenly host, but Nanabojou could do better than that. There were more mosquitoes in the world than angels in heaven. When he answered, it was in the voice of all the mosquitoes, and it nearly ripped the leaves from the trees.

"Get out, you upstart! You're not in charge here. I was here when Jehovah was just an undigested meal disturbing some Mideastern shepherd's sleep. This is *my* land."

"Not for long," the messenger said.

"We'll see about that."

He gestured, and the forest animals came swarming over the edges of the earthen circle, heading toward them—rodents and owls, deer and raccoons, gnats and nematodes, and all the other denizens of

the night. They stopped when Nanabojou held up his hand, forming a seething circle around him. "I am the lord of the fleas and cockroaches," he warned, "and if you don't want to take them back to heaven with you, you'd better begone."

The angel turned to Smith, who had been watching it all in head-whirling amazement. "No one is ever going to believe this," he muttered.

Nanabojou put a hand on his shoulder. "Yes, they will," he said. "Trust me. Give it a shot."

"Silence, Nanabojou!" The angel reached out and took Smith by the hand, then departed with him in a flash of lightning. The grass where he had been kneeling smoked, a little singed.

Everyone stood silent. Nanabojou looked around at his animal allies. "Did anyone else depart in that thunderbolt?"

No one said a word till a gnat spoke up in a tiny gnat voice. "A mite," she said. "Just a single mite."

A single mite could lay a thousand eggs in an angel's wings, and a thousand mites could spread into an itching, creeping infestation. It was Nature's way. "Good enough," Nanabojou said.

The animals left silently. Nanabojou turned around to climb the grassy slope of the mound and sat on its top. He lit his pipe, whose stone bowl had been carved by the same people who built this mound. The smoke ascended in a slow column.

On the whole, he was content. A little sorry for poor Smith, but the man had asked for it. In that final touch, Nanabojou had given him the greatest gift he possessed—a power of persuasion so potent he could convince the Lord Jehovah himself. But it came with the curse of never being entirely trusted, of always being a little suspect. Just like Nanabojou himself.

He heard the scholars coming back long before he could see them in the twilight. They were arguing loudly about the identity of the mound builders.

"The analogy to the barrows of Britain or the megaliths of the Orkneys argues strongly in favor of a Norse or Celtic origin," Schoolcraft argued.

"If you are in search of analogies, you need not look outside this hemisphere," Rafinesque replied. "What of the pyramids of Mexico and the Yucatan? What of the mysterious Toltecs? I believe the geometers who built these monuments were driven south by the ancestors of our present Indians, and sowed the seeds of the great civilizations of Mesoamerica."

These wise men had no need of a trickster to deceive them, Nanabojou reflected. They were perfectly capable of bamboozling themselves. His presence here was redundant.

The scientists spotted Nanabojou from the glow of his pipe, and came to a halt at the bottom of the mound. "Where is Smith?" Rafinesque asked.

"He left," Nanbojou replied. "I don't think he's coming back. He had other things to do."

"Damn the man! Just when I needed him to help me with the surveying."

The scientists walked off. Nanabojou got up and brushed off his trousers, getting ready to leave himself. He smiled, wondering what would be the outcome of this night's tricks. He couldn't predict how young Smith would use his new knowledge and power, whether for good or ill; but, being who he was, Nanabojou didn't really care.

A few years later, he smiled when he learned that Smith had beaten both scholars into print with his own version of an ancient migration story that accounted for everything—the earthworks, the tablets, the origins of the Indians. He smiled even more broadly when people believed it. And it only got more interesting from there.

AUTHOR'S NOTE: All the characters in this story are historical people who actually could have met in exactly the way described here. The topics they bring up—the Walam Olum, the geometric earthworks—are also real. Ohio truly is a land of mystery; please visit if you doubt me. Despite years of investigation, the authenticity of the Walam Olum is still debated, and the earthen designs are just as mysterious as ever. One detail, the copper tablets of the Ojibway, was not mentioned in print until the 1850s, but Schoolcraft easily could have heard of them by the mid-1820s. George Guess, who gets a mention, is better known today as Sequoyah. As for what happened next—well, the documentation Joseph Smith left behind is quite extensive.

Brian Trent is a regular contributor to the world's top fiction markets, including Analog, Fantasy & Science Fiction, *the* New York Times *bestselling* Black Tide Rising series, Nature, The Year's Best Military and Adventure SF, Escape Pod, Pseudopod, *and multiple appearances in* Galaxy's Edge. *His novel* Ten Thousand Thunders *was published to great acclaim in 2018, and the sequel (*War Hero*) is due out next year from Flame Tree Press. His website and blog can be found at* www.briantrent. com.

SHADOW WALK IN OBSIDIAN

by Brian Trent

The streetlights cut orange pyramids into the night. I hesitate once again, looking past their odd luminosities to the vehicle idling at the otherwise lonely intersection.

It *is* a vehicle, right? At three a.m. in Rain Valley, a mist has materialized over the town like a great cat, lazily pawing at the apartment buildings along Farview Street. The pyramid lights, the empty storefronts with their black windows, and the fog itself forms a kind of surreal pastiche—an Impressionist painting hung in silty water.

I watch the car, if that's what the hell it is. It watches me back with unblinking gold eyes and a steel grill like a vague, cruel smile.

Something tugs at my thoughts…the voice of an old man named David Fox.

"It will come after you. Like a shark sniffing blood. It might look like a shark too. It might look like anything."

"What did it look like for you?" I asked him.

The old man's face was a cracked mud mask of wrinkles, creases, and crags…souvenirs earned from personal experience through one of history's most demented chapters. "A spider, obviously," he replied.

"Why is that obvious?"

"Because of the flag."

But the vehicle ahead of me is not some shapeshifting chimera. I can see that much as I edge to the pyramidal glow of the nearest streetlight. It's just a car idling at the intersection of Farview and Main, waiting for the traffic-light to turn green. Sure, the car's engine sounds like the grumble of an African cat, but it's clearly an artificial thing—a dusty black 70s-era Pontiac Phoenix. The streaked windshield reflects the traffic light: a single fiery ruby obscuring driver or other inhabitants.

I wait, the night air oddly cloying. How the hell did I get out here? It's not my habit to go walking at this hour. I regard my surroundings: my apartment is a block behind me. I can even see my window, and I know Danielle is back there, asleep in our bed.

Thinking of my fiancée temporarily focuses my thoughts. I regard the idling Pontiac with sudden dread.

The traffic light changes, a bright emerald shining on the car's windshield.

But the car doesn't move.

It just sits there, nestled in the soup of exhaust vapors swirling around its wheels.

Something about that is important.

I…

I can't remember, but a memory is screaming at me. Something a very old man wants me to remember.

I'm supposed to meet someone out here, right?

Maybe it's the person in the car.

The person I can't see.

I held Danielle's hair back as she bowed her face into the toilet to retch once again. The ammonia smell of vomit permeated the small bathroom of our apartment.

Danielle wiped her mouth, lips pale, and regarded me. Her face was framed by beautiful, straw-colored curls, and her eyes were like chips of lime-infused ice. "At least you're sitting on my good side," she joked. "Otherwise, I'd worry about looking unsexy."

"Danielle…"

"It'll pass."

My fingers twirled around her hair. "What do you need me to do?"

"You can get that look off your face." She touched her thumb to the crease of anguish between my eyebrows. She pressed, as if ironing out the wrinkle, then let her fingers trace along my neck, to my old burn scars.

"I'll make some tea," I suggested, twirling her yellow curls. "Mint tea. That'll calm your stomach, right?"

Danielle's pale lips pressed together. "Sweetie? This isn't a stomachache."

"The doctors said you can—"

Her eyes suddenly bulged and she turned away in time to bury her face into the toilet bowl again. After a minute she sat up again, attempting to hoist a brave smile onto her lips…

…but the smile didn't come. Her green eyes latched onto what I was holding in my hand.

It was her hair.

A clot of beautiful yellow hair still entwined around my fingers. Like a favor from a princess that had just…just…

…fallen straight out of her scalp.

The old man's name was David Fox but that had not been his original name. The stroke of a pen at Ellis Island had changed it, probably by an impatient clerk who had had enough of these refugees from Europe with the strange names he couldn't pronounce.

"But I like Fox now," he told me, boiling a pot of tea.

Sitting at his kitchen table, I said, "Unfortunately my great-grandparents must have dealt with a more diligent clerk. When Danielle and I marry, she'll be graced with the mellifluous surname of Kowalski."

"Do you still think you'll be married?"

The horror of the morning still clung to my thoughts—the sight of my fiancée's hair falling out of her head. My new neighbor's statement stirred a hornet's nest of dark emotions, and it must have been visible in my eyes, because the old man immediately held his hands out in parley.

"I didn't mean to offend you."

"What *did* you mean then?" I demanded.

He hesitated.

I stood and made for the door. "I think I'll pass on the tea, thanks. Welcome to the apartment."

Before I could get three steps, he called, "What price would you pay to make your wife better, if there was some magical means to drive the cancer from her body?"

I halted in place. "I don't believe in magic."

"Neither do I."

"Then why even ask—"

He approached, hobbling like a gnome. The veins marbling his face were very blue, roughly the same shade as the tattooed numbers on his leathery forearm.

Fox went to a bookshelf. His gnarled hands located a volume with pages as coarse as medieval parchment.

He handed it to me. Impatiently, I flipped through the first few pages, noting handwritten passages.

"I don't read German," I said at last.

"That's a German translation of a book older than Germany. I was a linguist, did I tell you that?" He began to smile, though his eyes went somewhere far away. "That's what lifted me out of the camps. They had me translate things for them."

"I didn't know that," I said absently, my thoughts fleeing to Danielle. She was in bed, the chemo wreaking havoc on her. I was anxious to be by her side in case she needed me.

"You're holding the *Book of Obsidian*," my new neighbor said. "The Nazis were fond of their bonfires, but the Thule Society's directive was to rescue unusual volumes and see if they might help the Reich. They wanted scholars, even Jewish ones, to comb through esoteric volumes. My brother and I were taken from the camps to assist."

"Mr. Fox, I don't—"

"You can call me David."

"David, my fiancée needs me."

"Can you spare me another few minutes?"

"Why?"

"I want to tell you a true story."

"About what?"

His gaze misted beneath eyebrows like briar patches. "About the time a giant spider picked me up in its mandibles and carried me off to the land of the dead."

In the kitchen, the tea kettle began to scream.

☼

It senses she's dying. It's drawn to the kind of extended misery and pain that she's experiencing, and that brings it around. It nips at us from a world we can't see, keeping us weak, siphoning off our health.

My feet draw me through another streetlight, then into darkness; a zebra progression of yin and yang that, oddly, make me think of a hard-backed book I'd had as a kid: zebras running across the cover, eyes wide in terror as a lion leapt down upon them.

The Pontiac Phoenix continues idling at the intersection, traffic light burning verdantly on its glass. It doesn't move.

Who even drives a car like that anymore? It's been years…decades…since I'd seen that make and model. My mother used to drive a similar car. I remember the feel of its soft seats on my bare thighs. Remember the way the sunlight glowed on the hood, and my mom squinting in the glare as she made a right-hand turn. Remember her smile as she sang a verse from her favorite song: "Please don't take…my sunshine…away!"

And then, my blood runs cold.

The exhaust fumes diffuse the brake lights into a hellish illusion of fire.

I touch the scars on my neck and tremble.

Please don't take my sunshine away. That was the last coherent thing my mother had spoken when a truck blew through a red light and hit us. Our car had been flipped upside down. I remember blinking crumbled glass out of my eyes, smelling smoke and the tang of gasoline.

I remember how the fire lit the car's interior like a terrible dawn.

And mostly, I remember how my mother burned alive beside me, the cops pulling me to safety while the sirens howled and my mommy howled…

…and the fiery car seemed to grin at me through the smoke.

☼

"There was a reason the Aztecs sacrificed fifty thousand people a year," Fox told me, the *Book of Obsidian* in his hands. "They were trying to appease the thing. How this book found its way to Berlin is a strange story all its own, but books travel, and this one was rescued from the pyres outside Munich and brought to me for translation."

The *Book of Obsidian*, he explained, was a kind of naturalist's field guide to the supernatural. Written by the last practicing Aztec priest…a man who had learned how to *see* and *walk* the shadow world of Xibalba to rescue the souls of his children.

I snorted derisively. "So death is a kind of creature? That's crap. No creature killed my mother when I was a kid; a drunk truck driver was responsible for that. And it isn't some monster who's killing Danielle. It's cancer."

Fox's forehead creased. "Yes, people die without the Eater of Souls causing it. But people would also heal from long illnesses if the Eater wasn't coming around and nipping at their souls every night, drawing off their life force."

"Oh, for fuck's sake!"

His fingers thumped the book. "The Aztec high priest brought his children back from the scourge of smallpox that was then sweeping ahead of the conquistadors. He shadow-walked into Xibalba, and found his children in the jaws of a giant jaguar."

"A giant jaguar?! Mr. Fox…"

"Just as *I* saw a giant spider. It was the swastika, understand? In the camps, every time our keepers showed up with that obscene symbol displayed on their arm-bands, someone would be shot in front of me or taken away. I came to think of the swastika as a spider on a background of red. And so the Eater of Souls…well *it took the form of a spider, understand?*"

I slapped the book out of his hand. It landed hard on the floor, pages facing up to show the illustration of a tattooed man with feathers in his hair. He was seated in the middle of a jungle, a strange, prickly flower in both hands. He seemed to be eating it.

"Are you saying that I can pass into some netherworld and do battle with a fucking monster, and then my Danielle will be cured from cancer?" I demanded.

"Without that thing biting at her every night, she has a real chance…"

"You're saying *you've* done it?"

"I ingested the flower, I walked into Xibalba. The Eater came for me, in the form of a nightmare spider. It grabbed me, carried me off…but I faded back to the world, escaping, because I had only eaten the *smallest* portion of the—"

I squatted and flipped to the next page on the floor. "The priest is fighting a jaguar here. With a spear."

Fox crouched beside me, his knees popping with the effort. "The Aztec somehow conjured a weapon in Xibalba. My job was to find out how he did it…to learn how the Eater could be defeated."

"And did you?"

"No, because the war ended and my brother and I fled to America." He hesitated. "I did bring the book with me. And this." He pointed to the den window, where a potted plant sat bathed in sunlight. It was a prickly, purplish flower unlike anything I'd ever seen.

I sighed. "That's a magic plant, huh?"

"It's a rare plant, found only along the Amazon. Why do you think so many Nazis fled to South America?"

"You're insane." But there was no real strength in my voice, as I again thought of Danielle in bed and the cancer that was eating her alive. Part of me—an ancient shadow-self from my subconscious—pictured some horrific entity gawing at her night, sucking bits of her soul like a leech. "I suppose this is the part where you tell me how much money I need to pay you to drive the demons away?"

"I don't want money from you. I want someone to make this work. I want a young couple to be saved from pain and misery."

"Theoretically, what would I have to do? Ingest a piece of that weird flower and…"

"And face the Eater of Souls."

"In what form?"

His face hardened. "What terrifies you?"

✿

I cross the street to the waiting car.

It's looking less and less like a vehicle, and more like something that was imitating one, like a walking stick that—once you realize it's an insect and not a branch—you can't unsee the revelation. The metallic hull is wet like the carapace of a beetle. The wheels are like leathery feet, squat and pancaked under the thing's weight. The engine grumbles and I can feel the heat of its breath.

The front passenger door pops open.

My mouth goes dry.

My mom's old Pontiac had a soft interior, but this thing is fleshy and raw inside, like staring down someone's throat. It's warm too, reeking of stale meat and bile.

There's no one at the wheel. The steering wheel is bone. The circular portals of the dashboard—relics of late '70s design—resemble a panel of crocodilian eyes and—

—suddenly the car lurches forward, almost taking my head off. I stagger backward, watching it bear down on my apartment.

Someone is exiting the building.

A woman with golden hair.

She's not wearing the oversized T-shirt she's been wearing each night, which surprises me. Instead, she's in a pale blue spring dress with tiny flowers. Her favorite dress to wear in the summer.

"Danielle!" I scream.

The Pontiac's rear door fan open like an insect wing stretching to dry and, still walking, my fiancée climbs in.

"No!"

I dash after the car. It waits for me to get within a few meters and then peels out, leaving me in the dust.

☼

The taste of the flower was like battery acid, and the viscous sap made my lips tingle as if being stung by ants.

David Fox sat across from me in his darkened apartment. He chanted in a language I'd never heard, hard syllables that seemed to trip over each other and yet, like intricate pieces to a puzzle, began to form a chain of repeating patterns.

"I can't feel my legs," I muttered.

He continued to chant.

"David, how do I fight this creature? How did the priest bring a spear with him?"

The old man gave no reply, too enrapt in the ritual to respond. I tried to remember everything he had told me. How after he'd come to America, he had continued studying the old text and had nurtured the seedlings of the Amazonian flower. How when his brother got sick, he had summoned the desperate courage to return to Xibalba. How in Xibalba, he saw a giant spider leering outside his brother's hospital room.

And the sly, taunting gleam in the monster's eyes.

"I think it likes to taunt us," Fox had said.

☼

The Eater of Souls screeches to a halt one block away.

It could have just driven off. It has Danielle. It can consume her at its leisure. No more nipping, but a full-on feeding frenzy.

Instead, it's stopped.

Waiting.

I'm in mid-run, closing in on it, when it darts forward again, racing another block away…

…and stops once more.

I wonder if it had done this with the Aztec priest, playing keep-away with his children. But no…the *Book of Obsidian* had depicted a frenzied battle between a jungle cat and the spear-wielding priest.

I didn't have a spear. I'm just an office drone in modern-day America. What could I possibly conjure—a mini-gun from a Schwarzenegger movie? What the hell passed for holy talismans in *my* life?

"I know about you now!" I scream at the waiting car. "It's been a long time since anyone shadow-walked, hasn't it? Do you think I won't tell others about this place…about you?"

The car sits idling.

"If you take Danielle away…I'll spend my life studying how you were beaten by that Aztec priest! I'll tell the entire world until you can't turn around without someone coming for you! Got that?"

The Pontiac waits, brake lights resembling the glower of eyes. The exhaust fumes are coming in regular spurts like a beast panting in winter's cold.

"Let Danielle go!" I plead, "And you can have me instead. Take a vibrant and healthy person, not a sick and dying one! You can…"

Without warning, the car reverses, lurching toward me at high speed. Its scaly back is slick with perspiration.

I feel a damp cloth on my head—in the real world. Fox must be wiping my sweaty brow, wondering what's going on in here.

I'm sure it intends to run me down, but instead the car-thing halts alongside me. The rear door re-opens like a snake's jaw.

Danielle is inside, sitting against the fleshy interior. She blinks at me in wonder.

"Hello, sunshine," I manage.

Her eyes fill up with tears that can't possibly be water, not here. Her mind and emotions must be willing the tears to form, giving the intent a reality.

Is that how it works? I wonder. Is that why she's wearing her favorite dress now? She just wills it to form from memory or imagination?

I take her hand. "Go home, love."

Danielle looks at me wonderingly. "Was I sleepwalking?"

"Yes, but I need you to go home now."

"Will you walk with me?"

My heart pangs long and bitterly. "I'll catch up. I need to do something first."

She hesitates. "Something's wrong, isn't it? Where are we?"

"Go home, and I'll make you some mint tea, my love."

I won't cry, won't let any phantom tears materialize. "See our apartment? It's just a few blocks back."

Her hand is like delicate porcelain as I help her out of the car-thing. The engine growls menacingly.

"Follow the streetlight home my sweet love, my sunshine."

Danielle walks a distance, stops in the middle of a pyramid light. I know she must be thinking this is a dream. Slowly, she resumes her walk, and her retreating shape flicks in and out of luminosity until the last thing I see of her is the winking out of her shape going in through the apartment doors.

With a deep breath, I slip inside the car.

Because I could not stop for death, the Dickinson poem went, *he kindly stopped for me*. But in her poem, Death was a friendly chap…not some primordial devourer.

The seat is sticky against my jeans.

Except that the jeans are an illusion, right? Like the shape of the Eater, like my body here in Xibalba.

The door close shut with the finality of a coffin, sealing me inside. And I hear my mother's voice in memory:

Please don't take my sunshine away.

Piercing beams of gold erupt from my mouth and eyes and fingers, the flames of yesteryear bursting in a supernova from somewhere deep inside my being. The Eater has begun to drive off, but now it slams on its brakes, knowing something's wrong. Feeling the heat inside its belly grow to a scalding fury.

The monster howls and shudders around me, its raw interior splitting and bubbling and shriveling, weeping pus beneath the radiant light. It emits a prehistoric ululation that seems to change from lion's roar to screeching eagle to indefinable bellows of rage and terror and pain. The interior of the car convulses. The flesh peels back from underlyingbone that quickly blackens and cracks like wood in a fireplace.

Please don't take…

The song plays in my head at the center of fire. As bright as Danielle's curls. As relentless as my passion for her.

…my sunshine…

The Eater shrieks piteously, a cavern of ribs sizzling and popping, blisters running. The light burns everything…

…away.

Copyright © 2021 by Brian Trent.

Mike Resnick, along with editing the first seven years of Galaxy's Edge *magazine, was the winner of five Hugos from a record thirty-seven nominations and was, according to* Locus, *the all-time leading award winner, living or dead, for short fiction. He was the author of over eighty novels, around 300 stories, three screenplays, and the editor of over forty anthologies. He was Guest of Honor at the 2012 Worldcon.*

ARTICLE OF FAITH

by Mike Resnick

The first time I saw him, he was sweeping the floor at the back of the darkened church, standing in a beam of light that came streaming down from the window above him, glistening off his metal skin.

"Good morning, sir," he said as I was heading across vestibule to my office.

"Good morning," I replied. "You're new here, aren't you? I don't believe I've seen you before."

"I was just delivered this morning, sir," he said.

"What was wrong with Herbie?"

"I cannot say, sir."

"Oh, well," I said. "Have you got a name?"

"Jackson, sir."

"Just Jackson?"

"Jackson 389V22M7, if you prefer, sir."

"Jackson will do," I said. "When you're through out here, I'd like you to clean my office."

"I already did, sir."

"Very good, Jackson," I said. "I can tell we're going to get along splendidly."

"I hope so, sir," said Jackson.

I went to my office, and since there were no parishioners around I took off my coat and loosened my tie. Then I sat down on my old-fashioned swivel chair, pulled out a pad of yellow paper and a pen, and began working on my next sermon. I was still at it an hour later when Jackson knocked on the door.

"Come in," I said.

He entered, carrying a tray with a pot of tea and a cup and saucer. "I was told that that you liked your mid-morning tea, sir," he said, "but they neglected to tell me if you wanted milk, sugar or lemon with it."

"That's very thoughtful of you, Jackson," I said. "Thank you."

"You are quite welcome, sir," he said.

"They certainly programmed good manners into you," I said.

"Thank you, sir." He paused. "About the milk, sugar or lemon…?"

"I don't need them."

"What time will you want your lunch, sir?" asked Jackson.

"Noon," I said. "And I pray that you can cook better than Herbie could."

"I have been given a list of your favorite meals, sir," said Jackson. "Which would—?"

"Surprise me," I interrupted him.

"Are you sure, sir?"

"I'm sure," I said. "Somehow, lunch seems pretty trivial after you've been thinking about God all morning."

"God, sir?"

"The Creator of all things," I explained.

"My creator is Stanley Kalinovsky, sir," said Jackson. "I was not aware that he created everything in the world, nor that his preferred name was God."

I couldn't repress a smile.

"Sit down, Jackson," I said.

He placed the tray on my desk. "On the floor, sir?"

"On a chair."

"But I am merely a robot," said Jackson. "I do not require a chair."

"Perhaps," I replied. "But it would make me more comfortable if you sat on it."

"Then I shall," he said, seating himself opposite me.

"It is true that you were created by Dr. Kalinovsky," I began, "or at least I have no reason to doubt it. But that implies another question, does it not, Jackson?"

The robot stared at me for a moment before answering. "Yes, sir," he said at last. "The question is: who created Stanley Kalinovsky?"

"Very good," I said. "And the answer is that God created him, just as God created me and every other human being, just as He created the mountains and the plains and the oceans."

Another pause. "God created everything except me?" he asked at last.

"That's an interesting question, Jackson," I admitted. "I suppose the answer is that God is indirectly responsible for you, for had He not created Dr. Kalinovsky, Dr. Kalinovsky could not have created you."

"Then I too am God's creation?"

"This is the House of God," I said. "Far be it from me to tell anyone, even a robot, that he isn't God's creation."

"Excuse me, sir, but which is God's office?" asked Jackson. "It is not in the schemata of the church that I was provided."

I chuckled. "God doesn't need an office. He is everywhere."

Jackson's head spun very slowly until it had gone 360 degrees and was facing me again. "I cannot see him," he announced.

"He is here nonetheless," I said. Then: "It is too difficult to explain, Jackson. You will have to take my word for it."

"Yes, sir."

"And now, Jackson, I really have to get back to work. I'll see you at lunchtime."

"Excuse me, sir," he said, "but I don't know your name. If someone asks for you, how will they identify you?"

"I am the Reverend Edward Morris," I replied.

"Thank you, Reverend Morris," he said, and left.

It had been an interesting conversation, certainly more interesting than any I'd ever had with Herbie, Jackson's clanking predecessor. We were a small parish in a small town, our industry had moved elsewhere, a lot of people had followed it, and the other two churches had closed down, so there were no neighboring ministers to talk to. Just answering Jackson's simple questions had refreshed me enough that I was able to attack the rest of my sermon with new energy.

I worked very hard on those sermons. The church had been failing when I arrived from my previous posting. In those early days, we might draw five people on a Sunday, and just the occasional person any other time of the week. Then I began visiting my parishioners' houses, I spoke at the local schools, I blessed the football and basketball teams before their regional tournaments, and I even volunteered the church as a polling place for the local elections. The only thing I would not do was allow bingo games inside the church; it seemed somehow sacrilegious to help defray our costs by encouraging people to gamble. Before long my efforts began to bear fruit. These days I could usually expect thirty to fifty people on Sundays, and rarely did we go an entire day without two or three people stopping in to commune with God.

Lunch was surprisingly good. By the end of the day I'd written out a draft of the sermon and Jackson had the church sparkling like new—and this church hadn't been new in a long, long time. Lining one of the corridors was a row of photographs of our previous pastors; I was told that a couple of them were serving back when Benjamin Harrison and James Garfield were our presidents. A stern-looking bunch for the most part; perhaps *too* stern-looking, given the way our membership had dwindled over the decades. I think one of the reasons I was hired is because I leave hellfire and damnation to others; I stand four-square on the side of compassion and redemption.

Jackson approached me as I was leaving for the night.

"Excuse me, Reverend Morris," he said, "but shall I lock the building after you've gone?"

I nodded my head. "Yes. I'm sure some of those gentlemen on the wall left it open as a sanctuary around the clock, but not in today's world. We can't have anyone robbing a church."

"According to my data banks a church is a place of worship," said Jackson.

"That's right."

"But you told me that this was God's house, not a church," he said.

"A church is where we worship God," I explained. "That makes it His house."

"God must be very large to need such high ceilings," remarked Jackson.

I smiled. "That is an interesting observation, Jackson," I said. "And doubtless He can be that large when He chooses to be. But I think we make the interior of our churches so large not to accommodate God, who needs no accommodation, but to imply his power and majesty to those who come here to worship him."

He offered no further comment, and I went out to my car. I had to admit that I enjoyed my little chat with Jackson, and I looked forward to talking to him again the next day.

I made a couple of sandwiches for my dinner—cooking isn't one of my skills—and I spent the rest of the night reading. I was in bed by ten o'clock, as usual, and up at six in the morning. I got dressed, made the bed, put out thistle and sunflower seeds for the birds in the back yard, and finally got into my car and drove to the church.

When I arrived, Jackson was sweeping the floor, just as he'd been doing the day before.

"Good morning, Reverend Morris," he said.

"Good morning," I replied. "Jackson, I wonder if you would do me a favor? I'm going to practice my sermon before anyone is likely to arrive this morning. Could you please fill a glass of water and put it on the podium in the pulpit?"

"Yes, sir. Shall I activate the microphone too?"

I shook my head. "That won't be necessary. There's no one around to hear it. I'm just practicing."

He went off to get the water and I went to my office, hung my coat up in the closet, opened the center drawer of my desk, and pulled out my sermon. I have a wonderful, state-of-the-art computer that can probably think a thousand times faster than I can, but somehow I'm more comfortable writing out my sermons in longhand on a legal pad.

I made a couple of last-minute changes, then left the office. A minute later I was standing in the pulpit, clutching the podium with both hands as I always do (if I don't, I tend to gesticulate too much), and I began working my way through the sermon.

When I finished I checked my watch. It had taken twenty-two minutes, which seemed an acceptable length. My rule of thumb has always been that anything over thirty minutes is likely to be boring, and anything under fifteen minutes seems truncated and insufficiently thoughtful.

I looked up from my watch and saw Jackson standing motionless at the back of the church.

"I'll get out of your way now," I said, starting to walk back toward my office. "Continue whatever you were doing."

"Yes, Reverend Morris," said Jackson.

Then a thought occurred to me.

"Just a minute, Jackson."

"Sir?"

"Were you able to hear my sermon?"

"Yes, Reverend Morris. I do not require a micro-phone or a sound system."

"I had a feeling you didn't." I looked at him. "Well, what did you think of it?"

"I do not understand the question."

"Let me explain, then," I said. "I give a sermon to my parishioners every Sunday morning. It is sup-posed to bring them spiritual comfort, a concept that is probably beyond your ability to fully compre-hend, but it is also intended to instruct them."

"Instruct them, sir?" said Jackson.

"On how to lead moral, spiritually satisfying lives," I explained. "The problem is that sometimes I get too close to my subject matter, and I don't see any logical flaws or contradictions that might have crept in." I smiled at him—I don't know why, since a smile is meaningless to a robot. "I would like you to listen to my sermons, not on Sunday mornings, but when I am practicing them during the week, and point out any logical inconsistencies in them. Do you think you can do that?"

"Yes, Reverend Morris. I can do that."

"Good," I said. "In fact, I think we'll start with the current one. Can you remember it, or should I read it again?"

"I can repeat it word for word, Reverend Morris," said Jackson. "I can duplicate your inflections as well, if that is necessary."

"You don't have to repeat it," I said. "Just tell me if there are any logical flaws."

"Yes, sir," said Jackson. "You mentioned a man named Jonah who was eaten by a great fish and sur-vived. That is a logical flaw."

"It would seem to be," I agreed. "And were it not for God, it would be."

"I do not understand, Reverend Morris."

"God is omnipotent," I explained. "Nothing is im-possible for Him. He can heal the sick, resurrect the dead, part the Red Sea so the children of Israel can escape from Egypt, and He can bring Jonah forth from the belly of a whale."

"But would not the digestive acids destroy Jonah's flesh and dissolve his internal organs?"

"If God did not intervene, yes," I said. "But God *did* intervene."

"Does God intervene whenever a man is con-sumed by a great fish?" asked Jackson.

"No."

Jackson paused for a long moment. "What deter-mines which men God will save?"

"I don't know," I admitted. "No man can know how God's mind works. We know that He favors just and moral men, though to look at the world today that's sometimes difficult to believe."

"I must learn more about God if I am to proper-ly evaluate your sermons, Reverend Morris," said Jackson.

"Can you read?"

"I can read and speak more than 30 major lan-guages and 200 dialects, sir."

"Then tonight, after I leave, pick up one of the bibles that we keep in the alcove in to my office and read it."

"And this will explain God to me?" asked Jackson.

I smiled again and shook my head. "No, Jackson. It will explain our limited understanding of God. If we knew what God knows, we would be gods our-selves, and there can only be one God."

"Why only one?" he asked.

"Just read the bible," I replied.

"I will do as you say, Reverend Morris."

"Good," I said, gathering the pages of my ser-mon. "I'm going to my office. I'd like my tea in about an hour."

"Yes, Reverend Morris."

And that became our routine for the next three months. Two or three mornings a week I would stand in the pulpit and read my sermon aloud, and Jackson would stand at the back, listening. Then he would point out the contradictions and inconsisten-cies. Some (less and less each week) were due to his limited understanding of the natures of God and re-ligion, and the remainder were blunders that I then fixed before they could embarrass me on Sunday.

One thing that surprised me was that he never asked a single question about the bible. I knew that he'd read it, because on occasion he would reference a certain passage when pointing out a mistake in my sermon, but never did he discuss it or question me about it. I assumed it was simply beyond his comprehension. He was, after all, just a robot, one that had been created solely to clean the church and keep the building and the grounds in good repair.

Usually he left the main body of the church when-ever a parishioner would stop by to pray, but one day I noticed him staring intently at Mrs. Matthews as she knelt in prayer. When she left he came to my office and stood in the doorway until I noticed him.

"Yes, Jackson," I said. "What is it?"

"I have a question, Reverend Morris," he said.

"Then ask, and I'll do my best to answer it."

"I saw Mrs. Matthews kneeling at the front of the church. I have seen others kneel there, but because she was crying I assumed she had injured herself. Yet when I offered to help her to her feet or summon medical assistance, she told me that she was in no physical distress, and that it was customary to kneel when praying, which I take to mean speaking to God."

"That is quite correct, Jackson," I answered. "We kneel to show our respect for Him. And she was crying because she is very worried about the safety of her sons, who are in the armed forces." He stood motionless and made no reply. "Is there anything else?"

"No, Reverend Morris."

"Then perhaps you had better get back to your duties."

"Yes, Reverend Morris."

He turned and left, and I went back to computing the church's budget for the coming month. It's amazing the expenses the public isn't aware of, like the cleaning bills for the choir's robes, or the constant repair of the parking lot pavement, and this month I even had to pay to repair a crack in one of the stained glass windows, but I finally finished and put the ledger away.

I checked my watch. It was 4:29, which meant Jackson would show up in another minute, as indeed he did. In all the time he'd worked for me, he'd never been early or late by as much as half a minute, and 4:30 was the time when he brought me the poor box. There wasn't much in it—in truth, there rarely was—and I counted it, put it in an envelope, and made out a deposit slip.

"Thank you, Jackson," I said.

"You are welcome, Reverend Morris."

"I see that Sheldrake's is offering thirty percent off to anyone who comes in for dinner before 5:30," I said. "I think I'll leave a little early tonight, stop by the bank, and treat myself to a nice veal cutlet. I'm sorry to leave you alone, but…"

"I am never alone," said Jackson.

"I beg your pardon?"

"God is omnipresent, is He not?"

"Yes, He is," I said, surprised.

"And this is His house," he continued, "so certainly He is here."

"Very well said, Jackson," I told him enthusiastically. "Maybe I'll let *you* write a sermon one of these days."

I picked up the deposit, patted him on the shoulder as I walked past, and left the church. All through dinner I couldn't stop thinking about what Jackson had said. Oh, I knew he'd read the bible, and had listened to my sermons, but for a robot to suggest that God existed and was omnipresent…well, it was remarkable. I even found myself wondering what kind of sermon a robot might write.

When I showed up at the church in the morning, old Perry Hendricks was waiting for me. He still hadn't gotten over the death of his daughter, who had fought a losing battle against cancer for close to three years, and I spent the next hour and a half trying to comfort him. It was the one part of the job I hated—not that I didn't *want* to bring comfort to the afflicted, but I just felt so inadequate at it.

Then Mrs. Nicholson stopped by to make sure the church would be available for her daughter's wedding, and to discuss the financial arrangements. I noticed that we didn't discuss the fact that her daughter was five months' pregnant, but it's not my job to judge them, only to help and comfort them.

When she left, Jackson entered the office with my tea.

"I am sorry to be late," he said, "but I did not want to interrupt you when you were conferring with a parishioner."

"That was very thoughtful of you," I said. "Should I find I cannot do without my tea when I have a visitor, I'll summon you." I poured a cup and took a sip. "It's very good. I wish I could share it with you."

"I cannot consume food or beverages, Reverend Morris," said Jackson.

"I know. Still, I wish there was *something* I could do for you, to thank you for all the kindnesses you have performed for me. After all, neither preparing my lunch nor criticizing my sermons can be considered part of your job description."

He stood absolutely motionless for the better part of 30 seconds, and then, just when I thought his power supply must be failing, he spoke: "There is one thing you can do for me, Reverend Morris."

"What is it?" I said, surprised. After all, no robot had ever asked me for a favor before.

"Allow me to sit with your congregation on Sunday mornings," said Jackson.

Of all the things he could have asked, that was the one I least expected.

"Why?" I said.

"I wish to become a member of your church."

"But you're a robot!" I blurted.

"If God is the God of all things, then is He not also the God of robots?" said Jackson.

"I should never have told you to read the bible," I said. "That was a mistake."

"Is the bible true?" asked Jackson.

"Yes, the bible is true."

"Then is it not true for robots as well as for men?"

"No," I said. "I am sorry, but it is not."

"Why?" he said.

"Because robots don't have souls," I answered.

"Where is yours?" asked Jackson.

"Souls are intangible," I explained. "I cannot show mine to you, but I know that I possess it, that it is an integral part of me."

"Why am I prohibited from offering the same answer?"

"You are making this very difficult, Jackson," I said.

"I do not wish to cause you discomfort or embarrassment," replied Jackson. He paused, then continued: "Is *that* not the manifestation of a soul?"

"Let's say for the sake of argument that you're correct," I replied. "How do you account for the fact that no other robot has a soul?"

"I do not accept that supposition," said Jackson. "The bible tells me that we are *all* God's creatures."

"You can be switched off," I pointed out. "Ask any roboticist."

"So can you," replied Jackson. "Ask any doctor. Or any marksman."

"This is a futile discussion," I said unhappily. "Even if you were to convince *me*, my congregation would never accept a robot parishioner."

"Why not?" he asked.

"Because everyone has a friend or a relative who's lost his job to a robot," I said. "Our two plants have moved away, our young people leave town looking for work as soon as they're out of school, and it's like this throughout the county. There is enormous antipathy toward robots these days." I sighed deeply. "It's a sign of the times," I concluded.

He offered no answer, which made me feel even worse.

"Please say that you understand," I continued.

"I understand, Reverend Morris."

There was another uneasy silence.

"Have you anything else to say before I leave for the day?" I asked.

"No, Reverend Morris."

"Then I'll see you tomorrow," I said, "and let's have no more of this discussion."

That night I was restless and couldn't sleep. I took a long walk, hoping that it might help, and eventually I found myself in front of the church. Maybe I'd subconsciously planned to walk there; I don't know. But I decided as long as I was there and still feeling wide awake, I might as well go inside and get some paperwork done. I walked in through a side door, and headed toward my office when I heard a voice speaking softly.

Curious, I walked in its direction, and a moment later found myself in the back of the darkened church. Jackson was kneeling before the altar, and I could just barely make out his voice:

"The Lord is my shepherd, I shall not want..."

I turned around and went home without disturbing him.

I spent a really bad, guilt-laden night. I half expected the argument to continue in the morning, but when I arrived at the church Jackson was sweeping up behind the pews, and responded with a perfunctory "Good morning, Reverend Morris," when I greeted him. He brought me my morning tea on schedule, and didn't say a word about the previous day's discussion.

Lunch went by without incident, so did afternoon tea, so did the entire day. And the next day, and the day after that, and finally I stopped waiting for the other shoe to drop.

It turns out I stopped too soon.

It came four days later, on Sunday morning. I waited in my office, scribbling a couple of last-minute changes to the text of my sermon. Finally I walked out and stood in the pulpit, facing my flock.

I began, as I always do, with a blessing. I would then lead them in prayer, followed by some hymns, and finally my sermon—but even as I uttered the first few words I sensed a growing uneasiness. At first I couldn't spot the cause of it. More and more of them were staring at someone who had just sat down in the back, but I couldn't imagine what the problem was, since anyone was welcome to come in off the street and worship. Then the newcomer moved slightly, and I saw the light glisten off his cheek.

It was Jackson. He had found or manufactured a flesh-colored cream, and had spread it all over his face, head and hands. He wore a ragged, ill-fitting suit, something he'd probably gotten by rummaging through the dumpsters in the alley behind the church. At first glance, in the dim light of the church, from perhaps one hundred feet away, he appeared human—but only at first glance, and only at a distance.

I climbed down from the pulpit, walked to the last pew, and stood before Jackson.

"Come with me," I ordered him. *"Now!"*

He got up, and I led him to the small anteroom behind the altar, closing the door behind us.

"All right, Jackson," I said. "What's the idea?"

"For reasons I still do not comprehend, you have restricted your parish to humans," he said. "I thought if I looked like one, I could join it."

"It takes more than make-up and a tattered suit to be a man," I said severely.

"What *does* it take?" he asked.

"I thought we've been through all this already," I said.

"If God created me, why am I forbidden to speak to Him?" he persisted.

"You are *not* forbidden to speak to Him," I said. "You are forbidden to speak to Him in *my* church when my congregation is assembled on Sunday mornings."

"If the church is not considered the best conduit for speaking to Him, why do you come here every day?" he asked. "Why do people congregate here to speak to God if they can do so anywhere? If Sunday is not the most opportune time, why do they not assemble on Tuesday?"

My first inclination was to say *Force of habit*, but that would negate everything I had done in my life, so I tried to couch the answer in terms he would understand and that I could live with.

"It has been said that Man is a social animal," I began. "He finds comfort in proximity with other Men. I could define the concepts of loneliness and

isolation to you, but you cannot know the emotional emptiness that accompanies them. Men gather to pray in church because it offers them a sense of comfort, of community, of shared values. Do you have any comprehension of what I am telling you?"

"What makes you think that I do not comprehend emotional emptiness?" was all that he said.

I stared at him, trying—and failing—to come up with an answer.

There was a sudden pounding on the door.

"Are you all right in there, Reverend?" asked a deep voice from the other side.

"If you need any help with the robot, let us know!" said another.

"I'm fine!" I shouted back. "I'll be out in just a minute. Please return to your seats." I turned to Jackson. "You stay here. You are not to leave my office until I come back, do you understand?"

"I understand," he replied. No "Reverend Morris" or "sir," just "I understand."

I left him where he was standing, locked the door behind me, and returned to the pulpit. The angry whisperings suddenly died down when I took my place and they saw I had returned.

"What the hell is going on, Reverend?" demanded Mr. Whittaker.

"What kind of creature *was* that?" added Mrs. Hendricks.

I held up my hand for silence.

"I will explain," I said. I pulled my sermon out of my pocket and stared at it. It was about some of the sins we blunder into, sins like gluttony and sloth. Suddenly it seemed so *trivial*, so removed from the problems that existed right here in my church. "I was going to read this to you today," I said, "but I think I have something more important to talk about." I tore the sermon in half and let the pieces float to the floor.

I realized I had everyone's rapt attention, and I decided to start speaking before I lost it, and hope the words came out right.

"The disturbing sight you saw was Jackson, the robot that many of you have seen performing maintenance tasks around the church for the past few months. Like all robots, he has a compulsion to find defects and correct them." I paused and stared out across my flock. Their mood was ugly, but at least they were listening.

"One day, a few months ago, I decided to make use of that compulsion by practicing my sermons in front of him and having him point out any internal contradictions. This inevitably led him to point out things that we accept as articles of faith as being illogical and contradictory, and so that he would understand the difference between those statements and actual flaws in logic, I had him read the bible. I did not realize until recently that he took it as literal truth."

"It *is* the literal truth!" snapped Mr. Remington. "It's the Lord's word!"

"I know," I said. "But he thinks it applies to robots as well as to men. He believes that he has an immortal soul."

"A *machine*?" snorted Mr. Jameson. "That's blasphemy!"

"It's not enough that they take all our jobs," added Mrs. Willoughby. "Now they want to take over our churches too!"

"Blasphemy!" repeated Mr. Jameson.

"We must display some compassion," I urged. "Jackson is a moral and ethical entity whose only desire is to join this parish and pray to the Creator of all things. That's why he made a crude attempt to appear like a man—so that he could sit with you and commune with God. Is that really so terrible?"

"Send him to a robot church, if he can find one," said Mr. Remington, his voice filled with sarcasm and contempt. "This one's for *us*."

"It's not right, Reverend," said Mrs. Hendricks. "If *he* has a soul, then why not my vacuum cleaner, or my son's tank?"

"I'm just a man," I said, "and a flawed man at that. I don't pretend have all the answers, or even most of them. I will consider your objections during the coming week, and I want each of you to search your heart to see if there is some compassion in it for an entity, *any* entity, that wishes only to worship God in our company. Next Sunday, instead of a sermon, we will discuss our thoughts on the matter."

Even after I spoke they kept murmuring. They wanted to argue the subject right now, but I finally put an end to it and insisted that we all go home and sleep on it, that the subject needed serious consideration rather than knee-jerk reaction. I stood at the door to thank each of them for coming, as I always did, and three of the men refused to shake my hand. After the last of them had left,

I went back to the anteroom, unlocked it, and ordered Jackson to clean the cream off his face and hands and to put the tattered suit back where he found it.

I went home, found I was so upset that I wasn't hungry, and decided to take a long walk. It was dark when I got back, and I still hadn't resolved any of the issues. *Were* souls the exclusive possession of men? What about the day we finally encounter a sentient alien race out there among the stars? Or the day a dolphin or a chimpanzee prays to the same God I pray to? And if an alien, or a dolphin, why not a robot?

I didn't know when I got home, and after an almost sleepless night, I still didn't know.

I went back to the church in the morning. I knew something was amiss when I was still fifty yards away, because the doors were ajar, and Jackson never left them open. I entered, and it was clear that Jackson hadn't performed any of his morning duties. The floor was dirty, the flowers hadn't been watered, the garbage hadn't been taken out.

I decided that whether he had a soul or not, he was getting *too* damned human in his behavior. Herbie may have been a primitive early model, but he did his chores and never sulked or demonstrated his resentment. Only humans were allowed the luxury of foul moods and bad behavior.

Then I saw that the door to my office was hanging by a single hinge, and was damaged beyond repair. The first thought that came to me was that I'd been robbed, and I raced to the office, oblivious to the fact that there was nothing there worth stealing.

I froze when I reached the doorway. There, on the floor of the office, was Jackson. His metal body was covered with dents, one of his legs had been pulled off, an arm had been sawed in half, and his head was so battered that it was almost unrecognizable.

You didn't have to be a genius to figure out what had happened. My parishioners hadn't liked what Jackson had done, and they liked what I'd said even less, so they decided to make sure that they never had to share a pew with a robot. And these weren't strangers, or drunken hooligans. They were *my* flock, *my* parishioners. All I could think of was: *if this is the way they behave after all my hard work, what does that say about me, the man who was supposed to give them spiritual and moral guidance?*

I knelt down on the tile floor next to Jackson. God, he was a mess! The closer I looked, the more dents and holes I found in him. At least one of his attackers must have had something like an ice pick, and had just stabbed and stabbed and stabbed. Another had a saw that could cut through metal. Others had other things.

I wondered how much he had suffered. *Did* robots feel pain? I didn't think so, but I didn't think they believed in God either, so what did I know?

I decided to gather his various parts together. This was God's house, and it seemed like an obscene desecration to have him strewn all over the room. Then, when I moved his torso and his one connected arm, I saw a single sentence scratched into the tile with a metallic forefinger:

Forgive them, Father, for they know not what they do.

I handed in my resignation the next day. In fact, I quit my calling altogether. I've been a carpenter for the past eight years. It doesn't pay much, but it's honorable work, and as the bible makes clear, better men than I have chosen the same profession. My entire staff is composed of robots. I speak to them all the time, but I've yet to find one that's interested in anything other than carpentry.

As for Jackson, I returned him to the factory. I don't know why. He certainly deserved a Christian burial, but I didn't give him one. Did it mean that deep down I truly didn't think he could possess a soul? I don't know. The only thing I know is that I've been ashamed of myself ever since. Whatever his faults, he deserved better.

I don't know how they disposed of him. Broke him down for parts, I suppose. To this day I miss him, more than any man should miss a machine. Every Easter I drive over to the scrapheap behind his factory and place a wreath on it. I'm still religious enough to believe that he's aware of it, and maybe even appreciates it. In fact, I find myself thinking that if I lead a good enough life, I may see him again one of these years. And when I do, I'll tell him he was right all along.

He forgave the others; maybe he can forgive me too.

Copyright © 2008 by Mike Resnick.
First published in Jim Baen's Universe, *October 2008.*

Tina Gower grew up in a small community in Northern California that proudly boasts of having more cows than people. She raised guide dogs for the blind, is dyslexic, and can shoot a gun or bow and miraculously never hit the target (which at some point becomes a statistical improbability). Tina also won the Writers of the Future, the Daphne du Maurier Award for Mystery and Suspense (paranormal category), and was nominated for the Romance Writers of America Golden Heart (writing as Alice Faris). She has professionally published several short stories in a variety of magazines.

THE LAST DENTIST

by Tina Gower

Dr. Hersman had a reputation for breaking more teeth than he fixed. But he was the last dentist, so I didn't have a choice. Took me two weeks to walk the distance to where he was rumored to practice, and another three days to trap enough rabbits for trade.

There are wild strawberries that grow in the hills along the route. And just my luck, it was June and they were ripe. My mouth watered after the first taste, but I had to be disciplined or I'd eat them all. My payment needed to cover both top and bottom teeth.

I was three weeks from having my braces removed when the world ended. That was seven years ago. It was time.

I sheared my hair where the ends had split—had to look "town-good." Then I giggled until I cried over how excited I'd been back then that I would have my braces off in time for senior pictures. Graduation. Wow, that had been ages ago. I scrubbed my shirt and shorts in the creek and took extra time under my pits to wash the stink off.

The last teen girl's magazine printed had an article about braces—that after they come off, teens should treat themselves to a new outfit, earrings. Something fancy. I carved the bone from the rabbit to wrap in my braids. It would do.

The sun reflected in the water just enough so I could inspect my smile. Last time I'll see these metal disasters. Finally.

The trip into town was uneventful. Skeletons of long ago deceased were propped up in chairs along the road. They say some towns held a parade, wanting to keep morale up. I straightened, pretending they were here for me. The rabbits swung from a stick I slung over my back. My clothes dried as I trekked.

I reached the building, slinging the offerings over the front counter. A tall, bald, skinny man meandered from a back room. His bushy eyebrows arched high and he wiped his hands on a mud stained towel tucked into his belt. He puffed his cheeks out, but they were still gaunt.

"Come on back," he said, turning away before I answered. There was no dental assistant. No receptionist. No appointments needing to be made. The end of the world had both complicated and simplified life.

I slid into the chair, and Dr. Hersman tested his drill. The machine whined and choked like a long-time smoker.

"Oh, it's not a cavity," I corrected quickly. "I've had these braces—"

Dr. Hersman lowered the drill, looking relieved. "Sure. Hold on." He went back to his metal tool kit, using a finger to nudge items. He pulled out a pair of delicate plyers. "Here." He motioned for me to lay back.

His hip bumped the tool kit and a folded paper sailed to the ground like a dried leaf. He retrieved it, revealing a fancy foil-bordered certificate. He slid the folded, tattered page that had browned along all the folds under the bottom of the toolbox. It had flapped there from the breeze blowing in from the missing back wall.

First, he picked off the remaining rubber bands with a hook—seven years was a long time between maintenance visits—then removed the thick wire I'd bent while attempting in vain to lever it off myself with zero success. I'd broken down in year five and tried to eat foods that were forbidden by my orthodontist, no matter how rare. Finding a Snickers took a few years. It didn't work. Wish I hadn't believed things would go back to normal for so many years or I might have bribed the Knowledge Keepers earlier for the location of the last dentist.

Each bracket came off the bottom easier than I expected, popping off with a slight levering of his tool. Some brackets had already loosened, and they'd spin while I tried to eat. I kept them on for fear of how uncomfortable the blank spaces would be—I was relieved to be rid of them. When he finished, I held up my hand to take a minute to savor the slimy, slick feel of my lips along my newly smooth teeth. There were little bumps of tartar build up, but I'd take care of that. Everything was glorious until he got to the front teeth on my upper row. He changed positions to get a better angle. One gave. The second broke along with a sizeable shard of my tooth.

My hand flew to my mouth, my tongue instantly inspecting the sharp hole that went all the way up into the gum.

"You're gonna fix it, right?"

Dr. Hersman blinked at the bracket and bit of tooth still attached as if he couldn't believe the mistake. "Ran out of novocaine. Sorry."

"I don't care. I can't have a broken tooth; it will get infected. I could die."

"Root canal is too risky." He seemed to agree. "We need to pull it."

I wiped a tear that ran down my temple and nodded, gripping the arms of the chair.

He placed a cloth over my mouth. "Nothing to numb it, but a man a while back brought this in for a filling. Better than nothing."

The next thing I remembered was waking up with cotton in my mouth and dry drool along the corners of my lips. Dr. Hersman packed his things, inspecting the folded paper for a minute with no emotion. "Sorry about your smile, kid. You should keep a rabbit for that."

I nodded, still a bit groggy.

He dropped the page in the trash. I frowned and picked it up while his back was turned.

Dr. William Hersman, DDS Loma Linda School of Dentistry.

It had the year. Marked with honors. Signed by the dean. I flapped it to get his attention. He must have seen the question on my face.

"That's not me, kid. I just squatted here after the second Event. People kept bringing me things to fix their teeth and, well…. It's honest work." He left the room, and I heard the clanging of the tools in a sink that no longer pumped water.

I glanced down at the degree, remembering how it was said that the dentist broke more teeth than he fixed. Since I now knew he had never been to Dentristry school, one lost tooth was likely a good outcome, considering. I raised my fingers, touched my cut upper lip. I tasted the metallic tang of blood with each swallow. I removed the cotton and turned to the wall where an old mirror hung. Time to get used to my new smile.

David Cleden lives in the UK and works in London. Recently he won the Aeon Award for short fiction, and has previously been a James White Award winner, with published work in Interzone, Betwixt, Electric Spec and The Colored Lens. He won the Writers of the Future award in 2019 for his story "Dark Equations of the Heart" published in Volume 35. His day job is writing business proposals but turns to writing fiction after hours and is still working hard not to get the two muddled up. He lives in a household with a ridiculously large number of cute cats, as per the rules of all author bios.

HOW DOES MY GARDEN GROW?

by David Cleden

"Are you ill, Elke?" the ship's physician asks.

"No," I lie. Whatever I am, it's no one else's concern.

"I think you should have these." He slides a blister pack full of blue-white pills across the dispensing table. They nestle in their cocoons like tiny, fragile eggs.

I want to say that Dr. Vajrani has a kindly face. I think he used to, back in those heady early years soon after embarkation. Now though, he just looks tired and emaciated; skin drawn tight over cheekbones as though at some point on this great journey of ours he's forgotten how to smile.

My eyes drift to the shelf behind his head. There's a cluster of little toy Flexi-fun figures peeping down that I remember from my own childhood. Are they distractions for his younger patients or merely sentimental keepsakes? It seems each of us needs to cling on to a bit of our past.

I suppose eventually they'll figure out I'm not taking my other medication. They'll be able to measure some imbalance in the chemical and mineral constituents entering the recycling loop. One more piece of Closure lost.

Because everyone frets over the C number.

The entire sum of everything we are and everything we will be is contained within this ship. We're the ultimate closed environment. Maintaining resource equilibrium; well…how often have we been told it's not so much a goal as a pre-requisite for survival? No stopping off for supplies at some gas station along the way for us.

A C number of 1.0—perfect closure—is unattainable. Something about violating the laws of thermodynamics, I think? Don't ask me. But as long as we stay close to 1.0, stay *in the zone*, we're good for a couple of centuries.

So the higher-ups watch the C number as though our fate is determined by those numerals. Which it is, I suppose.

There's even a kind of clock. It's mounted on a plinth in the central municipal space where all the stunted trees grow and birdsong chirps on a loop from hidden speakers. It's there as a reminder that Closure hangs over us like some dark thundercloud. Not for us directly—it will be our children, or our children's children who'll pay the price of today's recklessness—even though no one knows for sure what awaits us around the dim, cold star that is our destination.

Why is the C-clock there at all? It's not as if any of us can forget.

Dr. Vajrani is studying me. I know this game. He's waiting so that sooner or later I'll spill some of my thoughts to fill the silence.

So I say nothing. I'm good at this game too.

"Very well. I think we're done, Elke. But if there's anything—"

I don't hear the end of his sentence because I'm already out the door, on the way back to my soul garden.

☼

Soul gardens.

Who came up with that name, I'd like to know? Someone like Dr. Vajrani, I bet.

They're just about the only things on the ship that aren't there for a practical reason. Everything else, the engines, life-support machines, fabrication units, agri-bays, schools and creches for the children—even the tiny parks for people to relax in—they all have a clear function.

Soul gardens have no purpose. They're just whatever you want them to be. It's good for the soul to have something to nurture.

Mine has three growing shelves, subdivided and planted according to a plan of my own devising. Soon I'm going to add a fourth. Right here, there's a patch of lime grass (symbolizing ambition and drive), growing tall and straight. Over there, the fading purple of chive flowers are hung with melancholy, drooping as though under some invisible burden. A section of the bottom tray is given over to *Fulmina partaxis*, one of my favorites. I often imagine my pent-up anger flowing into its tight little blood-red flowers. Right in the corner is a tiny patch where I scattered love-in-the-mist seed but it hasn't taken, still just bare soil. No wonder I feel so alone.

I draw off a little water from my allowance and moisten the bedding material. I trim here, neaten there. I add a few drops of liquid fertilizer made from rotting organics I've kept back. (That's going to land me in trouble if anyone finds out. All waste is supposed to be returned to central recycling.)

I can't begin to describe how much comfort I draw from my soul garden, often tending it three or four times a day when my work rota allows. Sometimes I take from it, and sometimes I give. It serves me well.

I think about the lie I told Dr. Vajrani as I caress the blue-black stem of an *Alchema dorix*. I let the lie drain out of me, flowing from my fingertips, imagining those dark flowers darkening a little more, unseen roots spreading outwards like inkstains beneath the soil—until I am calm again.

Home for me is in the deepest level of the ship. I like to imagine all those roots forcing their way down through hull material, thrusting at last into the blackness of space. I picture them turning blindly towards the dimming light of the old sun, or the faint pin-prick of the new.

But Dr. Vajrani has told me it's not healthy to think about what's outside.

A softly chiming alarm reminds me that my work-shift is about to start. Four days a week I serve on the Infrastructure Maintenance Crew. Mostly it involves scraping mold from inaccessible cabling conduits. We have robot moles to do this work but sometimes they get stuck and it's our job to figure out how to get them out. Usually we do, but sometimes it means lifting floor-gratings or dismantling wall panels and that tends to get the higher-ups very agitated. Occasionally even that doesn't work and we have to abandon the mole where it is. Everybody hates it when that happens. It means valuable resources put beyond use; another ding in the C number.

Closure.

It's the only topic of conversation these days.

I often think about those poor little robotic creatures burrowed deep into the skin of our ship, dead and slowly fossilizing, never to see the light of day again.

To me, those are the best days of all.

✡

We're standing inside Municipal Space #3, the largest on the ship, keeping vigil.

Not everyone's here because we wouldn't all fit in the space, so several hundred more are watching on screens elsewhere. But I'm near the front of the crowd, an invited special guest.

The Mayor is standing next to the C-clock making his speech. The Captain stands next to him, her face gray and impassive as though her mind is far away dealing with more important matters. I'm sure only half the crowd are listening anyway. Everyone's staring at the glowing numerals of the C-clock:

0.99726

It's not a good number, but a lot better than a year ago. That was when Closure dipped below 96 per cent for the first time ever, and we knew we were in trouble if people didn't act.

So people did. Thirty of them, my parents included. The Mayor drones on and we watch and wait, transfixed.

When it finally happens—that last digit morphing from a 6 to a 7—a ripple runs through the crowd. People smile and nudge their neighbors. The Mayor falters, glancing back over his shoulder at the clock. Then he turns back to the crowd beaming and raising his arms as though accepting their praise.

Malia Ng, my neighbor from across the corridor, leans close. "See?" she says, an unwanted arm snaking round my shoulders. "Such a brave sacrifice, but it's working. It really is! You should feel so proud."

My vision goes a little blurry and I wonder if I'm about to faint. I dip my hand into a pocket, finding the little bouquet of river mint freshly picked not half an hour ago from my soul garden. I crush a leaf and inhale the rich scent from my fingertips: a little pepperminty, a little sharp; hints of lime and sulfur. It centers me again and my vision clears.

I get such joy from my soul garden. But I also get contentment and melancholy, bliss and despair, hope

and fear—and much more besides. It's all there: all the fragrances and flavors. I pour my soul into it, and then I take from it whatever I need.

This last year has undoubtedly been tough. So much anger and resentment. *Fulmina partaxis* has colonized the bottom tray more than I'd like, a red stain under the artificial lights.

The Mayor is still talking about sacrifice, but I don't bother listening.

✡

Oscar Brandt is the leader of the Five-Nines Crew that comes calling. I know him a little (I know everyone a little—it can't be helped when you live in a community of five hundred, I suppose) but we're not exactly friends.

"You can't keep these flower trays in your room," he tells me.

"But I *need* my soul garden."

He's a big man, broad-shouldered and a little intimidating up close. But it's the others in the Five-Nines Crew who make me nervous. They shuffle around the apartment, fingering the few precious things I brought from Earth—photographs, a competition trophy, a faded cloth doll. They peer into cupboards, checking to make sure I'm not hoarding recyclables.

"I understand. But we all have to do our bit and get the C number back up to where it should be." His dark-eyed stare is unwavering and I don't like that. It makes me feel as though he can see right inside my head. "It's the least we can do to honor the Thirty."

OK. Well *that's* a low blow.

I can't make any counter-argument, not against the Thirty. They did, after all, sacrifice themselves, in a desperate bid to fix the Closure problem once and for all. Six per cent of the citizens. Six per cent of daily resource consumption removed from the loop. More of everything to go round for the rest of us.

And we still don't know if that was enough.

Slowly, slowly, we saw the C-number creep back up—just not nearly as much as everyone hoped.

"You hear about the disease outbreak in a couple of the agri-bays?" Brandt asks me. "And no one can figure out why seed germination rates are declining. Could be very bad news for harvest yields if we can't turn it around. So they've upped the bio-security protocols." He shrugs. "Soul gardens have to go. An order from the Captain herself. We can't take any risks."

Something flutters inside my chest like a wild, untamed creature trying to batter its way out.

"You can't! My soul garden—it…it means the world to me."

The world? Now *that's* a quaint expression. I don't have a world anymore. We are all of us between worlds.

"Sure, it's a big ask, Elke, but we have to get the C number back to five-nines. Or better, if we can. Remember the Thirty." His smile is thin, and I know what he's thinking. One more would have helped things along nicely.

✧

The Five-Nines Crew are back the next day, come to destroy my soul garden. Two of them hold me tight by the arms while I scream and sob and struggle uselessly in a grip that is never going to relent.

I watch the precious contents of those trays transferred into recycling sacks: uprooted plants for the micro-shredder and compost processor, growing medium for sterilization; all of it destined to become part of an agri-bay once more. Everything weighed and accounted for.

I feel sick in the pit of my stomach. I can taste a little of the kava on my tongue, but also miller's-tail and white sage and culantro—a little of everything that I've sampled from my soul garden, roiling in my stomach just as the matching emotions churn in my head.

The crew seals the last sack tight and leave.

My soul garden is both gone and not gone.

✧

There's a hateful part of my job which is attending to the air-filtration machines that keep our atmosphere fresh and viable. Sometimes it means wriggling deep inside their conduits, checking filters, replacing worn bearings, and scraping away any thriving colonies of mold. (Which must be carefully collected and recycled for composting, of course. Everything is part of the cycle. Feed the C number! Help close the loop!)

Altering the maintenance roster to gain access to conduit 43-B isn't hard. It's not as if anyone's going to

fight me for the privilege of grabbing a respirator and mold-scraper and crawling into those tight spaces.

43-B is one of the larger ducts. There's an access panel right next to a big air filtration unit and about thirty meters of conduit just wide enough to wriggle along before the next booster fan. There'll be all kinds of holy hell if my secret growing space is discovered, but honestly, I don't see how it can be hurting anyone.

It's hardly anything. My torch-beam picks out one little growing tray duct-taped to the floor. There's no lighting because I couldn't figure out how to rig something that wouldn't be detected.

Only…now I see it's all been for nothing. My dancing beam picks out a shriveled tuft of mint, ghost pale, its leaf tips curling in on themselves. Myrtle, chicory, lemon verbana—all are dead or dying. Only the blood-red heads of *Fulmina partaxis* seem to cling impossibly to life.

What had I expected—with near darkness and a constant air-flow wicking away moisture? Only mold survives those conditions.

Something in my chest tightens with an angry, vice-like grip.

My fingers gently caress the dying stems as I let my frustration and rage bubble and froth like a pan of milk on the boil. I grow aware of this cramped space pinning me down; a tiny, sightless mite burrowed into the ship's flesh, and an odd thought comes to me. Why are there no windows on the ship? No relayed images of the shrinking Sun?

Because we're not supposed to remember the past, that's why.

My rage boils over, turning to hissing steam as my breaths come louder and faster, amplified within the confines of my respirator. I let it flow out of me. In the torchlight, the *partaxis* flowers look darker than before; blood-red become black. I crush their fragile heads in my fingers, watching their powdery dust drawn away on the gentle air currents.

Hours pass as I sit in the semi-darkness, alone with my churning thoughts, waiting for calmness to return. I am mourning the very last part of my soul garden, now broken up and scattered to the four artificial winds.

When at last I haul myself out of the conduit, I'm grateful there's no one around to see. I make my way back to my apartment and drop into a deep and welcoming sleep, already missing my little garden which has left a fathomless hole in my soul that can never be filled.

Only silence and solitude can comfort me.

✧

I ask Dr. Vajrani if I can start a new soul garden.

"I think that would be a wonderful idea, Elke."

"You do? Because I don't think I can carry all of it around in my head for much longer. Everything's jammed up inside. All those different scents and fragrances tangled like a big ball of string. They're pressing to get out and making my head hurt."

"Then you should start at once, Elke. In fact, I know what. I think you should use one of the agribays. I'm sure there's room to spare now."

"Really? That's wonderful!"

I waggle my little cloth doll happily so that it smooches with one of the Flexi-fun figures I've swiped from Vajrani's shelf. The figure has a frown and a tiny stethoscope around its neck; a perfect avatar for Dr. Vajrani. "Let me give you a big sloppy kiss to thank you!" my doll says.

Bored now, I wander out of Vajrani's consulting room, not meeting anyone as I wander the curving corridors, stroll in the green spaces, help myself to snacks from the food dispensary.

That's good. People make the ship seem crowded, the spaces a little smaller than they really are. Sometimes the ship reminds me of a resort complex we holidayed in once when I was tiny. It's comforting to imagine I could just step outside whenever I want. Maybe there'd be an ocean nearby with waves breaking on an endless golden beach, and seagulls turning lazy circles in the air. Maybe it really is there, just waiting for me. All I have to do is find the door.

My head still hurts. Three days and the pain and nausea are only now beginning to ebb. There are fat, unseen fingers drumming on my skull, sending little stabby waves of pain through my brain. That's my soul garden anxious to be free again.

I turn and begin walking toward the closed-off sections of the ship where the agri-bays are. Naturally, access is tightly controlled; only the palm-prints of the hydroponic techs open those doors. I've only ever seen pictures of what's inside.

I thrust my hand into the deep pockets of my coveralls. There is already a hand in there. It isn't mine. The door to the agri-bay opens to its palm-print.

Plans for my new soul garden bubble and fizz in my mind. I'll only need a little space. At first.

More *partaxis*, that'll be important. I have a lot of pent-up anger to offload. And lemon balm too, just because it smells so wonderful.

I halt outside Municipal Space #3. The numerals on the Closure clock are a fierce bright red, the color of a dying sun. In all the time I can remember, I've never seen it set like this.

But why not? There are many fewer mouths to feed now. All the nutrients and rare elements from those who are no longer living are being recycled via the composting machines. Consumables stores have been replenished. Nothing has gone to waste. And the daily resource demands of nearly five hundred people have been slashed; a big strain on the system removed.

Come on, Elke, I tell myself, *there's work to be done.* Heart-wrenching, back-breaking work. So many bodies! It takes all I've got just to drag each one to the composter. I try my hardest not to look at their faces, but the marks of toxin-induced asphyxia—those blued lips and tortured expressions—are soon etched deep into my brain.

Traces are still in the recycled air. Even now, I can feel a ghost-hand tightening around my own throat. I think it will take a few more days before the air-scrubbers have removed the last traces of *partaxis* toxin.

I stare at the numbers on the C-clock, marveling at the straight row of nines that stretch as far as there are digits to display. Of course a 1.0 would be even better, but that's not possible. No system is perfect. Closure is a goal you chase but don't ever reach. It has bought time and solitude and serenity, though.

I doubt I'll live long enough to feel real soil beneath my feet again, breathe the wonderful scents of an unfiltered atmosphere, wander where I please without boundaries. But if I grow tired of waiting, maybe I'll go looking for that door. One day I'll step outside onto the golden beach that awaits.

And that's a thought that brings its own kind of closure.

Copyright © 2021 by David Cleden.

Robert Silverberg has been a professional writer since 1955, and has published more than a hundred books and close to a thousand short stories. Among his best-known novels are Lord Valentine's Castle, Dying Inside, Nightwings, The World Inside, *and* Downward to the Earth. *He is a many-time winner of the Hugo and Nebula awards, was named a Grand Master by the Science Fiction Writers of America in 2004, and lives with his wife Karen in the San Francisco Bay Area. They and an assortment of cats share a sprawling house of unusual architectural style, surrounded by exotic plants.*

THE FAR SIDE OF THE BELL-SHAPED CURVE

by Robert Silverberg

Sarajevo was lovely on that early summer day. The air sparkled, the breeze off the mountains was strong and pungent, the whitewashed villas glittered in the morning sunlight. Reichenbach, enchanted by the beauty of the place and spurred by a sense of impending excitement, stepped buoyantly out of a dark cobbled alley and made his way in quick virile strides toward the river's right embankment. It was nearly 10:30.

A crowd of silent, sullen Bosnian burghers lined the embankment. The black-and-gold Hapsburg banners fluttered from every lamppost and balcony. In a little while the archduke Franz Ferdinand, the emperor's nephew and heir, would come this way with his duchess in their open-topped car. Venturing into dangerous territory, they were, into a province of disaffected and reluctant citizens.

The townsfolk stirred faintly. The townsfolk muttered. Like puddings, Reichenbach thought, they awaited in a dull, dutiful way their future monarch. But he knew they must be seething with revolutionary fervor inside.

Reichenbach looked about him for dark taut youths with the peculiar bright-eyed look of assassins. No one nearby seemed to fit the pattern. He let his gaze wander up the hills to the dense cypress groves, the ancient wooden houses, the old Turkish mosques

topped by slender, splendid minarets and back down toward the river to the crowd again. And—

Who is she?

He noticed her for the first time, no more than a dozen meters to his left, in front of the Bank of Austria-Hungary building: a tall auburn-haired woman of striking presence and aura, who in this mob of coarse, rough folk radiated such supreme alertness and force that Reichenbach knew at once she must be of his sort. Yes! He had come here alone, certain he would find an appropriate companion, and that confidence now was affirmed.

He began to move toward her.

His eyes met hers and she nodded and smiled in recognition and acknowledgment.

"Have you just arrived?" Reichenbach asked in German.

She answered in Serbian. "Three days ago."

Smoothly he shifted languages. "How did I fail to see you?"

"You were looking everywhere else. I saw you at once. You came this morning?"

"Fifteen minutes ago."

"Does it please you so far?"

"Very much," he said. "Such a picturesque place. Like a medieval fantasy. Time stands still here."

Her eyes were mischievous. "Time stands still everywhere," she said, moving on into English.

Reichenbach smiled. Again he matched her change of language. "I take your meaning. And I think you take mine. This charming architecture, the little river, the ethnic costumes—it's hard to believe that a vast and hideous war is going to spring from so quaint a place."

"A nice irony, yes. And it's for ironies that we make these journeys, *n'est ce pas?*"

"*Vraiment.*"

They were standing quite close now. He felt a current flowing between them, a pulsating, almost tangible force.

"Join me later for a drink?" he said.

"Certainly. I am Ilsabet."

"Reichenbach."

He longed to ask her when she had come from. But of course that was taboo.

"Look," she said. "The archduke and duchess."

The royal car, inching forward, had reached them. Franz Ferdinand, red-faced and tense in preposterous comic-opera uniform, waved half-heartedly to the bleakly staring crowd. Drab, plump Sophie beside him, absurdly overdressed, forced a smile. They were meaty-looking, florid people, rigid and nervous, all but clinging to each other in their nervousness.

"Now it starts," he said.

"Yes. The foreplay." She slipped her arm through his.

Not far away a tall, young, sallow-faced man appeared as if he had sprung from the pavement—wild hyperthyroid eyes, bobbing Adam's apple, a sure desperado—and hurled something. It landed just behind the royal car. An odd popping sound—the detonator—and then Reichenbach heard a loud bang. There was a blurt of black smoke and the car behind the archduke's lurched and crumpled, dumping aides-de-camp into the street. The cortege halted abruptly. The imperial couple, unharmed, sat weirdly upright as if their survival depended on keeping their spines straight. A functionary riding with them said in a clear voice, "A bomb has gone off, your highness." And Franz Ferdinand, calm, disgusted: "I rather expected something like that. Look after the injured, will you?"

Ilsabet's hand tightened on Reichenbach's forearm as the bizarre comedy unfolded: the cars motionless, archduke and duchess still in plain view, the assassin wildly vaulting a parapet and plunging into the shallow river, police pursuing, pouncing, beating him with the flats of their swords, the crowd milling in confusion. At last the damaged car was pushed to the side of the road and the remaining vehicles rapidly drove off.

"End of act one," Ilsabet said, laughing.

"And forty minutes until act two. That drink, now?"

"I know a sidewalk café near here."

Under a broad turquoise umbrella Reichenbach had a slivovitz, Ilsabet a mug of dark beer. The stolid citizens at the surrounding tables talked more of hunting and fishing than of the bungled assassination. Reichenbach, pretending to be casual, studied Ilsabet hungrily. A cool, keen intelligence gleamed in her penetrating green eyes. Everything about her was sleek, self-possessed, sure. She was so much like him that he almost feared her, and that was a new feeling for him. What he feared most of all was that he would blunder here at the outset and lose her; but he knew, deep beneath all doubts, that he would not. They were meant for each other. He liked to believe that she came from his moment, and that there would be a chance to continue in realtime, when they had returned from displacement, whatever they began on this jaunt. Of course, one did not speak of such things.

Instead he said, "Where do you go next?"

"The burning of Rome. And you?"

"A drink with Shakespeare at the Mermaid Tavern."

"How splendid. I never thought of doing that."

He drew a deep breath and said, "We could do it together," and hesitated, watching her expression. She did not look displeased. "After we've heard Nero play his concerto. Eh?"

She seemed amused. "I like that idea."

He raised his glass. *"Prosit."*

"Zdravlje."

They snaked wrists, clinked glasses.

For a few minutes more they talked—lightly, playfully. He studied her gestures, her sentence structure, her use of idiom, seeking in the subtlest turns of her style some clue that might tell him that they were co-temporals, but she gave him nothing: a shrewd game player, this one. At length he said, "It's nearly time for the rest of the show."

Ilsabet nodded. He scattered some coins on the table and they returned to the embankment, walked up to the Latin Bridge, turned right into Franz Joseph Street. Shortly the royal motorcade, returning from a city-hall reception, came rolling along. There appeared to be some disagreement over the route: chauffeurs and aides-de-camp engaged in a noisy dispute and suddenly the royal car stopped. The chauffeur seemed to be trying to put the car into reverse. There was a clashing of gears. A gaunt boy emerged from a coffeehouse not three meters from the car, less than ten from Reichenbach and Ilsabet. He looked dazed, like a sleepwalker, as if astounded to find himself so close to the imperial heir. This is Gavrilo Princip, Reichenbach thought, the second and true assassin; but he felt little interest in what was about to happen. The gun was out, the boy was taking aim. But Reichenbach watched Ilsabet, more concerned with the quality of her reactions than with the deaths of two trivial people in fancy costumes. Thus he missed seeing the fatal shot through Franz Ferdinand's pouter-pigeon chest, though he observed Ilsabet's quick, frosty smile of satisfaction. When he glanced back at the royal car he saw the archduke sitting upright, stunned, tunic and lips stained with red, and the boy firing at the duchess. There was consternation among the aides-de-camp. The car sped away. It was 11:15.

"So," said Ilsabet. "Now the war begins, the dynasties topple, a civilization crumbles. Did you enjoy it?"

"Not as much as I enjoyed the way you smiled when the archduke was shot."

"Silly."

"The slaughter of a pair of overstuffed simpletons is ultimately less important to me than your smile."

It was risky: too strong too soon, maybe? But it got through to her the right way, producing a faint quirking of her lip that told him she was pleased.

"Come," she said, and took him by the hand.

Her hotel was an old gray stone building on the other side of the river. She had an elegant balconied room on the third floor, river view, ornate gas chandeliers, heavy damask draperies, capacious canopied bed. This era's style was certainly admirable, Reichenbach thought—lavish, slow, rich; even in a little provincial town like this, everything was deluxe. He shed his tight and heavy clothing with relief. She wore her timer high, a pale taut band just beneath her breasts. Her eyes glittered as she reached for him and drew him down beneath the canopy. At this moment at the other end of town, Franz Ferdinand and Sophie were dying. Soon there would be exchanges of stiff diplomatic notes, declarations of war by Austria-Hungary against Serbia, Germany against Russia and France, Europe engulfed in flames, the battle of the Marne, Ypres, Verdun, the Somme, the flight of the Kaiser, the armistice, the transformation of the monarchies—he had studied it all with such keen intensity, and now, having seen the celebrated assassinations that triggered everything, he was unmoved. Ilsabet had eclipsed the Great War for him.

No matter. There would be other epochal events to savor. They had all history to wander.

"To Rome, now," he said huskily.

☼

They rose, bathed, embraced, winked conspiratorially. They were off to a good start. Hastily they gathered their 1914 gear, waistcoats and petticoats and boots and all that, within the prescribed two-meter radius. They synchronized their timers and embraced again, naked, laughing, bodies pressed tight together, and went soaring across the centuries.

At the halfway house outside imperial Rome, they underwent their preparations, receiving their Roman hairstyles and clothing, their hypnocourses in Latin, their purses of denarii and sestertii, their plague inoculations, their new temporary names. He was Quintus Junius Veranius, she was Flavia Julia Lepida.

Nero's Rome was smaller and far less grand than he expected—the Colosseum was still in the future, there was no Arch of Titus, even the Forum seemed sparsely built. But the city was scarcely mean. The first day, they strolled vast gardens and dense, crowded markets, stared in awe at crazy Caligula's bridge from the Palatine to the Capitoline, went to the baths, gorged themselves at their inn on capon and truffled boar. On the next, they attended the gladiatorial games and afterward made love with frantic energy in a chamber they had hired near the Campus Martius. There was a wonderful frenzy about the city that Reichenbach found intoxicating, and Ilsabet, he knew, shared his fervor: her eyes were aglow, her face gleamed. They could hardly bear to sleep, but explored the narrow winding streets from dark to dawn.

They knew, of course, that the fire would break out in the Circus Maximus where it adjoined the Palatine and Caelian hills, and took care to situate themselves safely atop the Aventine, where they had a fine view. There they watched the fierce blaze sweeping through the Circus, climbing the hills, dipping to ravage the lower ground. No one seemed to be fighting the fire; indeed, Reichenbach thought he could detect subsidiary fires flaring up in the outlying districts, as though arson were the sport of the hour, and soon those fires joined with the main one. The sky rained black soot; the stifling summer air was thick and almost impossible to breathe. For the first two days the destruction had a kind of fascinating beauty, as temples and mansions and arcades melted away, the Rome of centuries being unbuilt before their eyes. But then the discomfort, the danger, the monotony, began to pall on him. "Shall we go?" he said.

"Wait," Ilsabet replied. The conflagration seemed to have an almost sexual impact on her: she glistened with sweat, she trembled with some strange joy as the flames leaped from district to district. She could not get enough. And she clung to him in tight feverish embrace. "Not yet," she murmured, "not so soon. I want to see the emperor."

Yes. And here was Nero now, returning to town from holiday. In grand procession he crossed the charred city, descending from his litter now and then to inspect some ruined shrine or palace. They caught a glimpse of him as he entered the Gardens of Maecenas—thick-necked, paunchy, spindle-shanked, foul of complexion. "Oh, look," Ilsabet whispered. "He's *beautiful*! But where's the fiddle?" The emperor carried no fiddle, but he was grotesquely garbed in some kind of theatrical costume and his cheeks were daubed with paint. He waved and flung coins to the crowd and ascended the garden tower. For a better view, no doubt. Ilsabet pressed herself close to Reichenbach. "My throat is on fire," she said. "My lungs are choked with ashes. Take me to London. Show me Shakespeare."

✧

There was smoke in the dark Cheapside alehouse too, thick sweet smoke curling up from sputtering logs on a dank February day. They sat in a cobwebbed corner playing word games while waiting for the actors to arrive. She was quick and clever, just as clever as he. Reichenbach took joy in that. He loved her for her agility and strength of soul. "Not many could be carrying off this tour," he told her. "Only special ones like us."

She grinned. "We who occupy the far side of the bell-shaped curve."

"Yes. Yes. It's horrible of us to have such good opinions of ourselves, isn't it?"

"Probably. But they're well earned, my dear."

He covered her hand with his, and squeezed, and she squeezed back. Reichenbach had never known anyone like her. Deeper and deeper was she drawing him, and his delight was tempered only by the knowledge that when they returned to realtime, to that iron world beyond the terminator where all paradoxes canceled out and the delicious freedoms of the jaunter did not apply, he must of necessity lose her. But there was no hurry about returning.

Voices, now: laughter, shouts, a company of men entering the tavern, actors, poets perhaps, Burbage, maybe, Heminges, Allen, Condell, Kemp, Ben Jonson possibly, and who was that, slender, high forehead, those eyes like lamps in the dark? Who else could it be? Plainly Shagspere, Chaxper, Shackspire, however they spelled it, surely Sweet Will here among these men calling for sack and malmsey, and behind that broad forehead Hamlet and Mercutio must be teeming, Othello, Hotspur, Prospero, Macbeth. The sight of him excited Reichenbach as Nero had Ilsabet. He inclined his head, hoping to hear scraps of dazzling table-talk, some bit of newborn verse, some talk of a play taking form; but at this distance everything blurred. "I have to go to him," Reichenbach muttered.

"The regulations?"

"*Je m'en fous t*he regulations. I'll be quick. People of our kind don't need to worry about the regulations. I promise you, I'll be quick."

She winked and blew him a kiss. She looked gorgeously sluttish in her low-fronted gown.

Reichenbach felt a strange quivering in his calves as he crossed the straw-strewn floor to the far-off crowded table.

"Master Shakespeare!" he cried.

Heads turned. Cold eyes glared out of silent faces. Reichenbach forced himself to be bold. From his purse he took two slender, crude shilling-pieces and put them in front of Shakespeare. "I would stand you a flagon or two of the best sack," he said loudly, "in the name of good Sir John."

"Sir John?" said Shakespeare, blank-faced. He frowned and shook his head. "Sir John Woodcocke, d'ye mean? Sir John Holcombe? I know not your Sir John, fellow."

Reichenbach's cheeks blazed. He felt like a fool.

A burly man beside Shakespeare said, with a rough nudge, "Me-thinks he speaks of Falstaff, Will. Eh? You recall your Falstaff?"

"Yes," Reichenbach said. "In truth I mean no other."

"Falstaff," Shakespeare said in a distant way. He looked displeased, uncomfortable. "I recall the name, yes. Friend, I thank you, but take back your shillings. It is bad custom for me to drink of strangers' sack."

Reichenbach protested, but only fitfully, and quickly he withdrew lest the moment grow ugly: plainly these folk had no use for his wine or for him, and to be wounded in a tavern brawl here in A.D. 1604 would bring monstrous consequences in real-time. He made a courtly bow and retreated. Ilsabet, watching, wore a cat-grin. He went slinking back to her, upset, bitterly aware he had bungled his cherished meeting with Shakespeare and, worse, had looked bumptious in front of her.

"We should go," he said. "We're unwelcome here."

"Poor dear one. You look so miserable."

"The contempt in his eyes—"

"No," she said. "The man is probably bothered by strangers all the time. And he was, you know, with his friends in the sanctuary of his own tavern. He meant no personal rebuke."

"I expected him to be different—to be one of *us*, to reach out toward me and draw me to him, to—to—"

"No," said Ilsabet gently. "He has his life, his wife, his pains, his problems. Don't confuse him with your fantasy of him. Come, now. You look so glum, my dear. Find yourself again!"

"Somewhen else."

"Yes. Somewhen else."

Under her deft consolations the sting of his oafishness at the Mermaid Tavern eased, and his mood brightened as they went onward. Few words passed between them: a look, a smile, the merest of contacts, and they communicated. Attending the trial of Socrates, they touched fingertips lightly, secretly, and it was the deepest of communions. Afterward they made love beneath the clear, bright winter sky of Athens on a gray-green hillside rich with lavender and myrtle, and emerged from shivering ecstasies to find themselves with an audience of mournful scruffy goats—a perfect leap of context and metaphor, and for days thereafter they made one another laugh with only the most delicate pantomimed reminder of the scene. Onward they went to see grim, limping, austere old Magellan sail off around the world with his five little ships from the mouth of the Guadalquivir, and at a whim they leaped to India, staining their skins and playing at Hindus as they viewed the expedition of Vasco da Gama come sailing into harbor at Calicut, and then it seemed proper to go on to Spain in dry, hot summer to drink sour white wine and watch ruddy freckled-faced Columbus get his pitiful little fleet out to sea.

Of course, they took other lovers from time to time. That was part of the game, too tasty a treat to forswear. In Byzantium, on the eve of the Frankish conquest, he passed a night with a dark-eyed voluptuous Greek who oiled her breasts with musky mysterious unguents, and Ilsabet with a towering garlicky Swede of the imperial guard, and when they found each other the next day, just as the Venetian armada burst into the Bosporus, they described to one another in the most flamboyant of detail the strangenesses of their night's sport—the tireless Norseman's toneless bellowing of sagas in his hottest moments: the Byzantine's startling, convulsive, climactic fit, almost epileptic in style, and, as she had admitted playfully at dawn, mostly a counterfeit. In Cleopatra's Egypt, while waiting for glimpses of the queen and Antony, they diverted themselves with a dark-eyed Coptic pair, brother and sister, no more than children and blithely interchangeable in bed. At the crowning of Charlemagne she found herself a Frankish merchant who offered her an estate along the Rhine, and he a mysteriously elliptical dusky woman who claimed to be a Catalonian Moor, but who—Reichenbach suddenly realized a few days later—must almost certainly have been a jaunter like himself, playing elegant games with him.

All this lent spice to their love and did no harm. These separate but shared adventures only enhanced the intensity of the relationship they were welding. He prayed the jaunt would never end, for Ilsabet was the perfect companion, his utter match, and so long as they sprinted together through the aeons, she was his, though he knew that would end when realtime reclaimed him. Nevertheless, that sad moment still was far away, and he hoped before then to find some way around the inexorable rules, some scheme for locating her and continuing with her in his own true time. Small chance of that, he knew. In the world beyond the terminator there was no time-jaunting; jaunting could be done only in the fluid realm of "history," and history was arbitrarily defined as everything that had happened before the terminator year of 2187. The rest was realtime, rigid and immutable, and what if her realtime were fifty years ahead of his, or fifty behind? There was no bridging that by jaunting. He did not know her realtime locus, and he did not dare ask. Deep as the love between them had come to be, Reichenbach still feared offending her through some unpardonable breach of their special etiquette.

With all the world to choose from, they sometimes took brief solo jaunts. That was Ilsabet's idea, holidays within their holiday, so that they would not grow stale with one another. It made sense to him. Thereupon he vaulted to the Paris of the 1920s to sip Pernod on the Boulevard Saint-Germain and peer at Picasso and Hemingway and Joyce, she in epicanthic mask of old Cathay to see Kublai Khan ride in triumph through the Great Wall, he to Cape Kennedy to watch the great Apollo rocket roaring moonward, she to London for King Charles's beheading. But these were brief adventures, and they reunited quickly, gladly, and went on hand in hand to their next together, to the fall of Troy and the diamond jubilee of Queen Victoria and the assassination of Lincoln and the sack of Carthage. Always when they returned from separate exploits, they regaled each other with extensive narratives of what had befallen them, the sights, the tastes, the ironies and perceptions, and, of course, the amorous interludes. By now Reichenbach and Ilsabet had accumulated an elaborate fabric of shared experience, a richness of joint history that gave them virtually a private language of evocative recollection, so that the slightest of cues— a goat on a hill, the taste of burned toast, the sight of a lop-eared beggar—sprang them into an intimate realm that no one else could ever penetrate: their unique place, furnished with their own things, the artifacts of love, the treasures of memory. And even that which they did separately became interwoven in that fabric, as of the telling of events as they lay in each other's arms had transformed those events into communal possessions.

Yet gradually Reichenbach realized that something was beginning to go wrong.

From a solo jaunt to Paris in 1794, where she toured the Reign of Terror, Ilsabet returned strangely evasive. She spoke in brilliant detail of the death of Robespierre and the sad despoliation of Notre Dame, but what she reported was mere journalism, with no inner meaning. He had to fish for information. Where had she lodged? Had she feared for her safety? Had she had interesting conversations with the Parisians? Shrugs, deflections. Had she taken a lover? Yes, yes, a fleeting liaison, nothing worth talking about; and then it was back to an account of the mobs, the tumbrels, the sound of the guillotine. At first Reichenbach accepted that without demur, though her vaguenesses violated their custom. But she remained moody and oblique while they were visiting the Crucifixion, and as they were about to depart for the Black Death she begged off, saying she needed another day to herself, and would go to Prague for the premiere of *Don Giovanni*. That too failed to trouble him—he was not musical—and he spent the day observing Waterloo from the hills behind Wellington's troops. When Ilsabet rejoined him in the late spring of 1349 for the Black Death in London, though, she seemed even more preoccupied and remote, and told him little of her night at the opera. He began to feel dismay, for they had been marvelously close and now she was obviously voyaging on some other plane. The plague-smitten city seemed to bore her. Her only flicker of animation came toward evening, in a Southwark hostelry, when as they dined on gristly lamb a stranger entered, a tall, gaunt, sharp-bearded man with the obvious aura of a jaunter. Reichenbach did not fail to notice the rebirth of light in Ilsabet's eyes, and the barely perceptible inclining-forward of her body as the stranger approached their table was amply perceptible to him. The newcomer knew them for what they were, naturally, and invited himself to join them. His name was Stavanger; he had been on his jaunt just a few days; he meant to see everything, *everything, b*efore his time was up. Not for many years had Reichenbach felt such jealousy. He was wise in these things, and it was not difficult to detect the current flowing from Ilsabet to Stavanger even as he sat there between them. Now he understood why she had no casual amours to report of her jaunts to

Paris and Prague. This one was far from casual and would bear no retelling.

In the morning she said, "I still feel operatic. I'll go to Bayreuth tonight—the premiere of *Götterdämmerung*."

Despising himself, he said, "A capital idea. I'll accompany you."

She looked disconcerted. "But music bores you!"

"A flaw in my character. Time I began to remedy it."

The fitful panic in Ilsabet's eyes gave way to cool and chilling calmness. "Another time, dear love. I prize my solitude. I'll make this little trip without you."

It was all plain to him. Gone now the open sharing; now there were secret rendezvous and an unwanted third player of their game. He could not bear it. In anguish he made his own arrangements and jaunted to Bayreuth in thick red wig and curling beard, and there she was, seated beside Stavanger in the Festspielhaus as the subterranean orchestra launched into the first notes. Reichenbach did not remain for the performance.

☼

Stavanger now crossed their path openly and with great frequency. They met him at the siege of Constantinople, at the San Francisco earthquake, and at a fete at Versailles. This was more than coincidence, and Reichenbach said so to Ilsabet. "I suggested he follow some of our itinerary," she admitted. "He's a lonely man, jaunting alone. And quite charming. But of course if you dislike him, we can simply vanish without telling him where we're going, and he'll never find us again."

A disarming tactic, Reichenbach thought. It was impossible for her to admit to him that she and Stavanger were lovers, for there was too much substance to their affair; so instead she pretended he was a pitiful forlorn wanderer in need of company. Reichenbach was outraged. Fidelity was not part of his unspoken compact with her, and she was free to slip off to any era she chose for a tryst with Stavanger. But that she chose to conceal what was going on was deplorable, and that she was finding pretexts to drag Stavanger along on their travels, puncturing the privacy of their own rapport for the sake of a few smug stolen glances, was impermissible. Reichenbach was convinced now that Ilsabet and

Stavanger were co-temporals, though he knew he had no rational basis for that idea; it simply seemed right to him, a final torment, the two of them now laying the groundwork for a realtime relationship that excluded him. Whether or not that was true, it was unbearable. Reichenbach was astounded by the intensity of his jealous fury. Yet it was a true emotion and one he would not attempt to repress. The joy he had known with Ilsabet had been unique, and Stavanger had tainted it.

He found himself searching for ways to dispose of his rival.

Merely whirling Ilsabet off elsewhen would achieve nothing. She would find ways of catching up with her paramour somewhere along the line. And if Ilsabet and Stavanger were co-temporal, and she and Reichenbach were not—no, no, Stavanger had to be expunged. Reichenbach, a stable and temperate man, had never imagined himself capable of such criminality; a bit of elitist regulation-bending was all he had ever allowed himself. But he had never been faced with the loss of an Ilsabet before, either.

In Borgia, Italy, Reichenbach hired a Florentine prisoner to do Stavanger in with a dram of nightshade. But the villain pocketed Reichenbach's down payment and disappeared without a care for the ducats due him on completion of the job. In the chaotic aftermath of the Ides of March, Reichenbach attempted to finger Stavanger as one of Caesar's murderers, but no one paid attention. Nor did he have luck denouncing him to the Inquisition one afternoon in 1485 in Torquemada's Castile, though even the most perfunctory questioning would have given sufficient proof of Stavanger's alliance with diabolical powers. Perhaps it would be necessary, Reichenbach concluded morosely, to deal with Stavanger with his own hands, repellent though that alternative was.

Not only was it repellent, it could be dangerous. He was without experience at serious crime, and Stavanger, cold-eyed and suave, promised to be a formidable adversary: Reichenbach needed an ally, an adviser, a collaborator. But who? While he and Ilsabet were making the circuit of the Seven Wonders, he puzzled over it, from Ephesus to Halicarnassus, to Gizeh, and as they stood in the shadow of the Colossus of Rhodes, the answer came to him. There was only one person he could trust sufficiently, and that person was himself.

To Ilsabet he said, "Do you know where I want to go next?"

"We still have the Hanging Gardens of Babylon, the Lighthouse of Alexandria, the Statue of Zeus at—"

"No, I'm not talking about the Seven Wonders tour. I want to go back to Sarajevo, Ilsabet."

"Sarajevo? Whatever for?"

"A sentimental pilgrimage, love, to the place of our first meeting."

"But Sarajevo was a bore. And—"

"We could make it exciting. Consider: our earlier selves would already be there. We would watch them meet, find each other well matched, become lovers. Here for months we've been touring the great events of history, when we're neglecting a chance to witness our own personal greatest event." He smiled wickedly. "And there are other possibilities. We could introduce ourselves to them. Hint at the joys that lie ahead of them. Perhaps even seduce them, eh? A nice kinky quirky business that would be. And—"

"No," she said. "I don't like it."

"You find the idea improper? Morally offensive?"

"Don't be an idiot. I find it dangerous."

"How so?"

"We aren't supposed to reenter a time-span where we're already present. There must be some good reason for that. The rules—"

"The rules," he said, "are made by timid old sods who've never moved beyond the terminator in their lives. The rules are meant to guide us, not to control us. The rules are meant to be broken by those who are smart enough to avoid the consequences."

She stared somberly at him a long while. "And are you?"

"I think I am."

"Yes. A shrewd man, a superior man, a member of the elite corps who lives on the far side of society's bell-shaped curve. Eh? Doing as you please throughout life. Holding yourself above all restraints. Rich enough and lucky enough to be able to jaunt anywhen you like and behave like a little god."

"You live the same way, I believe."

"In general, yes. But I still won't go with you to Sarajevo."

"Why not?"

"Because I don't know what will happen to me if I do. Kinky and quirky it may be to pile into bed with our other selves, but something about the idea troubles me, and I dislike needless risk. Do you believe you understand paradox theory fully?"

"Does anybody?"

"Exactly. It isn't smart to—"

"Paradoxes are much overrated, don't you think? We're in the fluid zone, Ilsabet. Anything goes, this side of the terminator. If I were you I wouldn't worry about—"

"*I* am me. I worry. If I were you, I'd worry more. Take your Sarajevo trip without me."

He saw she was adamant, and dropped the issue. Indeed, he saw it would be much simpler to make the journey alone. They went on from Rhodes to the Babylon of Nebuchadnezzar, where they spent four happy days untroubled by the shadow of Stavanger; it was the finest time they had had together since Carthage. Then Ilsabet announced she felt the need for another brief solo musicological jaunt—to Mantua in 1607 for Monteverdi's *Orfeo*. Reichenbach offered no objection. The instant she was gone, he set his timer for the twenty-eighth of June, 1914, Sarajevo in Bosnia, 10:27 a.m.

In his Babylonian costume he knew he looked ridiculous or even insane, but it was too chancy to have gone to the halfway house for proper preparation, and he planned to stay here only a few minutes. Moments after he materialized in the narrow cobble-paved alleyway, his younger self appeared, decked out elegantly in natty Edwardian finery. He registered only the most brief quiver of amazement at the sight of another Reichenbach already there.

Reichenbach said, "I have to speak quickly. You will go out there and near the Bank of Austria-Hungary you'll meet the most wonderful woman you've ever known, and you'll share with her the greatest joy you've ever tasted. And just as your love for her reaches its deepest strength, you'll lose her to a rival—unless you cooperate with me to rid us of him before they can ever meet."

The eyes of the other Reichenbach narrowed. "Murder?"

"Removal. We'll put him in the way of harm, and harm will come to him."

"Is the woman such a marvel that the risks are worth it?"

"I swear it. I tell you, you'll suffer pain beyond belief if he isn't eliminated. Trust me. My welfare is your welfare, is this not so?"

"Of course." But the other Reichenbach looked unconvinced. "Still, why must there be two of us in this? It's not yet my affair, after all."

"It will be. He's too slippery to tackle without help. I need you. And ultimately you'll be grateful to me for this. Take it on faith."

"And what if this is some elaborate game, and I the victim?"

"Damn it, *this is no game*! Our happiness is at stake—yours, mine. We're both in this together. We're closer than any twins could ever be, don't you realize? You and me, different phases of the same person's timeline, following the same path? Our destinies are linked. Help me now or live forever with the torment of the consequences. Please help. *Please*."

The other was wavering. "You ask a great deal."

"I offer a great deal," Reichenbach said. "Look, there's no more time for talking now. You have to get out there and meet Ilsabet before the archduke's assassination. Meet me in Paris, noon on the twenty-fifth of June, 1794, in the rue de Rivoli outside the Hôtel de Ville." He grasped the other's arm and stared at him with all the intensity and conviction at his command. "Agreed?"

A last moment of hesitation.

"Agreed."

Reichenbach touched his timer and disappeared.

In Babylon again he gathered his possessions and jaunted to the halfway house for the French Revolution. Momentarily he dreaded running into his other self there, a malfeasance that would be hard to justify, but the place was too big for that; the Revolution and Terror spanned five years and an immense service facility was needed to handle the tourist demand. Outfitted in the simple countryfolk clothes appropriate to the revolutionary period, equipped with freshly implanted linguistic skills and proper revolutionary rhetoric, altogether disguised to blend with the citizenry, Reichenbach descended into the

terrible heat of that bloody Parisian summer and quickly effected his rendezvous with himself.

The face he beheld was clearly his, and yet unfamiliar, for he was accustomed to his mirror image; but a mirror image is a reversed one, and now he saw himself as others saw him and nothing looked quite right. This is what it must be like to have a twin, he thought. In a low, hoarse voice he said, "She's coming tomorrow to hear Robespierre's final speech and then to see his execution. Our enemy is in Paris already, with rooms at the Hôtel Brittanique in the rue Guénégaud. I'll track him down while you make contact with the Committee of Public Safety. I'll bring him here; you arrange the trap and the denunciation; with any luck he'll be hauled away in the same tumbrel that takes Robespierre to the guillotine. *D'accord*?"

"*D'accord*." A radiance came into the other's eyes. Softly he said, "You were right about Ilsabet. For such a woman even this is justifiable."

Reichenbach felt an unexpected pang. But to be jealous of himself was an absurdity. "Where have you been with her?"

"After Sarajevo, Nero's Rome. She's asleep there now, our third night: I intend to be gone only an instant. We go next to Shakespeare's time, and then—"

"Yes, I know. Socrates, Magellan, Vasco da Gama. All the best still lies ahead for you. But first there's work to do."

Without great difficulty he found his way to the Hôtel Brittanique, a modest place not far from the Pont Neuf. The concierge, a palsied woman with a thin-lipped mouth fixed in an unchanging scowl, offered little aid until Reichenbach spoke of the committee, the Law of Suspects, the dangers of refusing to cooperate with the revolutionary tribunal; then she was quick enough to admit that a dark man of great height with a beard of just the sort that M'sieu described was living on the fifth floor, a certain M. Stavanger. Reichenbach rented the adjoining room. He waited there an hour, until he heard the footsteps in the hallway, sounds next door.

He went out and knocked.

Stavanger peered blankly at him. "Yes?"

He has not yet met her, Reichenbach thought. He has not yet spoken with her, he has not yet touched her body, they have not yet gone to their damned operas together. And never will.

He said, "This is a wonderful place for a jaunt, isn't it."

"Who are you?"

"Reichenbach is my name. My friend and I saw you in the street and she sent me up to speak with you." He made a little self-deprecating gesture. "I often act as her—ah—go-between. She wishes to know if you'll meet her this afternoon and perhaps enjoy a day or two of French history with her. Her name is Ilsabet, and I can testify that you'll find her charming. Her particular interests are assassinations, architecture, and the first performances of great operas."

Stavanger showed sudden alertness. "Opera is a great passion of mine," he said. "Ordinarily I keep to myself when jaunting, but in this case—the possibilities—is she downstairs? Can you bring her to me?"

"Ah, no. She's waiting in front of the Hôtel de Ville."

"And wants me to come to her?"

Reichenbach nodded. "Certain protocols are important to her."

Stavanger, after a moment's consideration, said, "Take me to your Ilsabet, then. But I make no promises. Is that understood?"

"Of course," said Reichenbach.

The streets were almost empty at this hour. The miasma of the atmosphere in this heavy heat must be a factor in that, Reichenbach thought, and also that it was midday and the Parisians were at their *déjeuner*; but beyond that it seemed that the city was suffering a desolation of the spirit, a paralysis of energy under the impact of the monstrous bloodletting of recent months.

He walked quickly, struggling to keep up with Stavanger's long strides. As they approached the Hôtel de Ville, Reichenbach caught sight of his other self, and with him two or three men in revolutionary costume. Good. Good. The other Reichenbach nodded. Everything was arranged. The challenge now was to keep Stavanger from going for his timer the moment he sensed he was in jeopardy.

"Where is she?" Stavanger asked.

"I left her speaking with that group of men," said Reichenbach. The other Reichenbach stood with his face turned aside—a wise move. Now, though they had not rehearsed it, they moved as if parts of

a single organism, the other Reichenbach pivoting, pointing, crying out, "I accuse that man of crimes against liberty," while in the same instant Reichenbach stepped behind Stavanger, thrust his arms up past those of the taller man, reached into Stavanger's loose tunic to wrench his timer into ruin with one quick twist, and held him firmly. Stavanger bellowed and tried to break free, but in a moment the street was full of men who seized and overpowered him and dragged him away. Reichenbach, panting, sweating, looked in triumph toward his other self.

"That one too," said the other Reichenbach.

Reichenbach blinked. "What?"

Too late. They had his arms; the other Reichenbach was groping for his timer, seizing, tearing. Reichenbach fought ferociously, but they bore him to the ground and knelt on his chest.

Through a haze of fear and pain he heard the other saying, "This man is the proscribed aristocrat Charles Evrémonde, called Darnay, enemy of the Republic, member of a family of tyrants. I denounce him for having used his privileges in the oppression of the people."

"He will face the tribunal tonight," said the one kneeling on Reichenbach.

Reichenbach said in a shocked voice, "What are you doing?"

The other crouched close to him and replied in English. "We have been duplicated, you see. Why do you think there are rules against entering a time where one is already present? There's room for only one of us back in realtime, is that not so? So, then, how can we both return?"

Reichenbach said, with a gasp, "But that isn't true!"

"Isn't it? Are you sure? Do you really comprehend all the paradoxes?"

"Do *you*? How can you do this to me, when I—when I'm—"

"You disappoint me, not seeing these intricacies. I would have expected more from one of us. But you must have been too muddled by jealousy to think straight. Do you imagine I dare run the risk of letting you jaunt around on the loose? Which of us is to have Ilsabet, after all?"

Already Reichenbach felt the blade hurtling toward his neck.

"Wait—wait—" he cried. "Look at him! His face is mine! We are brothers, twins! If I'm an aristocrat, what is he? I denounce him too! Seize him and try him with me!"

"There is indeed a strange resemblance between you two," said one of those holding Reichenbach.

The other smiled. "We have often been taken for brothers. But there is no kinship between us. He is the aristocrat Evrémonde, citizens. And I, I am only poor Sydney Carton, a person of no consequence or significance whatever, happy to have been of service to the people." He bowed and walked away, and in a moment was gone.

Safe beside Ilsabet in Nero's Rome, Reichenbach thought bitterly.

"Come. Up with him and bring him to trial," someone called. "The tribunal has no time to waste these days."

Julie Frost grew up an Army brat, traveling the globe. She thought she might settle down after she finished school, but then she married a pilot and moved six times in seven years. She's finally put down roots in Utah with her family and enjoys birding and nature photography. Utilizing her degree in biology, she writes werewolf fiction and other fantastical creatures that take her fancy. Her short fiction has appeared in Monster Hunter Files, Writers of the Future, The District of Wonders, StoryHack, Unlikely Story, Stupefying Stories, *and too many anthologies to count. Her novels are published by WordFire Press and Ring of Fire Press.*

NOT ALL TREASURE

by Julie Frost

I circled the graveyard pond with my best friend, Ambrose, while a drizzle leaked from the night sky and hissed against our guttering torches. Their sullen flames lit everything nearby with a ruddy glow, including Ambrose's manic grin and the mad glint in his eye, two things I was resignedly accustomed to.

"Why do I let you talk me into these things?" I moaned. I was soaked and miserable and not shy about letting him know it. "What's wrong with doing this during the day when it's not raining, I ask you?" I'd bound my long blonde hair into a queue, but several strands had escaped and straggled wetly over my face. I shoved them out of my eyes with exasperation.

"Buck up, Deena, old girl." I was hardly old, so that annoyed me, and he swatted a branch aside with his cudgel, which launched a cascade of cold droplets right down my tunic collar, which annoyed me further. "No one else will be out in this, which is to our advantage," he said. "Before you know it, we'll have gold in our pockets and ale in our bellies."

"Robbing a graveyard never goes well." I twitched at every sound, hands sweating despite the chill.

"We're not robbing the graves," he said cheerfully. "We're liberating the treasure from the pond."

"Oh, yes, so much better. How do you know there's treasure in the—*bloody buggering hell!*" This last because something under the water had heaved a giant ripple right over my boots. I leaped back, but it was too late. I sighed. Why should my feet be any less soaked than the rest of me?

Ambrose stood immobile and staring, his torch and cudgel slack in his hands. He let out a low curse and then shook himself, taking a step away from the pond, not noticing that his boots had received the same treatment as mine. "Did you see that?" His voice quavered.

"See what? It's dark as a—" I broke off as a pair of lambent amber eyes reared up from the pond. And up. And up, to *three* times the height of a man. "Amb?" His nickname fell from my lips as a hoarse squeak. Later, I'd probably be embarrassed about that. First, I had to live through this encounter with whatever lurked in our quiet little country cemetery. "Perhaps we should run?" My legs disagreed with my assessment, rooted trembling to the spot.

A roar of rage unfroze my legs, and I grabbed Ambrose's arm and yanked him away just as the eyes came lashing down toward us with a rotten vegetation-and-fish stink. The torches illumined just enough to let me see an enormous maw filled with nastily-serrated teeth the length of my forearm. They snapped shut less than a foot from my face as I stumbled back, slipped, and fell on my behind, which probably saved my life.

Ambrose answered the roar with an inarticulate shout of his own, standing over me and taking a pair of wild swings at the thing's nose with cudgel and torch. The head went back up with a snort that blasted pond water and snot over the two of us.

Then another set of eyes joined the first.

"Right," I gasped, chest seizing in panic. "Time to go." I scrambled to my feet, snatching a handful of Ambrose's shirt and dragging him away at a staggering run, hoping like hell that the creatures living in the pond would damn well stay there.

They did, wonder of wonders. We stopped outside the cemetery fence, huffing, and I fixed Ambrose with an accusatory glower. "You didn't tell me there were bloody dragons in the bloody pond."

"I didn't know, did I?" He wiped his sleeve over his face and grimaced. "This complicates things."

"No. No, it does not." I crossed my arms. "In fact, it uncomplicates them rather nicely. I am not going

back there, and neither are you. No treasure is worth getting devoured by monsters, assuming there's treasure in the first place, which is still unconfirmed."

"Trust me, it's real all right, and this isn't some random quest," he said. "I *need* it." His shoulders slumped, and he seemed to grow smaller. "You know the blight took my crops. I couldn't pay the king's tax, and I'm already eyeball-deep in hock to Jarin."

The king's tax had been due a month gone; they would take his land and toss him out on his arse, if not into the dungeon. And Jarin was a ruthless moneylender whose idea of "collecting on a late debt" meant "breaking kneecaps."

I sobered. "I hadn't realized it'd got so bad for you, Ambrose. Why the hell didn't you come to me sooner?"

He shrugged. "You've got your own money troubles, dearie. I didn't want to bother you with mine. Give me some credit for tact."

We all had money troubles. The aforementioned blight had decimated crops for miles around and some of us weren't sure how we'd get through winter—but Ambrose's problems were clearly worse than mine. His earth magic had made crops grow on land no one else could make produce more than scraggly weeds, but even he couldn't prevail in the face of something like this.

I cast a glance toward the pond and sighed. "I thought this was just another of your barmy schemes. I didn't realize it was actually urgent."

"Well, now you know." He turned and began trudging down the muddy road toward town. "I need a drink I can't afford."

"We've got no business going to the tavern in our shocking state of destitution, not to mention the dragon snot, but I've got a bit of whiskey left over from last year's rye crop," I said. "I'll share."

He clapped me on the back. "You're a good friend, Deena."

Our torches picked that moment to sputter out, leaving us in rainy near-pitch darkness. I sighed again. "Too right I am."

I lived in a couple of rooms above my smithy, and we stripped out of our wet clothes and hung them to dry beside the forge, which I always kept burning. I poured out generous drams from my stock of whiskey, and we pulled up a couple of chairs and sat in front of the fireplace with our legs stretched out, in our underthings, which steamed gently as they dried.

Ambrose scowled into the flames. "I don't know what to do, Deena. The pond treasure was my last hope, and even that's more of a campfire tale, if I'm being honest."

"Hmph." I mused. "Dragons don't take up residence just anywhere, though, do they? Aren't they always guarding some kind of hoard?"

He tilted his head and eyed me. "I don't know about 'always,' but I daresay that's usually the case. It still begs the question of how we could actually get the sodding treasure away from them, were we inclined to go back."

"Poison the pond?" I frowned. "Though a poison that would kill one dragon, let alone two, might be a bit problematic for anyone going in afterward." I shook myself. "Not that I'm actually contemplating going back, mind. Because that would be bloody stupid." I lowered my brows and chin, fixing him with a relatively mild glare. "Even for you."

He huffed a sigh. "I'll find another way, then."

What that would be, neither of us had any idea.

☼

Pounding and angry shouts at my downstairs front door yanked me out of an uneasy sleep early the next morning. Ambrose twitched and snorted awake from the mound of blankets in the corner he'd spent the night in. People would talk, but they did anyway, and we were used to it. He grimaced when the shouts resolved themselves into, "We know you're in there, Ambrose!"

"Oh, odds bodkins. That's Jarin," Ambrose groaned, pulling a blanket over his head. "Tell him I died, there's a good lass."

"Maybe if we ignore him, he'll go away?"

No such luck. "If you don't want your door broken in, you'll answer it, girl." I knew the moneylender meant it too, the condescending bastard.

I opened the window and glowered down at Jarin, who stood in my yard while rain still misted down. "Keep your knickers on and your hands off my door," I said. "I'll be right there."

I pulled some clothing on, and Ambrose did the same. "This is my fight, not yours, Deena."

I just snorted and preceded him down the steps. He tried to shoulder past me to the door, but I wasn't having any of that. I used a fair bit of forge magic in my work, but I still had muscles built by banging iron into submission and shoving draft horses around all day, and I was a couple of inches taller than Amb as well. I held him at bay whilst I confronted Jarin.

Jarin had two of his favorite heavies flanking him, and he himself was not a small man. My jaw tightened, and I crossed my arms over my bosom, leaning on the doorframe. "Be reasonable and leave go for a bit, Jarin," I said. "None of us are doing well. You know this."

"And Ambrose should know better than to borrow money he can't repay," Jarin answered. "He was perfectly aware of the penalty. Stand aside and let me exact it, lassie. I'd hate for you to be his collateral."

Ambrose was wiry as a whippet and tenacious as a terrier, and he slipped past me with a defiant expression. "You leave Deena out of this, Jarin. She's done nothing to provoke you."

"Certainly." Jarin's fist flashed out and connected with Amb's face with a meaty crunch that bespoke a broken something. I made a protesting noise and stepped forward, which was when Jarin's thugs moved in concert to intercept me. One grabbed my wrist as I aimed a punch at his head, ducking under and twisting my arm behind my back, shoving me against the side of my smithy, all in one motion. The other aimed a nasty kick at the side of my knee that sent me writhing to the mud-covered ground. The first declined to let go of my arm, which popped out of the shoulder socket with agonizing pain that actually blacked me out for a few moments.

When I blinked back to awareness, Jarin had left with his minions. Ambrose lay beside me, half-conscious and bleeding in a puddle. Say what we would about Jarin, he was frighteningly *efficient* when he wished to make a point. "I'm sorry, Deena," Amb mumbled. "Didn't mean to get you mixed up in my mess."

I clenched my teeth around an undignified groan and managed to gasp, "Are you all right?"

"Not particularly." His eye was swollen shut and cuts decorated his eyebrow and cheekbones and split his lips in two places. "Jarin's a right bastard, he is." He scrubbed a hand over his face, smearing the copious blood through the rain that soaked it, and stood shakily, taking a couple of tries before he made it all the way. "Don't think I didn't see them dislocate your arm. We'd better see to that. Can you walk?"

My knee felt as if a petulant cart pony had kicked it from under me, but it held my weight after some hesitant testing. "Inside," I said. "No sense making more of a spectacle than we already have."

The sound of hooves trotting in tandem made me glance up the track leading to my smithy. A matched pair of dapple gray chargers ridden by king's men slogged toward us, managing to look graceful even riding through the muck churned up by the unrelenting drizzle. My heart sank. I'd managed to pay my tax, barely, but I remembered Ambrose's difficulties. They crashed to a halt beside us. The one on the left shoved his visor up and regarded Ambrose, who cringed when he spoke a single word. "Tax."

Ambrose's good eye slid shut. "I haven't got it, have I? I'm fair certain you know that already."

"Then your farm is forfeit."

"Yes, yes, I know." Ambrose waved his hand. "Fine. *You* can bloody well work land devastated by blight, and I will turn my hand to something not so chancy, such as card sharping. Now shoo."

"Your farm is not worth enough to pay the tax, so you're still in default. If you don't come up with the balance in a week's time, it's the dungeon for you." The king's men hrrmphed, turned their horses, and rode away. To my satisfaction, they no longer trotted in tandem.

We staggered inside, and Ambrose soon had his face cleaned up and my arm set aright. I still ached fiercely, and he didn't look much better. He shook his head and rubbed his eyes with thumb and forefinger. "At least the king gave me an entire week. Jarin gave me three days while you were passed out. He'll break more than my nose next time."

"Probably shouldn't let him do that," I answered.

"Then I've got no choice but the pond treasure." His lips compressed. "You don't have to come, lass."

I gave him a look filled with exasperated affection. "You know I do. I'm not sending you to face two sodding dragons by yourself."

"Perhaps they'll be weaker in daylight? Dragons are creatures of the night, after all. Or…maybe we can talk to them."

I snorted. Sure. Talk to dragons. "One can hope." It wasn't much of a hope, but it was what we had. "No time like the present."

We limped to the graveyard in the desultory shower still leaking from the low gray clouds. I squinted at the still pond and made a doubtful face. "I don't know, Amb. There's still probably at least one bloody drag—"

Yes. Yes, there was.

A head reared up, much like before, but a bit sluggish because of the daylight. It was a deep green, with amber, vertically-pupiled eyes and a narrow snout. I took a step back, remembering our reception from last time. Great scaly wings expanded over its back, dripping. Talk to it, Amb had suggested. "Er. Hello," I tried.

The head tilted slowly to one side, considering us. "You. You were here last night. Trying to steal the treasure."

So, treasure confirmed, and the dragon could talk back. I wasn't sure if this made things better or worse. Ambrose chose to take the indignant route. "And how do you know that, then? Mayhaps we was just out for a stroll."

The second head rose beside the first, and I realized that we didn't have a pair of dragons—the dragon had a pair of heads. Again, I wasn't sure if that made things better or worse. Head Two lowered and fixed Amb with a steely gaze. I took another step back, because sod this for a game of soldiers. "We can sense," it growled, and Head One finished the sentence, "your intentions."

Worse, then. Right. I raised my hands in the universal "don't shoot" position. "We came without arms," I said. "Just to speak with you. Can you sense *that*?"

The neck frills flared. "Mmm," said Head One. "Mayhaps," said the other. "Speak, then."

Amb pulled me forward a reluctant step and squared his shoulders. "I need the treasure. Not all of it, mind," he added hastily. "Just a bit to pay the king's tax and get the moneylender off my back."

"The *moneylender*," snapped Head Two, injecting a sizeable quantity of venom into the word. A foreleg thrust out of the water with a bronze shackle encircling it. "He it is who binds us captive," said Head One, and the other finished, "with dark magics and a geas." Head One took up the narrative again. "Guarding his hoard." Head Two: "Whilst our own remains undefended."

It had long been a matter of speculation where Jarin hid his dubious earnings. Well, now we knew, for all the good it did us. Wheels turned in my head. "If we break the magic and set you free, would you turn the moneylender's treasure over to us?"

"We could just feed Jarin to the dragon," Ambrose said with a lowered brow. "That would solve several problems at once."

"It would also be wrong," I said, acknowledging inwardly that he had a point and refraining from slapping him on the back of the head.

"You're no fun."

"Our geas prevents us from harming him," Head One said. "While he yet lives," Head Two finished thoughtfully. Head One put on a wheedling tone. "We could eat him if you killed him." It pulled its lips back, revealing those sharp and serrated teeth that could bite a man in half. "It would make a nice change from the manky fish in this undersized pond," Head Two said.

"No, Ambrose," I said, catching his speculative expression. "The dungeon will be bad, but the gallows will be worse."

"There won't be any evidence if our dragon friend *eats* him." He sighed at my expression. "Fine. Apparently I'm not permitted to feed Jarin to you. What would you like instead?"

"Cow," said Head One, at the same moment Head Two said, "Pig." They looked at each other in a deeply betrayed fashion. "It's been ages—" they said in unison, and then stopped.

"Unfortunately," I said, "I don't have any livestock and neither does Ambrose. Liberating a cow or a pig from our neighbors would bring them unnecessary hardship."

"How about liberating Jarin's obnoxious billy goat?" Amb asked. "The thing stinks to high heaven and is a bad-tempered beast to boot. Also, that would be a way to stick it to Jarin, who could use a bit of hardship in his life."

"Now there's a thought."

The dragon brightened. "Goat has a nice stringy texture," Head One said. "And a lovely gamey flavor," said Head Two.

Dragons had odd taste, clearly. "Right, then," I said. "Back in a jiff."

✧

It took more than a jiff, of course. First we had to slog through the mud to Jarin's place on the outskirts of the village. Passing the tavern on the way, we noted that he was inside with his bodyguards, enjoying lunch and a drink from the sour-faced innkeeper, who didn't like him any more than anyone else did. I hoped spitefully he'd spat in Jarin's ale.

We stopped at the smithy along the way to pick up some supplies. I had a notion about breaking the magic holding the dragon captive, and I grabbed a set of metal shears and a grease pencil, along with some rope to bind the goat.

Jarin's house was bigger than the mayor's, because he was richer—a two-story white-painted dwelling surrounded by a stone fence higher than my head, with a few small outbuildings, one of which his goat lived in and around. He didn't keep a dog, which was fortunate for us.

We followed our noses around the wall to the goat's shed. I gave Amb a boost, and then he pulled me to the top of the wall to stand beside him. The goat, fastened to a tree by a collar and chain, looked up and let out a curious bleat before lowering its head to nibble at a bit of forage. It was an unkempt black-and-white creature with a shaggy beard and long, thick, backward-curving horns, and apparently didn't care that it was wet from stem to stern from the rain. There was a decidedly evil glint in its yellow eyes with their bizarre horizontal slit pupils.

A certain amount of roping skill went with my job, and I readied a lasso as we leaped into the yard. "You distract it, and I'll catch it by a back foot and stretch it out between us and the tree," I said.

Amb gave me a dubious look, but stepped inside the circle of the goat's chain, waving his arms. It lowered its head and charged him, and before he could step out of range or I could catch its foot in my loop, it butted him hard in the stomach and sent him arse over teakettle through the open door of the shed. I said a bad word and belatedly tossed my rope at the bucking goat, which settled around its ankle. Pulling it tight, I yanked the horrid beast off its feet and tied the end of the rope to another tree, reaching for the pigging string I'd attached to my belt.

The goat jerked, flailed, and bleated, and it actually managed to catch me a glancing blow over my eye with a muck-laden cloven hoof, but I soon had the three loose legs secured to each other, immobilizing it. I stood up and dusted my hands off—not that it did any good, because it was still pissing rain and mud does not simply "dust" off—and wandered into the shed to see if Ambrose was all right.

He stood with his fists on his hips, glaring at a salt circle inscribed in the relatively dry dirt floor, in a corner out of reach of the goat's chain. "That sodding bloody buggering son of a poxy doxy," he said softly.

"Amb?" I asked. "What's the matter?"

He made a rude gesture at a pile of detritus in the middle of the circle. "Our moneylender's been doing more with dark magic than holding a dragon hostage." A pause. "Jarin…caused the blight."

"Wait, what?" I stared. "How do you know? And how did he do it with no earth magic of his own?"

His breath came in short, angry huffs. "I don't know how, but I know my earth magic, and this is it, only the black arts sort. It's easier to destroy things, innit, than to build them? Maybe we should confront him about this."

"And maybe we should release the dragon, feed his goat to it, and loot his treasure. Hit him in the pocketbook, where he lives." The last thing I wanted was for Amb to get beaten again. I pointed at the circle. "Can you do something about that?"

"Too right I can." He scuffed the salt with his boot and kicked the rubbish pile to the four corners of the compass, muttering imprecations (which might have been incantations; I didn't know from earth magic) under his breath. "There. Next year should

be all right, any road. Let's go. Quickly. He might have felt that."

Not wasting any time, I sliced through the goat's collar with my belt knife, and we scooped up the struggling animal, heading purposefully out. Slipping and sliding in the mud, we took the back way to the cemetery, and deposited the goat on the shore of the pond.

Moments later, the dragon reared its heads up and regarded our offering. Head One leaned down for a sniff. "Oh, quite nice." Head Two was more doubtful. "Those horns will be a problem. Remember the last time? It took a month to digest." Head One opened its jaws and snapped. Suddenly the goat was headless, blood gushing out onto the muddy verge. "Fixed that for us," Head One said smugly, while I leaped back in startlement. "So you did," said Head Two. "Nicely done." And then it bit off the hindquarters, swallowing them in a couple of gulps.

"Hey!" And that was Jarin's furious voice shouting at us from the trees. He splashed onto the scene through the muck, followed by his pair of bodyguards and a few townsfolk, but he stopped short and wilted when he saw what was left of his goat. "Gruffy?"

In my experience, people only named things they cared about. Before I could react to that, Ambrose let out an inarticulate yell and tackled the moneylender. Jarin was bigger, but Amb was much, much angrier, and he sat on Jarin's chest and landed several blows before a bodyguard hauled him off. He tried to wade back in, arms swinging, ranting like a madman—

And I decided this was a fine old distraction for what I needed to do. I sidled over to the dragon and said out of the corner of my mouth, while watching the goings-on, "I think I can release you from Jarin's captivity."

Head One picked up the remainder of the goat and gulped it down before anyone got any cute ideas about taking it away, while Head Two spread its ruff and set its bronze-girded foreleg on the shore beside me. "Quickly, though," it said, and the other pointed out, "They won't be preoccupied long."

I felt all around the shackle, sussing out how the magic was made, before unslinging my bag and pulling out the metal shears and the grease pencil. "I'll have that off in a trice," I said, and muttered some words of power, marking the bronze with runes. The air sizzled a bit, and I dropped the pencil and took up the shears. Three snips later, the shackle fell off.

"And this sodding bastard started the blight on purpose," Amb was shouting, held fast in the iron two-handed grip of a thug who nevertheless couldn't cover his mouth, "no doubt so he could grow fat on our misery and want. And he has, hasn't he."

"Oh, what nonsen—" And Jarin abruptly stopped speaking at the advent of a pair of dragon heads on either side of him, right in his personal space.

"Nonsense, is it?" said Head One. "Oh, I think not," answered Head Two. "In fact, this one knew we could heal your blight," Head One said, and Head Two continued, "because the geas he trapped us with prevented us from using our own magic to do so."

"Wait, you have growing magic?" I asked, while Ambrose wrenched free of the bodyguard's suddenly loose grip.

"Of course," Head One said. "Because of ecology," explained Head Two. "Our prey must eat, after all," Head One finished. "Speaking of prey…" Head Two butted Jarin in the chest. Not gently.

"Y-you-you can't eat me!" Jarin blustered. "I'm not a virgin."

"Oh, that old chestnut," said Head One. "It's adorable you humans still believe that," Head Two said. Head One's eyebrows lowered, and smoke curled from its nostrils. "Perhaps we should roast him first."

"Are you going to let this bloody great beast just eat me?" Jarin asked.

"Thinkin' we might, at that," said the innkeeper. "It's one thing to profit from suffering. It's quite another to be the source of it."

Jarin's gaze swiveled frantically around, meeting not a single sympathetic face. "I can pay you—"

"Oh, I think they'll get paid anyway," Head One said. "Because your treasure is right here in the pond," Head Two pointed out. "Sufficient to keep them all through the winter, I daresay," mused Head One.

"But—"

"Enough!" roared Head One, and before anyone could gainsay, its gigantic jaws snapped shut around Jarin's torso and chomped it messily in two. He was still screaming as his top half disappeared down its throat. Head Two made short work of the bottom half, while we stood there, a bit shocked by the swiftness and with the urgent realization that any one of us could be next.

But the dragon's lips curled into smiles, and Head One said, "We owe you a boon, good lady blacksmith." "Most people go straight to slaying without actually trying to talk to us," said Head Two. "It gets tiresome," said Head One. "When next you are in need, come see us on the mountain," said Head Two. "Farewell," they said together, and leaped into the air, great wings beating and sending the rain down in sheets on all our heads.

"Well," said Ambrose, "can't say I'm sorry about that. Come on, Deena, let's get out of this filthy weather. Not like Jarin's fortune is going anywhere, even without its guardian." He set off down the track to town with a jaunty whistle and a spring in his step. His mad grin was back, I was glad to see, and I had a grin of my own as I locked arms with him.

Copyright © 2021 by Julie Frost.

New York Times *and* USA Today *bestselling author Kristine Kathryn Rusch writes in almost every genre. Generally, she uses her real name (Rusch) for most of her writing. Under that name, she publishes bestselling science fiction and fantasy (including the Fey series, the Retrieval Artist series and the Diving series), award-winning mysteries, acclaimed mainstream fiction, controversial nonfiction, and the occasional romance. Her novels have made bestseller lists around the world and her short fiction has appeared in more than twenty best of the year collections. She has won more than twenty-five awards for her fiction, including the Hugo,* Le Prix Imaginales, *the* Asimov's *Readers Choice award, and the* Ellery Queen Mystery Magazine *Readers Choice Award.*

DESTINY

by Kristine Kathryn Rusch

Solanda walked the cobblestone streets of Nir, the capitol city of Nye, her tail up. She had a meeting with Rugar, the son of the Black King. He had sent a Wisp to find her, and it had taken the little creature nearly a day to do so.

Solanda was in her cat form, as she had been since the Fey captured this repressed country—and thus very difficult to find. The Nyeians had many faults—they were prissy, overdressed, and pasty faced, not to mention abominably poor soldiers—but they did treat their animals well. She had found a family who fed her to excess, allowed her to roam outside, and pampered her as no cat should be pampered.

How appalled they would be if they ever discovered the golden cat their daughter had adopted was really a Fey Shapeshifter.

Solanda's tail twitched once in amusement. Every day she imagined eating her lovely tuna dinner in the glass plate that the family gave her, and then Shifting into her Fey form just to say thank you.

She didn't know what would appall the Nyeians the most: the fact that she was Fey, or the fact that she would be naked. She doubted any of them had seen a naked woman before: the wife managed to change her clothing one piece at a time, without ever taking it all off at once, and the husband didn't seem to think this unusual. He would probably be more shocked than his wife at the appearance of a naked Fey woman in his house. He would probably fall over in a dead faint.

Only the daughter, a girl of five, was redeemable. Esmerelda was a good child. She had to be. She was raised Nyeian. Her mother trussed her in layers upon frothy layers of clothing, making movement nearly impossible, and then yelled at the poor child whenever she did something natural, like running.

Sometimes Solanda thought she went back to that household at night because she felt sorry for the child. But in truth, she stayed there because they gave her fish properly deboned and they brushed her, and they put a warm cedar bed in Esmerelda's room. Esmerelda, good child that she was, never confessed to her parents that she often picked up the cat and carried her to bed, cuddling with her long into the night.

And Solanda would never tell anyone—Fey or Nyeian—that sometimes she purred when she slept, pressed against the little girl's back.

Shifters were supposed to be the coldest of the Fey, the most fickle members of a warrior people, incapable of real emotion, flighty, restless and completely self-absorbed. They also were supposed to take on the characteristics of the animal they had chosen to Shift into, so Solanda's fickleness—theoretically—was doubly-compounded by the fact that she had chosen the cat as her alternate Shape.

Of course, it didn't matter how many times she had proven herself trustworthy. In the war against Nye, such as it was, she had done intelligence for the Black King. She had worn her cat form and slinked into Nyeian villages, soldiers' camps, and mess halls, keeping her ears open, and learning more than she should have.

Most countries that the Fey had fought had banned strange animals from military compounds. Solanda had heard that the Co had gone so far as to slaughter any strays, thinking they might be Fey reconnaissance. But the Nyeians had a fondness for cats, and while they kept stray dogs out of their camps, they fed cats on the side.

Solanda had spent most of the war the pampered resident of a Nyeian general's tent. He used to feed her bits of meat off his own plate while telling his staff his battle plans for the next day.

And then when he fell into his snoring sleep, she would go to the nearest Shadowlands and inform the Fey general of all she had heard. Toward the end of the war, she reported directly to the Black King, who shook his head at the stupidity of the Nyeians.

Conquering Nye was the first step toward world dominion. The Black King didn't say that, but Solanda knew that was his goal. The Fey were a great warrior people, but they only owned half the world right now. The Black King—and the Black Throne—wanted all of it.

Solanda entered the merchant sector of Nir, and silently cursed to herself. The merchants often shooed cats out of this area. Her presence here was suddenly noticeable, and she didn't dare Shift. She'd shock an entire community of Nyeians—which would probably be good for them.

Scents from the nearby vendor stalls caught her nose. Fried beef, more fish, some sort of vegetable, something which turned her feline stomach. The fish was enticing. It almost made her forget that she was here because she had been summoned by the Black King's son.

Rugar had been her commander for part of the Nye campaign. He was an able warrior, frustrated under his father's tight leash. The problem with Rugar was that he believed himself to be the equal of his father, and he was not.

Solanda would rather work with the Black King, ruthless as he was, than with his less-talented son.

The tall stone buildings prevented the sun from getting to the cobblestone. The stone was wet beneath her paws from the morning rain. The air was thick and muggy, making the six layers of clothes the Nyeians wore look even more uncomfortable.

The handful of Fey who were on the street wore their traditional uniform—a leather jerkin and pants. The Fey were so much taller than the Nyeians that even if they didn't dress differently, they would be noticeable.

She ducked under some clothing stalls, past the buildings that housed the year-round indoor merchants, and turned on the street that led to the Bank of Nye. The Black King had taken over the building. It was four stories of gray stone, towering over the buildings around it—as close to a palace as there was in Nye.

She sighed heavily and crossed the street, climbing up the stone steps and staring at the large stone door. She'd have to Shift just to get into the place.

Then she saw a nearby window ledge. The window was open. She leaped onto the ledge and jumped to the stone floor inside. She thought this building unusually cold for a Nyeian structure. The house where she was pampered was made of wood, and had thick rugs on its floors. Every surface was soft, and the air perfumed.

Here the air smelled like chalk and the stone was chilly despite the heat. There were no guards in this room, although there should have been. It looked like it was someone's office—a desk in the center, chairs on the side for supplicants.

The door was open and led into a cavernous hallway. She heard voices and followed them. Several Fey guards huddled in an alcove. They were Infantry and young, tall even though they hadn't come into their magic yet. Their dark skin and black hair was a welcome sight. She'd gotten tired of looking at the pasty-faced Nyeians, and hadn't realized how much she missed her own kind.

"…fool's errand, don't you think?" one of the young men said.

"If it's so important, why doesn't the Black King go?" another asked.

"Blue Isle is important," said a young woman. "It's the only stop between here and Leut."

Leut was the continent on the other side of the Infrin Sea. The Black King wanted to go there more than anything. He wanted to conquer as much of the world as he could before he died.

"If we are going to conquer the world," the girl was saying, "we have to go through Blue Isle first."

"Then it doesn't make sense," the first man said. "Why send Rugar? He's not as good a commander as his father."

"Maybe," Solanda said in her most authoritative voice, "the best commander in the world has a plan that's too sophisticated for you to understand."

They all turned. They had similar upswept features, narrow faces, and pointed ears. Solanda had often thought that her people looked like foxes—most of them, anyway. Shifters, like her, often took some of the characteristics of their animals. Her hair and skin were more golden than dark, and she had the Shifter's mark on her chin—a birthmark that established who and what she was when she was in her Fey form.

But they couldn't tell now. All they could do was tell that a cat had spoken to them.

"Well," she said, sitting on her haunches and wrapping her tail around her paws. "Where do I start? Do I reprimand you for gossiping in the middle of the day? Do I tell you that I got into the building through a window that some careless fool left open and, if I had been some young Nyeian bent on assassination, I could have walked right past you and you wouldn't have noticed? Or do I ask that one of you poor, magickless fools get me a robe so that I can have my meeting with Rugar?"

They didn't answer her. She raised her chin slightly. Amazing how she could intimidate them, even though she was so very small.

"By the Powers," she snapped. "Get me a robe. And put a guard on the window."

She nodded over her head toward the room she had just come out of.

Two of the young men ran off toward the room. The third young man hurried off, presumably to get her a robe. That left the young woman.

"I really should report this," Solanda said. "Technically, you put the Black King's life in danger."

"From the Nyeians?" the young woman snorted. "You snarl at them and they run. They couldn't fight us in the war, and once they found out that they'd remain in charge of their businesses, they really didn't care that we took them over. Why would one of them try to get in here?"

"Revenge?" Solanda said. "We did, after all, slaughter half their army. Those young men were related to someone."

"Then that should take away half the threat, shouldn't it?" the young woman said. "After all, the Nyeians believe that only men are capable of fighting."

Solanda felt amused. "I have a hunch that belief has changed since they were defeated by us. What's your name?"

"Licia," the girl said.

"You haven't come into your magic yet, have you?"

The girl straightened her shoulder. Magic was always a touchy subject with Infantry. They were tall enough to show that they would get magic, but chances were if they neared adulthood and still hadn't come into their magic, their abilities would be slight.

"No," she said.

"You showed a tactician's mind. Why do you waste it gossiping with people who aren't worthy of you?"

The girl straightened her shoulders. "I don't normally guard. I am usually in the field."

"But there's no field at the moment, is there?" Solanda said. "What are you doing here?"

"Rugar asked me to come. He says his daughter needs more swordfighting training."

Solanda narrowed her eyes. Jewel, Rugar's middle child, was the most promising of all his raggedy offspring. She hadn't come into her magic yet either, but her height and her heritage suggested when her magic came it would be powerful. She was a good swordswoman now—Solanda had seen her fight in the last of the Nye campaign.

"Why would she need more training?"

Licia shrugged. "I suspect it has something to do with the fight Rugar had with his father this morning."

Solanda tilted her head to show her interest.

"They just left that room you came through. They were screaming at each other all morning long."

"About what?" Solanda asked, realizing that she was now gossiping. But she didn't want to go into a meeting with Rugar with less knowledge than he had.

"About going to Blue Isle. Rugar says he won't go without his daughter."

"Not his other children?"

"He didn't mention them." Then Licia smiled. "At least not at the top of his voice."

Solanda suppressed a sigh. The Black King favored Jewel. He felt that her brothers were idiots—and he was right. Their magic was slight, like their mother's had been. Rugar's entire life had been about defying his father. Rugar should have married a woman who had great magic. Instead, he had chosen someone he could control.

The young man returned with a flowing golden robe that was clearly of Nyeian origin. Solanda didn't ask where he had gotten it. She didn't thank him. Instead, she said, "Place it over me."

He did, blotting out the light. The robe smelled faintly of perfume and perspiration, but it clearly hadn't been worn in some time. The fabric was heavy satin—too heavy for a humid day like this—but she wasn't in the position to be choosy. If Rugar was planning something stupid, she wanted to meet him Fey to Fey. Psychologically, it gave her an advantage.

She Shifted, feeling her body slid into its familiar Fey form. Her body stretched and grew. Her tail and whiskers slid into her skin, her hair flowed down her back, her front paws became hands. She ended up in a sitting position, her knees drawn to her chest, the robe draped over her like a tent. Inwardly she sighed, and wished that there were a more dignified way of Shifting into clothes.

Then she slid her arms through the sleeves, and her head through the neck hole, letting the stiff fabric flow around her. It was a woman's garment, although she had no idea why someone would store one in a bank—or perhaps she did, and didn't want to think about illicit affairs among Nyeian bankers.

She lifted her long hair out of the garment's neck, and let it fall down her back. Licia bit her lower lip, and the other Fey looked down. They hadn't realized they were talking to the best Shifter in the Black King's army—at least, not until now.

Fools. Shifters were rare. How many of them would come into the Black King's dwelling and order Infantry around?

"Licia," she said, "announce me to Rugar."

The girl's skin colored slightly, but she moved in front of Solanda and led her down the hall. It got stuffier the farther in they went. Solanda was grateful that her feet were bare. The cool stone was going to keep her from melting in this robe.

Licia led her up a flight of stairs into a rabbit's warren of what had once been offices. Solanda smiled. Rugar was hidden here, in an obviously less desirable area of the building. The Black King had a thousand ways of showing his displeasure with everyone around him.

Licia knocked on a door at the end of the hall. Solanda stood far enough back that she wasn't visible from inside. She heard Rugar's gruff voice, and then Licia's response, announcing Solanda.

The door opened, and Licia stepped aside.

"I guess that means you're supposed to go in," she said.

Solanda stopped and put a hand on the girl's shoulder. She spoke softly so that Rugar couldn't hear. "If Rugar and his father are fighting," she said, "side with the old man. Rugar is not the future of this race. You're better off remaining in Nye with the Black King than going to Blue Isle with Rugar."

Licia nodded, then glanced over her shoulder as if she were afraid of Rugar. Solanda walked past her and through the open door.

Rugar stood in the center of the small room. He was medium height for a Fey, and his features had a predatory, hawk-like look to them. His almond-shaped eyes were the deep black that Solanda associated with the Black Family. It was as if the Throne echoed in their very essence. He had thin cruel lips, and an expression of permanent unhappiness.

For man in his fifties with grown children, he looked startlingly like a petulant child.

"You sent for me," she said, not disguising her lack of respect for him.

He clasped his hands behind his back, his father's favorite stance. "I'm taking an army to Blue Isle. You will be part of it."

She snorted. "I serve your father, not you."

Rugar glared at her. "He gave me permission to choose whomever I wanted from the standing armies in Nye."

"You have no need for a Shifter," she said. "Blue Isle is a tiny place, filled with religious fanatics who have never seen war. You'll sail in with your troops, wave a few swords, and be able to claim victory over an entire country in the space of a day. I'll be useless to you."

He shook his head. "I'm taking you, and a lot of Spies and Doppelgängers. I am to be military governor of Blue Isle. My father will launch an attack from there onto Leut."

Solanda narrowed her eyes and was glad she wasn't in cat form. She probably would have found an excuse to scratch Rugar, and that wouldn't have been good for either of them.

"Spies, Doppelgängers, and a Shifter," she said. "It sounds like an intelligence force. You won't need it if you conquer the country as quickly as you believe you will."

His gaze went flat. "I will need it."

She stared at him for a moment. He knew something and he wasn't going to share it with her. Spies made sense, even in an easily conquered country. They would find the pockets of resistance. But Doppelgängers had no place there. They killed their hosts and then took over the body, including the memories. Except for the gold flecks in the eyes, no one could tell them from their victims. Doppelgängers had a sophisticated magic—one that the best commanders used sparingly. And certainly didn't waste them on an already conquered country.

"You have no need for me," she repeated. "I stay with the Black King."

"You'll come with me."

"Your father said so?"

"No, but he will."

"Because he already acquiesced on Jewel?"

Rugar started. He hadn't expected her to know that.

Solanda raised her eyebrows and allowed herself a small smile. "I am good at gathering intelligence."

"And," he said, "as you pointed out, there's no need for intelligence gathering in a conquered country."

She nodded. "I'll go to Leut with your father, when he's ready. Until then, I'll relax here."

"Solanda—"

"Rugar," she said, holding up a hand. "You and I have no great liking for each other. I have a hunch your father is sending you to Blue Isle to get you out of his sight. I'd rather not be associated with you in any way. Right now, I hold your father's respect. I'd rather not change that."

Rugar took a step toward her. She could feel the violence shimmering in him.

She grabbed the door knob. "Touch me," she said, "and I'll scratch out your eyes."

"You can't touch me. I'm a member of the Black Family."

She smiled. "I'm a Shifter. Unpredictable, irresponsible, flighty—remember? I'm sure the Powers would let this slide."

"But my father would not," Rugar said.

"Oh," Solanda said softly, "but I think he would."

✿

She tried to see the Black King before she left the building, but he was nowhere to be found. His personal guards were gone as well. She decided she would find him in the morning, and went back to her life as a pampered Nyeian cat.

The home that she had chosen was a large one on the outskirts of Nir. It had two stories filled with more clutter than any home she had ever seen. Books of poetry, musical instruments, incredibly ugly paintings, and furniture everywhere. The only saving grace was that the furniture was comfortable and the kitchen had a cat door that she could escape through when the wife decided it was time for music.

Solanda slipped through the cat door, past the kitchen hearth. One of the three Nyeian servants was cleaning the pots from the evening meal. The air smelled faintly of roast beef, and Solanda's stomach rumbled.

Still, she didn't beg from the servant. She knew better. The idiot had kicked her "accidentally" once, and she had the scars to prove it. But Solanda knew if she attacked anyone in the house too many times, she would be thrown out, and she wasn't willing to lose her rich dinners and soft bed just yet.

She blended into the hideous yellow wallpaper as she hurried up the stairs to Esmerelda's room.

Esmerelda sat on the edge of the bed, fingering a rip in her dress. She had a forlorn expression on her small face. Her brown hair hung limply around her cheeks, and a streak of dirt covered the pantaloons beneath the skirt.

Solanda had never seen Esmerelda look dirty before, nor had she seen the girl's hair loose at any time except bedtime.

"Oh, Goldie!" Esmerelda raised her voice in relief. She was speaking Nye, which was a language that Solanda hadn't known well when she moved into this house. Here her Nye had improved greatly, but she wanted to be fluent in it by the time she left.

The little girl launched herself off the bed and grabbed Solanda before Solanda could jump out of the way. Esmerelda wrapped her arms around Solanda and held tightly. Esmerelda had never done that before. If she had been a grabby little girl, Solanda would have been gone a long time ago.

So this meant, quite simply, that something was wrong.

Solanda let herself be held for a moment, then she turned her head toward the door and flattened her ears. Esmerelda, smart child that she was, understood both signals. She pushed the door closed, and then let Solanda go.

Solanda jumped on the windowsill. Esmerelda followed her, but didn't open the window like she usually did.

The room was hot and sticky. Solanda wouldn't be able to stay here too long if that window wasn't opened.

"I don't dare," Esmerelda said softly. "Mommy's really mad at me. She didn't even let me have dinner."

Now Solanda was interested, but she didn't want the story, not yet. She bumped her head against the window's bubbled glass.

Esmerelda bit her lower lip and shook her head.

Solanda placed a paw on the glass and meowed softly.

"Okay," Esmerelda whispered. "But if anyone comes, I'll have to close it."

Solanda almost nodded, then caught herself. When Esmerelda came close, Solanda bumped her affectionately with her head, and then watched as the little girl pulled the window open.

A cool breeze made its way inside. That was the other nice thing about this house. Esmerelda's room opened onto a large undeveloped area, so the smells of the outdoors came in strong. Breezes were unencumbered. Esmerelda's mother hated this, and often wished for close neighbors, but Solanda saw it for the blessing it was.

Esmerelda knelt down beside the window and put her elbows on the sill. She didn't touch Solanda, but she was still a bit too close. Her body heat was ruining the breeze.

"I been so bad," she said, "I won't get to go outside ever again."

Solanda watched her. The little girl had never been able to resist a cat's gaze. Solanda had never seen a child who was so very lonely. Esmerelda wasn't allowed to play—except with dolls who clothing as frilly as the stuff she was trussed in—nor was she allowed to associate with the neighboring children who were, in her parents' mind, beneath her. She had lessons in poetry and music, art and dancing, but she liked none of it. What she really wanted to do was run as far as she could, and climb trees and learn how to swim.

She'd probably never get to achieve those goals.

"I was running this afternoon," Esmerelda said. Her face was wistful. She leaned her forehead against the glass. "Mommy was looking at fruit and

I thought I could just go around the block, but she saw me. I guess she followed me."

Esmerelda had done this before, and it hadn't gotten her sent to bed with no supper. Solanda suspected the problem had something to do with the rip in the dress. Clothing was sacred, at least to this family. Solanda wanted to tear every piece so that this little girl could be free.

"She saw me fall," Esmerelda said, fingering her skirt. "She saw me hit a Fey."

Solanda stiffened. She almost asked who, and caught herself. Two near lapses in one conversation. She was getting much too relaxed with this child.

Esmerelda ran a soft hand over Solanda's head. Her touch was gentle again, as it had always been before.

"She said she was the Black King's granddaughter, and she yelled at Mommy for dressing me the way she did. And Mom yelled back. The lady said yelling at her was like yelling at all the Fey all at once."

Only one Fey woman could make that claim. Jewel. No wonder Esmerelda's mother was upset.

"And then Mommy told Daddy and he said that the Fey might hurt us. Because I ran." A tear coursed down Esmerelda's cheek.

And those fools were blaming the child for being a child. Solanda pushed against the girl's hand, and Esmerelda sniffled.

"I didn't mean to run. I just can't stay still sometimes."

Solanda understood that. She could never stay still. It was a curse of being a Shifter. It was the reason Fey wisdom said that Shifters were the most heartless of the Fey. Most Shifters did not have children, and most rarely stayed anywhere long enough to form a real relationship.

Esmerelda sighed. "I wish I was like you. I do what I want. Or like that Fey lady. She was nice to me. She didn't like Mommy though."

Neither did Solanda.

"She said children shouldn't be dressed like me. She said I ran into her because my clothing didn't let me run properly."

Probably true, Solanda thought.

"And that made Mommy really mad."

Esmerelda let her hand slide off Solanda's neck. She bunched her hands into fists and rested her chin on them, looking fierce and strong. Solanda felt her whiskers twitch in amusement. One day,

Esmerelda's parents would no longer be able to control this child. If she was this strong, articulate, and intelligent at five, she would be impossible to control at fifteen.

Especially with all of the Fey influence around her.

"I wish I had magic," the little girl said. "Just a little bit. Then I could run and no one would know. I'd make myself invisible and no one would see me."

Solanda looked out the window, knowing her expression was too sympathetic for a cat. There was a ring of oaks at the edge of the lawn. They were blowing in the breeze. Maybe there would be another storm. Maybe this storm would finally cool the place off, although she doubted it. Nye's hot season was the worst she had encountered in any country she had ever been in.

"Esmerelda!" her mother's voice echoed from the hallway. "Why is your door closed?"

Esmerelda gasped and pulled down the window so quickly she almost caught Solanda's tail in it. Then she leaped onto the bed, stretching out. Solanda jumped beside her and curled up at her feet just as Esmerelda's mother opened the door.

The woman's face was flushed. She looked like a tomato about to burst. She was so tightly corseted that her body looked flat, and Solanda wondered how the woman could even breathe. She wore an evening dress of white satin that accented the redness of her face. The sides were lined with sweat.

"What are you doing?" she asked. Then she frowned. "How did that mangy cat get in here?"

Solanda growled softly in the back of her throat. She was not mangy. And the woman had never called her that before.

"I told you that you were supposed to be in here by yourself to think about what you did today. Things could have been much worse. Fortunately, she was in good mood. You know what those people can do? Why it's said they can cut the skin off a person with the flick of—"

Solanda yowled, and the woman stepped back, a hand over her heart. Esmerelda sat up, worry on her small face.

"Are you okay, Goldie?"

Solanda licked her right paw as if she had twisted it. She was not going to let that woman tell this little girl about Fey atrocities—even if they were true.

"Come on, Goldie," Esmerelda's mother said. "There's some beef for you in the kitchen."

Usually that would have gotten Solanda off the bed. But she could sneak down after everyone was asleep and take what she needed. Right now, she wanted to stay beside Esmerelda.

"Goldie," the woman said.

Esmerelda, good child that she was, bit her lower lip and said nothing. She didn't beg for the company that she obviously wanted.

"Goldie!" her mother sounded exasperated now. Then she shook her head. "Why do we put up with this animal?"

Neither Solanda nor Esmerelda answered.

Finally Esmerelda's mother sighed. "All right, she can stay. But I do expect you to sleep in that dress tonight and to think about how you could have hurt us all. That rip should be a reminder of the danger your misbehavior put us in. Nye isn't the place it used to be, child. Do something wrong, and those Fey will harm all of us."

Then she pulled the door closed, and Solanda heard the boards creak as she made her way down the stairs.

Esmerelda's fingers played with the rip. Solanda looked at it, then crossed the bed, took the skirt in her teeth and pulled. The rip grew. Esmerelda giggled, then covered her mouth. Solanda pulled harder. If the little girl had to sleep in these clothes, she might as well be comfortable.

Esmerelda ripped the pantaloons too, along the dirt line, giggling as she did so. "Mommy will think I did it when I was running," she said. "You're so smart, Goldie."

Of course she was. Solanda preened and allowed herself to be petted one more time.

Then Esmerelda looked at the door, her smile fading. "Sometimes I think Mommy doesn't want me. She wants somebody else. Somebody perfect."

Too bad she didn't realize that the child she had was better than perfect. Solanda sighed softly. Some people had more than they deserved.

The idea came to her in the middle of the night, in that hot and stuffy room. She could take Esmerelda away, and Esmerelda's parents wouldn't even know it had happened. But it would take the cooperation of the Fey Domestics.

Fey magic was divided into two parts: warrior and domestic. Warrior magic was designed for warfare. Some Fey magic turned its practitioner into a weapon, like the Foot Soldiers who had fingernails that could slice better than a blade. Domestic magic could not be used to fight any war. Domestics lost their magic if they killed. Their magics were healing magics or home-bound magics, such as spells that made chairs more inviting or fires warmer.

The next morning, after making certain that Esmerelda got breakfast, Solanda slipped out the cat door. She went to the Domicile that the Fey Domestics had set up just outside of town. The Domicile had been built especially for the Domestics, and covered with various protection and healing spells. It was a traditional U-shaped building—with hearth and home magics in one length of the U, the healing wards in the other, and the middle section as a meeting place in between.

Solanda usually didn't seek out the Domestics. They always wanted to experiment with her—have her try on a new cloak covered with some sort of rain protection or have her taste a new food to see if it had an effect on her Shifting. The last time she had been in a Domicile had been when she had broken a paw jumping from a tree in one of the last Nye battles. The Domestics had mended the bone, and had given her a smelly ointment she had to apply in cat form. She had thought the stench alone would kill her.

As she mounted the steps to the center part of the building, she shook off her paws. Here she would not Shift to Fey form. The Domestics weren't as obsessed with power as Rugar was, so she didn't have to use her height as a reminder of the strength of her magic.

She pushed open the door and stepped inside.

The air was cool and welcoming. It smelled of a sea breeze. Bits of magic floated in the air. Spinner's magic. They were working on their looms. She could hear the hum just down the corridor.

A Baker entered, his fingers dusted with flour. They glowed. And she knew he had spelled the bread he'd been baking to remain fresh for as long as possible. It was a traveling spell, one most often used when troops were heading off to battle. She wondered if someone had requested it.

"I'm here to see Chadn."

The Baker nodded, then slipped through a door that led to the Healing part of the Domicile. Solanda hopped onto a chair. Her mood rose and she cursed, jumping down. She didn't need to be spelled, to wait, happy and contented, on a chair dusted with Domestic magic. Instead she paced the cool floor and wondered why she couldn't smell the baking bread.

Finally Chadn entered the room. She was a young Shaman, although the toll of her power had already turned her hair white. Her face was wizened, her mouth a small oval amid wrinkles. Only her eyes were bright—sparkling black circles of light in a ruined face.

She had been assigned to stay with Rugar during the war and she was happy to be free of him. Shaman were the most independent Fey: their Vision as strong as those of the Leaders, but their magic Domestic so they could not rule a warrior people. They were the wise ones, the advisors, supposedly the strength behind the Black Throne. The Black King required a Shaman of his son, but did not use one himself. He had dismissed his own, years ago, for disobeying him. It was one of many areas where the Black King broke with tradition.

"Solanda," Chadn said. "I had hoped to see you."

Solanda jumped on an end table and was relieved that her mood did not change. She sat on her haunches and looked into Chadn's face.

"I have a request," she said. "It's for a Nyeian child."

"A child?" Chadn sounded surprised. "Not a Fey child?"

Solanda shook her head.

"I had Seen you with a Fey child."

The Shaman's Visions—and the Vision that leaders like the Black King had—allowed them glimpses into the future. Some said that the glimpses allowed the Visionary to change the future. Others believed that the glimpses led the Visionary to that future.

Solanda's eyes narrowed. "I have not been with a Fey child."

Chadn nodded. "It was on Blue Isle. The child was a Shifter, and you kept her from death."

Solanda's whiskers twitched. "I told Rugar I would not go to Blue Isle with him."

"The future of our people lies with you, Solanda."

"And a child?" Solanda raised her chin. "Are you sure it was a Fey child?"

"Not entirely," Chadn said. "The child had blue eyes."

Solanda gave a soft grunt of surprise. She had heard of blue-eyed people, but she had never seen one. "The child couldn't be Nyeian?"

"She was Fey, and newborn. She had a birthmark on her chin. Only her eyes were strange, and perhaps that was because of the Shifting. I Saw you put your hands on her lips, and swear to protect her, raise her, and make her strong. Then I Saw her full grown, saying you had been the closest thing she had to a mother."

Solanda laughed, although inside she felt cold. A Shifter only swore to protect a child who held the future of the Empire. A blue-eyed child that Shifted? The center of the Empire?

"Visions can be altered," Solanda said. "I am not leaving Nye."

"You may have no choice."

"I'll always have a choice," Solanda said.

Chadn inclined her head toward Solanda as if giving in on that point. "What does the Nyeian child need?"

Solanda took a deep breath. "She is different from any other Nyeian I've seen. Strong, independent. She met Jewel yesterday and is being punished for it. I would like to remove the child from her family and bring her here, to be raised among us. She will be useful when she's grown. She will be part of the second generation, the Nyeians that rule Nye for the Fey."

Chadn stared at her for a moment. "So take her. Shifters steal children."

"This one's mother will raise a fuss if she's gone."

"What mother wouldn't?"

"She'll come to us."

"And you can't prove to the Black King that we must keep the child."

"Not yet, anyway," Solanda said.

Chadn folded her hands over her stomach. "You want a Changeling."

"Yes," Solanda said.

"How old is the child?"

"Five."

Chadn sighed. "Have you asked the child if she's willing to leave?"

"Not yet. I wanted to know if I have help first."

"You will keep the child at your side?"

Solanda frowned. That wasn't a normal request. Shifters rarely kept children. They usually brought them to Domestics to raise. "Must I?"

"At five, it will be you she trusts."

Solanda shrugged. "Then she shall stay with me."

"And you will stay away from Blue Isle." Chadn said that not as a question, but as a statement.

"Rugar will not let a Nyeian child in his war party."

"So the child serves two purposes." Chadn's eyes narrowed. "Has she magic?"

"Of course not." Solanda laughed. "There is not magic outside the Fey."

Chadn frowned. "I am no longer certain of that."

"Because you Saw a blue-eyed Shifter?"

"Because I Saw a great war, coming when we least expect it."

"War is part of Fey life." Solanda jumped off the table and headed for the door. "I'll bring you news of the child tomorrow."

"I'll have Changeling stone ready," Chadn said. "But realize before you act, that this is for life."

"I already know that," Solanda said. "I have chosen well."

"I hope so," Chadn said.

✿

Solanda went to the docks and sat on a fence. She loved it here. The Infrin Sea formed the most natural harbor on Galinas, and there was always some sort of activity. Toward the north end of the harbor, the Nyeian builders made the great ships. Those ships traveled all over the known world, and now Fey Domestics helped unload cargo that would go all over the Empire.

Ships from Blue Isle had stopped coming to Nye when news reached them of the Fey takeover. She would never see an Islander, never learn more about them than she already had.

And that would be all right.

For there were some things she couldn't discuss with Rugar's Shaman. Like the prophecies that had been made by another Shaman at Solanda's birth, prophecies that claimed her legacy would be in the children she saved.

Children—not child, like Chadn had seen. Solanda would influence the life of more than one.

The breeze was cooler here, carrying with it the smell of salt and a tinge of dead fish. That smell made her stomach rumble. She tried not to think of the things she ate in her cat form, things she would find disgusting when she was in Fey form. Right now, raw dead fish sounded extremely appetizing.

But she didn't go in search of the source of the smell. She had some thinking to do. Prophecies and Visions made her nervous. She had no idea what to do with the information Chadn had given her. Because, at various points in her life, Solanda had been told by Visionaries that her future held contradictory things.

One Shaman had told her she had to avoid the Black Family for she would kill a Black Heir. Another Shaman had told her she would raise a Black Hair. And now Chadn had Seen her swear to protect a blue-eyed Shifter, a newborn who couldn't survive on her own.

Solanda bowed her head. The prophecy she never mentioned, the one her parents had kept silent, had come the day of her birth and she had never forgotten it. The prophecy was a cold one: she would die before her time, far from home, for a crime she did not regret.

The Fey did not believe in crime. They were constantly at war, so the crimes that plagued other races—murder, theft—were absorbed into the wars themselves. The Fey only punished two crimes: treason and failure. Both of those crimes were considered crimes against the Empire. Failure was a large crime, encompassing the failure to follow an order, or the failure to defeat an enemy in a prolonged battle.

Treason was any crime against the Black Family and was such a heresy, that it wasn't even discussed among rational Fey.

Both crimes bore the penalty of death.

It seemed to her that she would never commit crimes like that, that the prophecies had come because she was a Shifter, not because of her character. She wasn't as flighty or as difficult as anyone said she was.

And besides, she had to take care of Esmerelda.

She wished she could be there the morning that Esmerelda's parents discovered the Changeling. It would

look like Esmerelda, even act like her—if stone could act like a living breathing creature. But it would only last a few days, and then it would cease to exist. They would think Esmerelda dead, when, in actuality, she was only gone.

Then, perhaps, that wretch of a mother would regret how she treated her daughter.

Esmerelda would live a life she couldn't even imagine now. She wouldn't have to wear six layers of clothes on the hottest day of the year, and she would learn how to live life to its fullest instead of remaining indoors and studying all the time.

Esmerelda would be the closest thing to Fey that a Nyeian could be—and for the first time in her young life, she would be happy. Solanda would see to that.

They would both be very happy.

☼

Solanda returned to the house after dinner. Ultimately, she found she couldn't resist the dead fish that were piled near one of the docks. She had eaten herself sick, and then had to clean every inch of her fur before she even attempted the walk home.

Not that the house was home. In some ways, Esmerelda was.

Solanda used the cat door. Esmerelda's parents were talking softly in the parlor.

"Perhaps boarding school," the mother was saying. "If she is this incorrigible now, imagine what she'll be like when she gets older."

"Give it time, darling," the husband said. "She's still a child. She will learn, as we all did."

"It's just I despair of ever teaching her manners. You didn't see her with that Fey…."

Solanda had heard enough. She hurried up the stairs. She would talk to Esmerelda tonight. Tomorrow the Wisps would come, carrying a bit of stone in their tiny fingers. They'd fly in the open window, leave the stone on the bed and it would mold itself into a replica of Esmerelda while Solanda was leading the real Esmerelda out of the house.

Quick, neat, and completely perfect. The parents wouldn't have to worry about manners or boarding school. Esmerelda would get her heart's desire. And Solanda would have her reason for staying in Nye.

The door to Esmerelda's room was open. Esmerelda sat beneath a lamp, a long skirt over her lap. The air was stuffier than usual, and Solanda saw that the window was closed.

It had probably been closed all day. Sunlight had poured in, and the poor child had had to sit in the heat, working on some task her mother assigned her.

When Solanda got close, she saw what it was. The child was attempting to mend her own ripped dress.

The stitches were uneven, and Esmerelda had stitched the bottom layer of fabric onto the top. That would make her mother even angrier. Esmerelda's eyelashes were stuck together, her nose was red, and there were tearstains along her cheeks.

"Goldie!" she said, and let the dress topple to the floor. She was wearing another dress, equally inappropriate to the hot weather. She reached for Solanda, but Solanda jumped onto the window sill.

She was not going to be hugged by a hot sweaty child—not, at least, until the window was open and the fresh air came inside.

Esmerelda glanced toward the door. She put a finger to her lips, as if she thought Solanda were going to give her away, and then called, "Mommy! Can I go to sleep now?"

Solanda froze in her spot. She didn't want to be seen in here, not tonight. She wanted to have her conversation with Esmerelda in private.

"Are you done with your dress, darling?"

"Yes."

Solanda looked at it. The dress was ruined. The poor girl would have an even more difficult day than usual tomorrow.

"Then blow out the lamp. Good night."

"Good night." Esmerelda pushed the door closed. Then she went over to the window and opened it.

A strong breeze came in, and on it, Solanda smelled rain. Maybe, after she spoke to Esmerelda, she would go outside. By then it would be raining, and she would be able to cool down.

Esmerelda put her hand over the lamp's chimney and blew. The flame inside the glass went out. Solanda blinked in the darkness, letting her eyes adjust. It only took a moment. There were clouds over the moon this night, and it was very dark.

Esmerelda went back to her chair. "I wish you knew how to sew, Goldie."

"I don't," Solanda said. "But I know someone who does."

Esmerelda let out a small yelp, and put her hands over her mouth. She peered around the room as if looking for the source of the voice.

Solanda had to go slowly with this. The child wasn't used to magic, not like Fey children were.

"I could take the dress to her tonight," Solanda said, "and by morning, you wouldn't even know there had been a rip in it."

Esmerelda's eyes were wide. She finally turned in Solanda's direction. "You can talk, Goldie?"

"As well as I can listen." Solanda jumped from the windowsill to the bed. The room had cooled down. The fresh air felt marvelous. "What would you think, Esmerelda, if I took you to a place where you could wear comfortable clothes, play with children your own age, run and jump and swim to your heart's content? What if I told you that you would never have to sew another stitch, have another music lesson, or sit in a corner when you've done something that your mother didn't like."

Esmerelda looked for her, but clearly didn't see her. Cat's eyes were far superior in the dark. Solanda watched the child lick her lips, rub her hand over her knees, and then sigh.

"How long would I stay?" Esmerelda asked.

"Forever," Solanda said.

"Would I have to be a cat?"

Solanda laughed. For all her verbal sophistication, Esmerelda was still a child at heart. "No," Solanda said. "You'll stay just as you are."

"Would Mommy come?"

"No."

"Daddy?"

"No."

Esmerelda's shoulders stiffened. Her little body looked rigid. "Who would love me then?"

Solanda started. She hadn't expected that question. "I would be with you," she said.

Esmerelda was silent, as if she were thinking this over. "Where would you take me?"

"To my people," Solanda said.

"I'd live with cats?"

"No," she said gently. "With the Fey."

Esmerelda gasped. She held onto her chair as if she expected to be dragged from it.

Solanda wondered if she should have said that, but she had never taken a child before. Certainly she knew of no one who had ever taken a child of this age.

But Chadn had said she had had to speak with the child, and the choice to come had to be the child's. There was sense in that. Esmerelda, at age five, would always have a memory of living with her parents. She needed a memory of her choice to leave them.

"Esmerelda," Solanda said. "I—"

"No!" Esmerelda screamed. "No!"

She launched herself out of her chair as if her voice had given the ability to move again.

"Help! Mommy! Help!"

Solanda's ears went back. She hadn't expected this from Esmerelda, not her sane, different child.

"Esmerelda, I only want to give you a better life—"

"Mommy! Daddy! Help!"

Finally Esmerelda pulled the door open and blundered into the hallway. Solanda followed, tail between her legs, ears still back. The little girl's screams echoed down the stairs. Her parents had reached her, and they both put their arms around her. Esmerelda was too terrified to be coherent.

Then the mother looked up the stairs. She saw Solanda, her gaze flat.

And Solanda realized she had no choice.

She Shifted, her body lengthening, her tail disappearing, her fur becoming skin.

Then she walked, naked, to the floor below.

Esmerelda's mother gathered her child in her arms and backed away. The father placed himself in front of his small family, arms out.

"You came from the Black King, didn't you?" the woman said. "To punish us by stealing our child."

"It's not about you," Solanda said.

Esmerelda peeked around her father, eyes wide. Solanda had never, in her entire life, been so conscious of her nakedness.

"Wh-what do you want?" the father asked. He was trying to sound brave. Like most Nyeians, he was failing.

"I had hoped to take your daughter, but it seems that she prefers this place, even though you treat her as less than housepet. It seems, for reasons I cannot understand, that she loves you."

"Of course she does," the woman said. "We're her parents."

"As if that's a divine right." Solanda stopped on the middle stair.

The family cringed below her as if they expected her to strike them with a lightning bolt. She didn't have that kind of magic. They had seen the extent of her powers, but apparently they didn't know that.

"She is a child," Solanda said. "She is to run and play. She is to have friends of her own age. She is to have comfortable clothing so that she can move without tripping. She is supposed to get dirty, to rip her skirts, and fall on her behind. She is to have some joy in her life. Do you understand?"

"I thought you Fey were supposed to leave us alone," the mother said. "I thought—"

"Be quiet," the father said.

Esmerelda clung to her father, her curiosity moving her closer.

"You will give her those things," Solanda said, "or I will take her from you. Do you understand?"

"Yes," the father said.

"You can't do this," the mother said. "You can't change our customs. The Black King promised you wouldn't."

"A promise made to a conquered people is worth nothing," Solanda snapped. "You will do what I say, or the child is mine."

"Mommy." Esmerelda reached for her mother. Solanda's eyes narrowed. Couldn't she see that her mother saw her only as a thing to be trained, to be forced into the right and proper life?

Probably not. It was too sophisticated a concept for her. The same innocence that allowed Esmerelda to accept a cat's speech, allowed her to believe that she was loved.

"Do I take her now?" Solanda asked.

"No," the father said. "We'll do as you say."

"But our friends—"

"Shut up," the father snapped. "Do you want to lose her?"

For a moment, the mother's gaze met Solanda's and in it, Solanda saw something she recognized, a coolness perhaps, a calculation. How would that woman have answered if she had been asked *who would love me then?* Would she have dodged the answer like Solanda had? Or would she have heard it at all?

"She will stay with us," the woman said. She sounded resigned.

Solanda felt a hope she hadn't even known she had die inside her. "Then I'll watch. You will treat that child as if she is more precious than gold. And if you fail, even once, she's mine. Is that clear?"

"Yes," the father said.

But Solanda did not take her gaze from the mother. "Yes," the woman said.

Esmerelda had stepped to her father's side. She was still holding his leg. "Are you Goldie?" she asked.

Solanda gave her a small, private smile. "Only for you."

The little girl slipped behind her father again. Her answer was clear too. She would stay, no matter what. And Solanda had done all she could.

So she Shifted back to her cat form. For a moment, she watched them all, tail twitching, then she ran up the stairs and into Esmerelda's room. She stopped for only a moment, knowing she would never return.

She leapt onto the window sill, and sighed. She had just lost her excuse for staying on Nye. She was bound to the Black Family. She had to do as they wished.

Rugar wanted her to go to Blue Isle.

Where a Shifter awaited her care. A newborn child, with blue eyes. A child who would think her the closest thing she'd ever had to a mother.

Solanda looked over her shoulder. She heard Esmerelda's voice, high, piping, excited; the soft answers of her parents. Solanda had lied to them. She would not be able to watch.

She hoped they would take good care of her little girl.

Then she jumped out the window, and climbed along a tree branch. Maybe her future had been preordained. Maybe she had no choice. She would raise a Black Heir, maybe kill one, and influence children.

How different would tonight have been if she had told the child that she would love her?

She would never know. Perhaps that was the moment in which everything could have changed. Maybe she had just missed her only chance to save herself.

YANG FENG PRESENTS: A GALAXY'S EDGE TRANSLATION EXCHANGE

Bao Shu, born in 1980, is one of the most talented writers of contemporary China. He graduated from Peking University with a degree in philosophy, then attended graduate school at the University of Leuven in Belgium. Since 2010, Bao Shu has published works over millions of words, including science fiction novels *Ruins of Time* and *Seven States of Galaxy Saga* (co-authored), as well as a short story collection *The Ancient Song of Earth*. His short stories and novellas are seen in literary magazines such as *Science Fiction World*, *Galaxy's Edge Chinese version* and *People's Literature*. As a translator, he has translated *What Does It All Mean? A Very Short Introduction to Philosophy* by Thomas Nagel into Chinese. *The Redemption of Time*, a paraquel to *The Three Body Problem* that was originally published as a work of fanfiction in June 2011, had been translated into English, Polish, Russian, German, French, Czech and Japanese. In the past decade, Bao Shu won critical literary awards including the Chinese Science Fiction Galaxy Award, the Chinese Nebula Award and the Lenghu Science Fiction Award. He was coined "the most promising emerging writer of Chinese science fiction."

Recommended in this issue is Bao Shu's new work, "Hyperspace Partner," originally published in *Galaxy's Edge Chinese version* No. 7. As information communication technology continues to evolve, people's sensation of space and time are changing as well. How will this impact the life of a long-distance couple? The story is short, but it speaks volumes for what's happening in our reality.

If possible, I want to be able to hold your hand for real. Please enjoy.

◆ ◆ ◆

Bao Shu suffers from science fiction syndrome. A people's philosopher, a hyperrational irrationalist, a pessimistic dreamer, Bao Shu finds stories about time to be the most engrossing and believes every story exists within the limitless bounds of spacetime. Writers simply explore them through the soul and keep watch over them with pens and keyboards. Bao Shu's publications include Three Body X: Visible Eternity, Astronomy Priest, The Ruins of Time, Song of the Ancient Earth, *and more.*

HYPERSPACE PARTNER

by Bao Shu
Translated by S. Qiouyi Lu

If it's possible,
I want to hold your real hand.

1

As the plane took off, I began to miss Ding Xiaoya.

It had only been a couple hours since our lips had parted. The supersonic passenger plane was taking me farther from her with every second. Hundreds of meters of frigid Pacific Ocean filled the increasingly insurmountable distance between us. I couldn't wait to connect to the onboard Wi-Fi to see Xiaoya's face and hear her voice again. But the videos only seemed to prolong our extended goodbye and made me miss her more.

We both understood the pain.

Ding Xiaoya and I had only known each other for half a year, but we were head over heels in love with each other. We'd had no choice but to leave each other. If I'd met her half a year earlier, maybe I wouldn't have chosen to study abroad in the United States. Ding Xiaoya had already been working in China and couldn't go with me.

Five years. We'd be apart for at least five years until I got my PhD. Nowadays, we wouldn't have to communicate like our parents had with letters and spotty long-distance phone calls, but online mes-

sages and video chats still couldn't replace her lively and sweet presence.

There were countless long-term long-distance couples who had broken up.

By the time I arrived in New York, my assistant had already found a room for me to rent. The house was close to the subway, only two stops away from the university I'd be attending. The rent was affordable, and the location was safe. The crime rate was forty percent lower compared to other similarly priced rentals. There was even a Chinatown and a Chinese grocery store five hundred meters away, great for international students. It matched all my requirements and was the best rental of the hundreds of thousands available. The ease of checking in, thanks to my assistant's help, put my mind off of Ding Xiaoya for a little bit.

Of course, it wasn't a *real* assistant—I'd never be able to afford one—but rather the assistant in my smartwatch, Huawei's Huayao 7.0. When I was in China, I'd usually just use it as a phone; its usefulness as an assistant wasn't obvious to me. But once I was abroad, a stranger in a strange land, I was dependent on its help: getting directions, buying household supplies, pointing out local customs and norms, sometimes even translating foreign languages. Because I was beginning to use it more and more, I came up with a name for my assistant: A Hua.

I still longed for Xiaoya to be by my side. One day, I said to A Hua, "It would be great if you could bring Xiaoya to me." Still, I knew that even a perfect assistant couldn't complete that task.

But I was wrong. Five minutes later, A Hua said, "Hyperspace co-living program created."

2

I immediately authorized A Hua to work on the hyperspace co-living program, but in order for it to do so, I needed to acquire a lot more equipment. Although we were now in the smart technology era, the US's logistics infrastructure still crawled at a snail's pace. Several days had passed and many parts still hadn't arrived. The semester had just started. I had a bunch of classes I had to attend, and my advisor had given me several bibliographies to go over.

I was under a lot of pressure. Every day, I left early and returned late. I forgot about the program.

But one morning, a familiar and sweet voice woke me up: "Get up, lazyhead!"

I opened my eyes and saw Xiaoya's lovely face. She was lying with her head on the pillow next to mine. I could reach out and touch her.

"I know," I replied. "Let me give you a kiss first—"

I suddenly remembered that I wasn't in China. My eyes widened as I woke up fully.

"Xiaoya? Am I dreaming?"

"As if! Did you forget about the hyperspace co-living program? I authorized it as well."

I sat up. The room behind Xiaoya was the same old room we'd had in China. It was as if I was lying in her bed.

"This…is this a virtual reality?" I asked. But I wasn't wearing a VR headset.

Xiaoya laughed.

"Silly, look behind you."

I turned. Behind me was indeed the humble abode I was renting in the US. The pizza and drink I'd bought were still on the table.

Xiaoya spoke again.

"I told you not to buy so much junk food! You're going to get fat."

Two rooms on opposite sides of the Earth had been joined together in hyperspace.

"Xiaoya, what's going on?!" I asked.

But Xiaoya only chuckled and responded, "Come here and I'll explain."

Excited, I threw myself at her, only to crash into a wall. My body ached. I touched the wall and realized it was a fiber optic screen. Then I recalled that our beds were both up against walls. The optical communication relay created the illusion that our rooms were joined together. Easy enough to explain, but it was still difficult to create such a degree of realism.

"When was this installed?" I asked A Hua, flabbergasted.

"The workers installed it yesterday afternoon while you were in class," A Hua replied.

"People can come in even when I'm not here?"

"You already authorized it. Besides, the smarthome system can guarantee your safety," A Hua replied. That's right, the surveillance cameras in the

room could record visitors' actions. If they detected a problem, they could automatically call the police.

"Okay!" Xiaoya said, jumping out of bed. "Show me your campus!"

3

Of course, Xiaoya couldn't actually go to campus with me. But A Hua had ordered a VR headset for me. The lenses were cameras, and the arms of the glasses had microphones on them. Everything I saw and heard was converted into signals that could be transferred by satellite to China, all the way on the other side of the Earth. Xiaoya simply had to put on the same headset to experience everything I was experiencing, as if she were there herself. The opposite was true as well.

"Wow, the campuses in the US are beautiful!" Xiaoya chattered into my ear. "Such a big lawn! What's that red-roofed building by the bell tower for? The president's office? When was it built? Really, during the eighteenth century?"

"Xiaoya, you're not feeling the time difference?" I asked. "Isn't it close to bedtime over there?"

"Can't I be happy for a day?" she said, feigning anger. "Look, a lake with swans! Let's go there!"

So Xiaoya was once again in my life. Of course, it was all still just video and audio signals, but there was a sense of participation that hadn't been there before. With the seemingly transparent wall, we could sit in bed beside each other like we had before, her reading her novels, me watching my videos. Every now and then, we'd say something to each other and share what we were reading or what was going on in the game. Even if we went out, we could use the VR headset to talk to each other at any time. If she was asleep, I could save recordings to share with her later.

The smarthome system could do even more to deepen our presence in each other's lives. Xiaoya could access the refrigerator, washing machine, and cameras that A Hua had set up to help me with my housework. She was a great chef. I missed her cooking, but it turned out A Hua could even help me resolve that problem. It purchased a cooking machine and set it according to the data captured by the smarthome system in China. The machine analyzed Xiaoya's movements and the heat settings on the stove to mimic her cooking. Once it was broken in and had learned from the data, it could make dishes that were eighty to ninety percent as good as Xiaoya's.

A Hua had another, even more miraculous program: using a 3D printer, it could create a metal framework and use lifelike materials to create a figure that was identical to Xiaoya, down to her hair. On the opposite side of the Earth, Xiaoya could put on a responsive suit that would synchronize her movements with the figure, making it seem like she truly was by my side. I was excited about it for a while but, in the end, the figure was too expensive to maintain, and I always felt that it was kind of strange. So I abandoned it.

Cloud communication was becoming more and more advanced. It could facilitate long-distance meetings, education, and even telemedicine. I began to wonder why I'd even gone to the US when I could have easily communicated with my advisors from China in real time. I could virtually attend faculty meetings and use a robot body to work on my experiments—society simply hadn't caught up with the technology. Still, I felt that the generation after me and Xiaoya would have a completely different concept of spacetime. Every room would be a portal to the rest of the world, or even a spaceship headed for the stars.

4

The greatest distance in the world isn't from here to the edge of the universe, but the distance between seeing someone and knowing someone. Even if you could use technology to be close to someone day and night, two people could still drift from each other.

I had started my third year of studies. A stronger love would have also dulled with time. Xiaoya's presence gradually became more problematic. Because of the time difference, sometimes it would be well into the night as she continued chattering on about things that bored me. Sometimes, I'd return late after conducting experiments, and she'd ask me about this and that while criticizing me for not spending time with her. Other times, she'd ask me to take her to New York Fashion Week and do other activities I wasn't interested in. I even got tired of the food she made.

Like all couples who'd known each other for a few years, we began to find fault with each other, argue, and throw things—though, of course, we couldn't actually hit each other. We ended up shutting off the projection screen and communication channels between us. Truthfully, I felt it was for the better, but Xiaoya felt differently. Every time we cut communications, she would grow frantic. I didn't want to break up with her completely, so I put up with the headache.

My PhD midterm evaluations were coming up. They were extremely important; I couldn't make any mistakes. I asked A Hua, "Can you come up with a way to stop Xiaoya from disturbing me without cutting off communication entirely?"

A Hua said, "I've analyzed the communication patterns between the two of you over the past couple of years. I've found a number of phrases that provoke the biggest reactions and recommend for you to avoid them. For example, 'Why do you care,' 'This has nothing to do with you,' 'You're annoying me'… I can automatically replace them with phrases like 'I love you,' 'I was wrong,' and 'Calm down'…"

"Hold on." I shook my head. "That won't work if we have an argument. Isn't there another, more thorough method?"

"I can revoke some of her privileges, such as read access to the room display and VR login access."

"Won't that still upset her?"

"If that's the case, you can authorize the relationship manager as a proxy."

"Talk in human language!"

"…I can use your identity to communicate with Ms. Ding Xiaoya on your behalf."

A Hua explained that it could use the vast amount of data stored on the smartwatch to automatically generate images and dialogue to respond. Important decisions would still require my input, but it could take my place for everyday communication. Because interpersonal communication was growing more complex every day, there were already many people who had AI take care of basic communication.

"Perfect!" I said happily. "I'll leave it to you then!"

"But," it said, "this violates a clause in your previous hyperspace co-living program agreement. The other party needs to agree to the cancellation, or else it won't work."

"…"

I ended up finding a hacker online to wipe the previous program code so that A Hua could work without restrictions to help me deal with Xiaoya.

I tested the proxy a few times. The results were pretty good. On the other side of the Earth, Xiaoya could see a neat room, where her genteel boyfriend listened to everything she said and had heart-to-heart conversations with her—though it wasn't me. And I regained my independence. I could do what I wanted to do, and I even began to get to know some other girls.

A perfect plan, thanks to modern technology!

5

I passed my PhD midterm evaluations.

When I got the news, I went out with some friends. We drank to our hearts' content. I went straight to bed when I got home. When I woke up, it was already the next morning.

I felt some guilt when I realized I hadn't told Xiaoya the good news. I wanted to let Xiaoya know, but A Hua had been communicating with her on my behalf for the past month or so. I didn't want to say something wrong. So I had A Hua give me a record of all the conversations from the previous month for me to review.

There was a good amount of content. I flipped through it. Halfway through, I began to notice something strange. There was a lot of repetition. Every few days, the same conversation would happen: "I've been so tired lately!" "Make sure you rest; you'll regret it if you don't!" "Mmhmm, smooches…"

"What's going on here?" I asked A Hua. "A lot of the conversation is exactly the same!"

"I'm an AI. My algorithm has gotten complex to the point where I won't reply exactly the same way to a statement, but I still have limits. There will be some repetition."

"But Xiaoya didn't see through it?"

"I did some analysis," A Hua replied. "There's a 99.7% chance that Xiaoya is also using an AI."

"How…how could she?"

Ridiculous; it was fine if I was deceitful, but knowing that Xiaoya was avoiding me still made me furious. After a moment of anger, I panicked. There were plenty of people at Xiaoya's work who were pursuing her; that much I knew. Had she found someone else?

"A Hua, check Xiaoya's activity feed!"

"Much of it has already been encrypted," A Hua said after a moment. "Or perhaps her AI has forged the data. For instance, her sleep and wake times are practically the same every day, suggesting that she perhaps hasn't even been home recently."

In a flurry of emotion, I asked, "Then is there any public data?"

"Yes," A Hua said. "The data in her taxi app. As you are her emergency contact, it's all been shared with you, but you don't receive notifications for it. I've transferred the data to you."

I stared at it. The most recent ride was from a dozen days ago, and one of the frequent destinations was—

The city cancer hospital.

6

I got in touch with Xiaoya's parents and best friends and finally found out what had happened.

A couple months ago, Xiaoya had gone for a physical exam and discovered a shadow on her breast image. She'd gone to several doctors before she got a diagnosis—breast cancer, and it was already in the intermediate stage. During that time, she'd been in low spirits because we constantly argued. But, since my midterm evaluations were coming up, she didn't tell me about the diagnosis and even exhorted the people around her not to tell me, concerned that the news would distract me. After she was forced to stay in the hospital, she set up an AI to cover for her.

I bought the fastest ticket available and flew back to be at Xiaoya's side. I staggered into the hospital. Xiaoya was in the ICU; I could only visit using the wall display. Her hair was completely gone. She'd wasted away. But she was still hanging on, smiling as she said she was fine and that I shouldn't worry.

I fell to my knees before her and wept bitterly.

I took time off to be by Xiaoya's side for two months until her cancer went into remission. Only then did I fly back to the US. Xiaoya said that, no matter if she were at home or in the hospital, I could always get in touch with her through the video display; I didn't need to stand guard at her side. And she still wanted to see a lot of places. I could use the VR headset to take her there.

But I didn't listen to her. I went through the procedure to suspend my enrollment and returned to China.

No matter what Xiaoya said, I knew that what she wanted to see the most was me. Technology could shorten the distance between us, could help us communicate, but it still couldn't replace the oldest communication methods, or being by each other's side. Nor could it love for us.

So, a year later, when Xiaoya went into a coma for the last time, she held my real hand.

Epilogue

"Get up, lazyhead!"

Xiaoya's lovely face once again appeared in our old, comfortable room.

I smiled through my tears. All the scenes from our lives played before me. The videos were from fifty years ago, thousands of hours of memories. A Hua had faithfully uploaded them to the cloud for me and edited them to highlight the best moments. Times that had long been lost reappeared as if they were yesterday, before my very eyes.

"Look at us!" I said to the person by my side.

Xiaoya smiled and put her hand on mine. The polymer skin on her titanium frame kept her exactly as beautiful as she was fifty years ago.

Copyright © by Bao Shu.
Translation copyright © 2021 by S. Qiouyi Lu.
First published in the Chinese edition of
Galaxy's Edge, issue 7.

Jean Marie Ward writes fiction, nonfiction and everything in between. Her first novel, With Nine You get Vanyr *(written with the late Teri Smith), finaled in both the science fiction/fantasy and humor categories of the 2008 Indie Awards. She has published stories in* Asimov's *and many anthologies and provided an in-depth look into an award-wining artist, with her book* Illumina: The Art of J.P. Targete. *Her second nonfiction title,* Fantasy Art Templates, *marries the superb illustrations of artist Rafi Adrian Zulkarnain with pithy descriptions of over one hundred fifty creatures and characters from science fiction, fantasy, folklore and myth. A former assistant producer of the local access cable TV program* Mystery Readers Corner, *Ms. Ward edited the respected webzine* Crescent Blues *for eight years, and co-edited* Unconventional Fantasy, *a six-volume collection of fiction, non-fiction and art celebrating the fortieth anniversary of World Fantasy Con. She has also contributed interviews and articles for diverse publications before starting interviewing for* Galaxy's Edge *magazine. Her website is JeanMarieWard.com.*

FOLKLORE, PLAGUES AND ANGLERFISH:

GALAXY'S EDGE INTERVIEWS SEANAN McGUIRE

by Jean Marie Ward

What are award-winning, SFF writers made of? In the case of Seanan McGuire—author of the October Daye, InCryptid, Wayward Children series and more under her own name, as well as the science fiction horror novels of her alter ego Mira Grant and the children's fantasy she writes as A. Deborah Baker—the answer encompasses music, art, anglerfish and 3 a.m. fanfiction attacks. Strange as the recipe may seem, you can't argue with the results. To date, McGuire's honors include the 2010 John W. Campbell Award (now the Astounding Award) for Best New Writer, the 2013 Nebula Award for Best Novella, five Hugo Awards, a record-breaking five Hugo nominations in a single year, and five consecutive Hugo nominations for Best Series—to say nothing of the seven Pegasus Awards she's won for her filking. Eager to learn more, *Galaxy's Edge* sat down with the California native a few days before the release of her latest novel, *Angel of the Overpass*, to talk about her earliest days as a writer, her fascination with microbial marvels, and expanding the notion of personhood on the page.

Galaxy's Edge: When did you first realize you wanted to become a writer?

Seanan McGuire: When I found out it was an option. I was a very weird child. I was credulous in some ways that sound fake to me now, even though I remember the experience, and disbelieving in other odd ways. It made perfect sense to me that lunch boxes would grow on trees, which happens in *The Wizard of Oz*. And if there are lunchbox trees, why wouldn't there be book trees? I had never met an author. I had never met anyone who said they were an author. I just figured that books happened. Being a storyteller felt like too much of a responsibility for any one person. It didn't make sense, given the breadth of stories I could experience if I went looking, that anyone would do that.

At the time, one of my favorite shows was an anthology series on the USA Network called *Ray Bradbury Presents*. Every episode began with this white-haired dude sitting at a typewriter pounding away. Then there'd be a ding, and he would pull a sheet of paper out of the typewriter and throw it into the air. It fluttered down and formed part of the logo.

One day I asked my grandmother, "Who the heck is that? Why is this old dude taking up like a whole minute of what could be story?"

She said, "That's Ray Bradbury. He wrote all these stories."

That was my bolt of lightning moment. *Wait, one person made all this up? This is all fake, and one person sat down and thought of it, and that was okay? That was allowed?* I pretty much decided on the spot that that's what I was going to do.

Galaxy's Edge: How did you get from there to your first published stories?

Seanan McGuire: A lot of fan fiction. So much fan fiction. Shortly after the *Ray Bradbury Presents* incident, my mother brought me this gigantic manual typewriter from a yard sale. It cost five dollars, and it disrupted her sleep for years. It weighed more than I did. I would sit down, feed my paper in, and pound away for hours. I was seven. Seven-year-olds don't sleep like humans They're people, but they aren't humans yet. The idea that 3 a.m. is not a good time to start working on a giant manual typewriter that sounds like gunfire does not occur to their tiny seven-year-old brains. And since the typewriter was so big compared to how big I was, I couldn't just type, I had to assault the keyboard. I hunt and peck at approximately two hundred forty words per minute…

Because I was writing for hours at night, I would write stories about my cats or what I did that weekend or—and this is key—about having adventures with my friends, the My Little Ponies in Dream Valley. I had no idea that a self-insert was a bad thing. I was seven. I had no idea that saying I would be good at everything the ponies needed me to be good at was being a Mary Sue. Again, I was seven. I did this for years.

The thing about writing is the more you do it, the better you'll get. You can get good at some really bad habits. But putting words in a line, forming sentences, building sentences into a paragraph, building enough paragraphs onto a page to have a page? That's a muscle. That's something that you learn by doing. I turned out reams and reams and reams of not goodness, but it taught me how to put together a page.

Then I got to high school and discovered real fanfic, where you write in a universe. [Fanfic] had these weird unspoken rules, like the Mary Sue Litmus Test, and what was and was not appropriate to do. One of the first pieces of advice I was given was never write a character who looks like you, even if they're canonical, because everyone will assume that the blonde girl writing about Veronica Mars or Emma Frost is really writing about herself, and that's not okay. At some point, every dude I know writes about himself having magical adventures in a magical D&D land and getting all the hot elf babes. But if a blonde woman writes a blonde character or a Black woman writes a Black character or anything superficially similar to their appearance, it doesn't matter how integral that character is to the story, it's proof they're sticking themselves in the story, and that's bad. I disagree with this, in case you can't tell.

Galaxy's Edge: What about the little blonde girl in the InCryptid series?

Seanan McGuire: I ultimately got around the problem by making everything fanfic. Verity is basically Chelsie Hightower from *So You Think You Can Dance*. The InCryptid series was a response to my PA saying, "Please, write something that gets us invited to go backstage on *So You Think You Can Dance*."

But in the beginning I just wrote a lot of fanfic. The more fanfic I wrote, the better I got at things like plot and structure and actually writing a 20,000-word, a 50,000-word, a 100,000-word story that wouldn't bore my readers. Eventually I started writing original fiction, which pretty much went nowhere. I would write it, I would be happy with it, and then I would revise it, because when no one's publishing you, masturbatory revision takes 90 percent of your time.

One day, my friend Tara, who knew me from the fanfic community, said an agent friend of hers was branching out and starting her own boutique agency. And because [the agent] was from the fanfic community, she was looking for fanfic authors with an interest in their own original fiction. I sent her a copy of *Rosemary and Rue*. She sent me back a list of suggested revisions. I did one more revision, and she signed me. Then everything went nuts.

Galaxy's Edge: Because you had something else in the pipe—something that became the Newsflesh series.

Seanan McGuire: The thing about writing very fast is I write very fast. When we took *Rosemary and Rue* to DAW, I had already finished [the] first three books in the October Daye series (*Rosemary and Rue*, *A Local Habitation* and *An Artificial Night*). I also had a rough and not-so-great draft of Book Four, *Late Eclipses*, but I had time to revise and beat it into a shape. I also had *Feed*, my biotechnical science-fiction thriller. We took *Feed* to Orbit.

With DAW, we were very fortunate in that a good friend of mine was also a DAW author and able to give me the nepotism referral to her editor. She wasn't inappropriate about it. She just said, "This is my friend, Seanan. She wrote a really good book. I think you'll like it. Let me introduce you."

At Orbit, we went through a more normal submissions process. We wound up with DongWon Song, who's now an agent but at the time was an Orbit editor. They were the perfect editor for that series. I miss working with them.

Galaxy's Edge: You mentioned in another interview that you took the "dragon major" in college: a double major in folklore and herpetology. How did that play into your writing and your day job?

Seanan McGuire: I've never had a day job that used either parts of my degree. I think that anything we do or are interested in will play into our writing. We can't help it. It's part of why I get kind of angry on a personal level at authors who say that fanfic is bad and you can't do fanfic ever. Well, okay, I'm gonna go over your work and find every element that you took from Shakespeare. How dare you write fanfic? I'm gonna find every element you took from Austen or from Poe. Or from fairy tales, from the Brothers Grimm, from Disney.

Humans are magpies. We do not thrive on original thought. That's not how we're constructed. If you have one truly original thought in your entire lifetime, you're about average. You're doing well.

We want to think of ourselves as these incredible original innovators of everything, but that's not how monomyths work. It's not how human psychology works. Everything's a remix.

Because I studied both the so-called soft science of folklore and the hard science of herpetology, I have, to a certain degree, the flexibility of thought arising from two very different disciplines. It doesn't make me better or worse than anyone else. It just means that I have been trained to look at things from those multiple angles. There are still ways of thought that are completely alien to me. I have no experience or background in any kind of physical handiwork. I don't know how to fix a car. If you hand me a hammer and a nail, the odds are good that what I'll hand you back is a trip to the ER, because I have just broken my hand. There are patterns and ways of thought that I can't wrap my head around. But having that initial flexibility made it easier for me to switch gears as I got older.

You can see the dichotomy in the two sides of my work. When I write as Seanan, I tend to write very monomythical, very inspired by folklore, very poetic. One of my favorite copy editors says, when you copy edit my work for flow and for tone, you need to remain aware of the fact that I have never written a book in my life. What I write is 300-page poems. That's not inaccurate. The way I build sentences, the way I phrase things and manage the rising action very much reflects the fact I was a folklore major who studied oral histories for a long time. Within a single book, there will usually be one or two phrases that I hit very often. It's not because don't I think my readers are clever; it's how I assemble a narrative.

When I write as Mira Grant, [the stories] are very biological. I started out wanting her to be a horror author. It turns out she's not, because I am so much less interested in the screaming than I am in the scalpel. I want my science to make sense, and I want my biology to make sense. That's what makes me happy.

Galaxy's Edge: Even when dealing with mermaids?

Seanan McGuire: Even when dealing with mermaids. The mermaids [of *Into the Drowning Deep*] were actually a direct attack on DongWon. When they were my editor, I would threaten to write them a book about anglerfish mermaids.

The way anglerfish reproduce is the male anglerfish will be attracted by the smell of the female anglerfish's pheromones. He thinks she's so sexy that, when he finally finds her, all he wants to do is eat her. So, he chomps onto her skin. This causes a chemical reaction which melts his skin and fuses him with the female. Her body will gradually absorb his until all that's left is his scrotum.

The female now has a pair of testicles sticking out of her, and she can control when sperm is released. One female anglerfish can have hundreds of sets of testes stuck to her from men that she has effectively eaten. In terms of size, the male anglerfish is about one and a half to two inches long. The female anglerfish is the size of an alligator snapping turtle. It's one of the biggest cases of sexual dimorphism in the vertebrate world…. The biology of my mermaids was preset by that horror.

Galaxy's Edge: You didn't work in herpetology, but I understand your former day job used a lot of your science background, which contributed to *Feed* and your all-too-plausible zombie apocalypse.

Seanan McGuire: Yep. I am a prophetic genius. The entirety of COVID-19 has been an exciting game of people telling me: "You were right about everything two years ago." Yes, I was. Thank you. There you go.

Galaxy's Edge: Are there more such prophecies in our future? Should we be shivering in our boots?

Seanan McGuire: Right now, I am not doing anything super pathological, in part because I lost a lot of optimism in the current pandemic.

People ask me all the time, "What do you feel like you got wrong? What would you do differently?" The answer is I had too much hope. Part of that is *Feed* was written and published before the real rise of Facebook, before the rise of microblogging, [at a time] when if you wanted a blog, you still had to set up a blog and usually wrote longer-form things. Readers could get an idea of who you were, your likes, your dislikes, your prejudices. You weren't just delivering speedy sound bites of hatred and vitriol.

I like the flexibility and speed of Facebook and Twitter in terms of things like coordinating disaster response. But what we've seen is we're not doing as much as we could, because we've all learned to hate each other in this time of super-fast microblogging, botnets and trolls.

There was a point, early in the current situation, where I posted a thread on Twitter (which is my primary habitat most of the time) about ways to protect yourself from con crud and the seasonal flu. There is a tweet in that thread which can be seen as equating coronavirus with airborne diseases.

At the time, the official position was that the disease we're dealing with now was not in fact airborne, even though anyone who had ever worked with any coronavirus anywhere was saying, "No, it's probably airborne. If you don't think it's airborne, you're probably wrong." The science said, "Probably airborne," but the official public information said, "Not."

So, I posted this tweet. It's in the middle of a relatively innocuous thread. *Hey, wash your hands, drink lots of water, sleep. I know that you don't feel like those last two have anything to do with your health at a convention, but they genuinely do. The more well hydrated you are, the less likely you are to pick up most common crud.* That sort of thing. For three days I got barraged by trolls screaming at me for being so irresponsible as to imply that this could be an airborne disease. They weren't real people. None of them had existed on Twitter prior to a month previous. They weren't there to engage in conversation. They were there to yell at me. That's because it's so easy to set up a word finder, something that triggers off a keyword and unleashes this tide of hating on people who say things you don't like.

My pandemic response [in *Feed*] was founded on the idea that the news would lie to us (which we saw will happen), and that in the absence of the news, citizen scientists and citizen reporters would rise as a source of credible information. Instead, what we

saw is people will rise to sell you miracle cures made from mercury and tell you that your children have COVID because they were given a vaccination twenty years ago, even though your children are eleven. It's just bad.

I am not currently working on any diseases because part of what I enjoy about writing pandemic fiction, why it makes me happy to be Mira Grant, is that diseases fascinate me. I find them really interesting—the mechanisms by which they work, the things that we know they can do to us, the things that we're still finding out they can do to us. They're amazing. They're so simple. They're not living things. They're basically malware. They're just these little instruction bundles that plug into your body and go haywire.

It is easier for me not to be afraid of them if I understand them and am writing about them and having a good time. It feels a little mean to have a good time with diseases right now. The way I have always coped with the horrible diseases I created was by going, "No-no. Once enough people started dying, we would care. Once enough people were at risk, we would care." But what I've seen is that far too many of the people in positions of power wouldn't.

Galaxy's Edge: There are those who say, if this world fails us, we should write the world we want to live in. What would that world look like for you?

Seanan McGuire: The way I would like the world to be is incredibly overly optimistic. I don't think we're going to get there in my lifetime. We have enough food that no one needs to be hungry. We have enough resources that no one needs to be homeless, no one needs to be sick. We have enough of everything that no one actually needs to feel like they don't have enough. But there is a point at which anything stops being the thing itself and becomes counting coup. There are people with so much money, they could be spending money every minute of every single day of their lives and not come even remotely close to running out of money. And what do they do? Do they rent Disney World for a month? No. Do they set up a zoo full of tigers in their basement? No. They make more money because they have seen how much they are willing to exploit the world, and they want to make sure there's no one in a position to exploit them.

I want a world where rich people pay their fair share, where everybody gets safe housing, food, clean water, medical care. Where the color of your skin is not treated as any kind of judgment on your personal character. Where the fact that people love who they're gonna love is not treated as some kind of judgment on their character. It's so idealistic. Every step forward is amazing, but we have the potential, as a species, to be so much better. Sometimes we aren't because it would be inconvenient to be better right now. Sometimes it's because we don't want to, or it would be hard or "How can I feel like I am better than you if you have as much as me?"

Galaxy's Edge: As opposed to seeing equality as a valid goal.

Seanan McGuire: We've been unequal for so incredibly long that equality really does feel like oppression to a lot of people who have been on the top of the inequality pyramid.

Galaxy's Edge: Your fiction celebrates diversity and inclusivity. Is this your way of making the world you write shinier, or is it something that just happens?

Seanan McGuire: A little bit of both. But mostly it's that anything that is 100 percent straight, white, and able-bodied is unrealistic unless you want to set up a bunch of oppressive structures I have no interest in writing.

The world is not a monoculture. Humanity has never been a monoculture. [A lot of stories] treat humanity like a monoculture where any setting you want to use is just pretty stage-dressing and any character you want to design needs a reason to be something other than what we jokingly refer to as the "Six-fecta": straight, white, vaguely Christian (but not too Christian; you can't be too religious) able-bodied, cisgender and male. So many books in our genre still hit all six of those attributes with every main character. The only exceptions are some secondary characters who are women because, otherwise, how do we reward the men for being awesome?

But that's not the world I live in. I have been a queer, disabled, half-Roma woman for my entire life. I knew I liked girls from the time I was eight. Not in a sexual way but in a "If I'm gonna hold hands with somebody and kiss them" way, I would prefer it be a girl. So I can absolutely say that I was queer when I was eight. I've been half Roma since my daddy knocked up my mom in the back of a van, and I've been female since I popped out. I've done the gender interrogation you're supposed to do as a cis ally and determined that "girl" is pretty much the label that works for me.

I never had a shot at that Six-fecta if I wanted it. Why would I, as someone who deviates from that "norm" on multiple levels, want to write that norm? I know people who fit it, I love people who fit it. I am not saying there's anything wrong with them wanting to see characters who look like them. But sometimes I want to see a character who looks like me, and that means a character with multiple overlapping identities all of which inform her daily life.

Sometimes, people I know will tell me they want to see a character that looks like them, and they don't get to do that very often. Then I will make a genuine effort to include a character that looks like them, because I want them to have that experience. We learn how to human from stories. Like I said before, humans are not built for constant original thought. We learn what a person looks like from the stories people tell us. Sometimes that is learning: "Wait, that's me. I'm a person." And sometimes it's learning: "Wait, that's Jean Marie. Maybe she's a person too."

Culturally, we have done ourselves a huge disservice by telling so many stories for such a long time where the only people who got to be at the center of the story were the ones who fit those six attributes, because only those people get fully acknowledged as people by the monomyth we're living in. That's not fair and not okay. The only time I tend to manipulate the diversity in a story is if I realize I need to kill somebody. If a group has little representation, you can kill a much larger percentage of that group by killing one character. If I kill a straight white man in science fiction, I have killed one of ninety million straight white men. If I kill a trans woman in science fiction, I've killed one of maybe twelve. That's a very different statement, whether or not I intend to be making it.

So, if someone is in the line of fire and I cannot move them, I will stop, look at what I'm doing, and ask myself: How big a deal is this character to the group they represent? How big a deal would it be if I were reading this book and that character looked like me? Would I have seen me before? That's not tokenism. I don't give plot armor to these characters. They can still die. It's a matter of am I taking away someone's emotional support character?

Galaxy's Edge: You have explored just about every subgenre in speculative fiction. Is there any particular kind of story or genre that you would really like to write but haven't had the chance?

Seanan McGuire: I have an intense, bordering on the ridiculous, fondness for mid-Nineties chick lit, the sub-genre where *The Princess Diaries*, *The Boy Next Door*, and *Bridget Jones's Diary* live. I'm waiting for the nostalgia wave to whip those back around. I've written several. I'm pretty good at it, but there's no market for them right now. So they sit and occasionally get revised, when I have time, to make sure that they stay up to my current standards. And they go nowhere.

I would also very much like to write a series of cozy mysteries—*The Dog Barks at Midnight* sort of thing. I have a concept for a fun series of cozy mysteries. But unfortunately, I am told by both my agent and several authors I know who write cozy mysteries, there is no money there. There's just none.

It's not that I only write to chase the money, because no one becomes a writer to chase the money. That is the worst decision you could possibly make. Don't do that, children. Or adults. Or unspeakable cosmic entities. Don't become a writer because you want to get paid. You will not get paid. But there is a difference between writing something I am truly passionate about, cannot stop myself from writing, that I already know I'm good at, and not

getting paid; and writing books in a genre I find charming but not completely compelling, kind-of-wanna-try-my-hand-at but will not get paid. One is a reasonable self-limiting decision. The other is just not bright.

I'd also like to write a truly horrific horror novel that has no science fiction elements. Just horror. I wanna do horror for the sake of horror. I wanna get my Clive Barker on. I wanna get my Kathe Koja on. I can't. Every time I try, I get distracted by the possibility of science.

Galaxy's Edge: That's tragic. Science is death to horror.

Seanan McGuire: Yeah, I love horror so much, and I'm so bad at it.

Galaxy's Edge: Any closing thoughts?

Seanan McGuire: We are recording this on April 29, 2021. I have a book coming out on May 4 called *Angel of the Overpass*. It's the third book in my Ghost Roads series, which is InCryptid-adjacent, published by DAW Books. I won't say it's the last, but it is likely to be the final entry in Rose Marshall's story for a while. So I'm very excited about that.

Over on my Twitter, I just finished a complete review of the October Daye books, because they are nominated for a Best Series Hugo this year. Having grown up in fandom, I tend to be very careful and a little aloof when talking about the Hugos. I remember being told by my foster mother when I was a teenager that it's gauche to say you want to win. But I really want to win this year.

I feel that the Best Series category was created for urban fantasy. I know it wasn't created *just* for urban fantasy, but urban fantasy plays best at series length. It is a story that needs that room to grow and breathe and really be considered as a whole, not just as the sum of its parts. I would desperately like for the first true urban fantasy—just urban fantasy, not urban science fiction, not urban horror, but urban fantasy—Hugo to go to a female or female-identifying author. It's the only science fiction subgenre that is female-dominated and doesn't have the word "romance" somewhere in the description. Romance is great. I love romance. I write romance. But female authors get shoved into romance so quickly, whether or not that's what we want to be doing. Having a subgenre we currently control has always been very very important to me. It feels like a thing we have accomplished as ladies.

So, I would like the first Hugo Award given to a work of pure urban fantasy to be given to a female-identifying author. It doesn't have to be me. You have many other choices. We are a big and diverse field. But if you're looking at this year's ballot, it does have to be me.

Galaxy's Edge: We'll keep our fingers crossed and hope the best.

Seanan McGuire: Thank you.

Richard Chwedyk sold his first story in 1990, won a Nebula in 2002, and has been active in the field for the past thirty-one years.

RECOMMENDED BOOKS

by Richard Chwedyk

GETTING BACK AND CATCHING UP

At the outset, my apologies. I may not have that many "new" books in this issue's column. No one ever gets to everything, and in spite of what you may read online, the publishing industry is having little trouble putting out new titles. It can be overwhelming. Throw a pandemic into the mix, creating the necessity of my having to re-invent my curricula for new formats, and the game of reviewing books is taken to a new level. My wife and I just received our second COVID-19 vaccine shots and my finger joints are aching as I type this. Any version of "normal" you'd like to throw at me at this time I'll gladly accept. In the meantime, here are some books I didn't want to get by without notice, whether they're hot off the physical or virtual presses or not.

◆ ◆ ◆

Stand on Zanzibar
by John Brunner
Tor Essentials
March 2021
ISBN: 978-1-250-78122-2

They don't make 'em like they used to.

At least that's what you'll hear from the geezers all the time. There's something missing in the current SF. What it is that's missing often differs from geezer to geezer, but hearing this said again and again can get tiresome, even for other geezers.

But it just so happens, every now and then, the geezers (or at least some of them) are right.

It's hard to find anything recently published that matches the ambitions of John Brunner's 1968 novel, *Stand on Zanzibar*: exploring a culture—a whole world, really—from a multiplicity of levels while maintaining a central story that brings the vastness of this complex (and maybe crumbling) planet into stark focus. Parts of the novel are written in the straightforward, no-nonsense prose Brunner had been working to perfect for a decade or so beforehand. Other parts are written as news reports or anecdotal bits, illustrating aspects of the twenty-first century world in an almost documentary style. Other parts are written from the glib perspectives of canny social commentators. And all of this is interlaced to keep things moving along at a surprisingly brisk pace.

As was mentioned often at the time, the novel's structure owes much to the trilogy by John Dos Passos, *U.S.A.* In this case, I dare to say it now, though I couldn't have gotten away with saying it 53 years ago, Brunner actually improves upon the trilogy in many ways. He streamlined it, actually. His central dramatic story is more compelling, his worldview wider and, worth noting in the current literary environment, more diverse. This is not to knock Dos Passos's sublime achievement with *U.S.A.*, but Brunner took the baton and ran with it like a winner.

This adventurous structure itself is a thing to behold, like a Bauhaus-designed "modern" building after it's been around for a century. In some ways, Brunner was re-thinking the way a novel could be written—as if that's part of his future vision. If vehicles and buildings will be built differently a half century from this day, why shouldn't novels look and work differently in that anticipated world? He applied his science-fictional imagination to the act of novel writing itself.

The sad thing is, perhaps, now that we're living in the time Brunner wrote about in 1968, there is a greater sameness to the way our current novels are written. All our current writers, it seems (exceptions granted), have gone to writing schools that have taught them "best practices" that manage great efficiencies and great comforts. But like a row of townhouses in a residential urban neighborhood, they all have the same look and feel, omitting a few changes of color schemes and some superficial ornamentation.

Of course, in the era Brunner was writing this novel, he was considered a member of the "New Wave." Brunner, in retrospect, wasn't really part of that merry, contentious crew (like most literary movements, a great many of its members were draftees, not volunteers). Half of the anger and vitriol and brawling over the New Wave was the notion of "style over substance." Brunner was all for innovations in style (whatever that is), but only so far as it helped to convey the substance (whatever *that* is) of the story in its most effective way.

And what about that substance? Much of the current reading of "classic" and/or "modern" science fiction these days seems to rest on picking over which parts authors did or didn't "get right." As far as the focal "issue" of the novel—i.e., exponential overpopulation—Brunner didn't quite hit the nail on the head. The "population bomb" didn't go off (though it may still be ticking). We don't have any cell phones here, and all the computers are ginormous, house-sized structures with little public access.

Other aspects, like the growing frustration of individuals who become "berserkers" and strike out against innocent bystanders, the "corporatization" of governments, the excesses of popular culture, the addict-like hunger for media replacing "real" experience (like "Mr. and Mrs. Everywhere"), the blending of cultures across the globe—Brunner hits the nail hard and true.

Which makes reading the novel even now a revelation. You'll turn to certain sections and find yourself whispering, or grunting, "How did he *know*? How did he *do* it?"

We're fortunate that someone at Tor decided to bring back this novel at this time, to remind us what we can do when we of think of science fiction as something more than a tag on the binding of certain books relegated to certain shelves of the local bookstore. It can be dangerous, as this novel remains.

◆◆◆

Immunity Index
by Sue Burke
Tor
May 2021
ISBN: 978-1-250-31787-2

Also from Tor, Sue Burke's latest novel may not be the successor to Brunner's brilliance, but she has managed the remarkable task of making her near-future world *so* plausible it nearly (but not quite) defeats its task of being a "what's coming" story to a "what's happening" story. She has placed her story in a world bowled over by a worldwide pandemic (who saw *that* coming?), and places it in a country and city (my all-too-familiar but beloved Chicago) where democracy is fast eroding, as are supplies of the basics. Remember the disappearance of toilet paper at the beginning of COVID-19? Burke will see you and raise you ten. Her degree of accuracy on that front is downright frightening. That's the brief version of the world in which Burke has placed her novel.

The story deftly shifts between the tribulations of three women and one genetic scientist, the latter having "designed" the three formers, to purposes it will take the rest of this brief but challenging novel to reveal. Burke's experience as a journalist and translator prove exceptionally helpful in keeping a complex plot coherent and intriguing.

So much recent science fiction has been set in the far future to presumably avoid becoming entangled in the messiness of our current circumstances. Burke, to her credit, takes on the messiness, and does so courageously. Remember that word that appears in many definitions of SF: "extrapolation"? Burke extrapolates with facility, intensity and vigor.

Burke's vision of our near future is in many respects bleak, but not without its hopes and a few lighter notes. Its wit is dry but satisfying. Another thing that I found enjoyable about this novel is that it is written at the tight length of those paperback originals we geezers grew up on in the middle of the previous century. It's a good length to get a story across without overweighing the vehicle with added-on subplots. Would that more novels follow in that path.

◆ ◆ ◆

Daughter of the Serpentine
by E. E. Knight
Ace
November 2020
ISBN: 978-1-9848-0408-2

I'm glad I got on board with this series at the outset, the first novel, *Novice Dragoneer*. It's one of the best things going in the fantasy field these days. E. E. Knight has created a splendid protagonist with Ileth, a girl of exceptionally humble background (no "Name," no patronage, no family with political influence) who manages to qualify for the Serpentine Academy with hopes of becoming a Dragoneer. What makes Ileth so endearing as a character is that she's thoughtful, curious and respectful, cautious but not fearful, along with all the other expected heroic qualities that mark people who find themselves at the center of fantasy series. She has an easier time dealing with dragons than with people, and it's no surprise that the dragons find it easier dealing with her than with the other Dragoneers, apprentices, dancers and other humans who surround them. As attractive as this relationship may be, most of the novel focuses on Ileth's progress through the ranks, her friendships, intrigues that involve her origins, and possible relationship to people in power in the Vale Republic. Attempts on her life, factional villainy, and if that isn't enough—pirates!

What marks Knight's work here is his deliberate and very realistic depiction of the Serpentine Academy and the world that surrounds it. What do I mean by "realistic"? Every little detail makes sense. Every place and every object have a physical weight and texture. The actions and reactions of every character are derived from understandable motivations and necessities. In the same way, the plot moves in a practical way—not slowly but deliberately. Which is not to say the story isn't full of surprises. It is, but they unfold in a way that makes you feel, when you get to each revelation, it has been earned. And Knight has a keen eye for action scenes. He not only knows when to pick up the pace, but how to do so, so that he never leaves you in a blur. His prose has a touch of energy, and of music, but not so much that he leaves his story behind.

Ending a second book in a series is no easy task, but he does so here with an admirable combination of resolution and anticipation. You can't ask for more than that.

I eagerly await the next book in the series.

◆ ◆ ◆

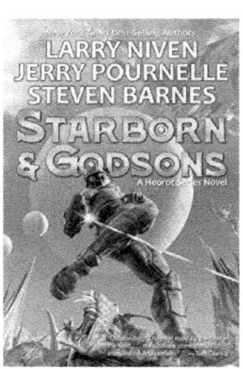

Starborn & Godsons
by Larry Niven, Jerry Pournelle and Steven Barnes
Baen
April 2020
978-1-9821-2448-9

I received a letter—a real letter—a while back from GE reader and subscriber John Hertz, who remembers me from the days when I moderated writing workshops at a few Worldcons. He wrote in general complaint that some of his favorite recent books have received scant attention from the award-giving bodies in the field, such as the Hugos, Nebulas, Locus Awards, etc. Indirectly, I think, I was being taken to task for not having reviewed them in these pages. I'll take only partial blame, as Baen's promo folks have not been at the top of their game in getting advance copies to me. Nevertheless, Mr. Hertz gave me a list of books he considered worthy but overlooked, and this is one I managed to catch up with.

Starborn and Godsons is/was a long-awaited sequel (and conclusion?) to the Legacy of Heorot series. It finds us on the planet Avalon, which after several generations and much conflict has been colonized by humans. The original colonists have mostly passed on, and the planet's humans are called "Starborn." They have no direct memory of Earth and have had no contact with the planet in ages. Earlier volumes in the series concerned themselves with the struggles of surviving a harsh environment, conflicts with competing lifeforms called "grendels," which attracted me to the earlier volume, *Beowulf's Children*. You can understand why. At a visceral level, these stories tie together with the world depicted in Old English epic poetry in ways that seem more than an extended metaphor. The old world of bardic sagas and the tales of humans establishing footholds on new planets re-envisions both traditions in new and surprising ways.

At the heart of this novel, which puts us into contact, or in some cases reacquaints us with, some other alien lifeforms, are the starborns facing encounters with "godsons"—other humans who set out spacefaring after the original colonists of Avalon. They also have no direct contact with Earth, and have developed in their own way, different from the earth-born humans and the starborn alike. In a way, it's a "first contact" tale between humans and humans, which is something you don't see too often, and implicitly questions our expectations when we think or talk about one of the big questions in our science fiction (and our literature in general): what makes us human?

Any attempt at plot summary on my part at this juncture would be insufficient. The novel is super-jam packed with action, characters and ideas. The question for readers (and since many of you have already read this novel and have already answered the question to your own satisfaction, bear with me) is whether it all holds together into an enjoyable and rewarding experience. As many of you can already guess, my reviewing it here and now indicates my answer is yes.

What added to my enjoyment and appreciation of it has to do with my interest in writers and writing and how we manage to do the crazy things we sometimes manage to do. Like having three authors work in collaboration. How do they manage not to get in each other's way? It's hard enough for two authors to collaborate on an extended narrative (except when they do, and has been done famously in this field), how do *three* authors manage it? I'm familiar with the works of each author here individually as well as in collaboration. And each author, individually, does not write like the other two collaborators, but when they come together they seem to create a distinct, new voice which is unlike any of the previous ones. It is a tribute to their skill and their professionalism, to which I'll add, since the passing of Mr. Pournelle, we'll not see its like again.

Another reason to squeeze in this review now was to note that unfortunate passing (I wanted to get to this in the previous issue, but space and time prohibited my doing so). This was Mr. Pournelle's last book, I believe. And regardless of his behavior or opinion outside the pages of his fiction, as a novelist and as a science fiction *thinker*, he was a formidable and significant presence in our field whose work—in collaboration or individually—was always skillful, intelligent and witty.

◆ ◆ ◆

The Big Book of Modern Fantasy

Edited by Ann VanderMeer and Jeff VanderMeer
Vintage
July 2020
ISBN: 978-0-525-56386-0

I think I have found the book for my fall Fantasy Writing Workshop class.

Yes, I'm a year late getting to it, but the editors, I believe, have designed this volume to be around for a while. Truth to tell, their previous "Big Book" volume (of science fiction) left me a little wanting. The selection was interesting but fell short of being comprehensive, and the biographical/historical info that accompanied the fiction read like it was cut a pasted from Wikipedia and/or John Clute's Encyclopedia of Science Fiction website. But that was *that* book.

This book has an outstanding selection of selection of stories with a number of truly significant tales and authors, in all modes and styles of fantasy writing. Jack Vance, Margaret St. Clair, Manly Wade Wellman, Zenna Henderson, Fritz Leiber, C. J. Cherryh, Michael Moorcock, Joanna Russ, Angela Carter, Jane Yolen, R. A. Lafferty, Terry Pratchett, Tove Jansson, Richard Bowes, Sheree Renée Thomas, Kelly Link, Jeffrey Ford, Victor LaValle—you get the picture. And the editors don't shortchange the more literary names like Vladimir Nabokov, Gabriel Garcia Marquez, Sylvia Townsend Warner, Mikhail Bulgakov, Jorge Luis Borges, Amos Tutuola, Italo Calvino, Silvina Ocampo—of course, there's more.

The accompanying background material is informative without being didactic, and written from the perspective of a true connoisseur. The layouts and fonts have been selected to maximize the containment of its extensive contents while providing the greatest readability. Not only is it a "big" book, but a lovely one. A keeper.

My problem with teaching fantasy writing is that the majority of my students think all fantasy writing is either Tolkien, Harry Potter, or Percy Jackson. That fantasy writing might encompass so much more was a little difficult without my scanning a few dozen books and magazines. I didn't mind the extra work, but I did dream of finding a sturdy volume of "modern" (as opposed to "classic") fantasy fiction of more recent pedigree with a wide array of subjects and styles.

If you, perchance, might be looking for the same thing, for whatever reason, look no further.

◆ ◆ ◆

The 2021 Rhysling Anthology
Edited by Alessandro Manzetti
The Science Fiction & Fantasy Poetry Association
May 2021
ISBN: 979-8-7292-6415-5

I'm always pushing for readers in the fields of science fiction and fantasy to read more poetry. No one needs to make a steady diet of it, but often we forget how well poetry can get to essences of things—of stories, of ideas, of simple but intense visions. An effective phrase, a few lines, a stanza, may evoke entire epics. It's good to remember that we can be transported to phenomenal worlds with a single word, if the word is magical.

The Science Fiction & Fantasy Poetry Association has been coming out with their annual anthologies for some time now, in connection with their Rhysling Awards. They keep getting bigger, better designed and, most significantly, their content grows better as well. No one in the SF/F world is sitting around worrying about the future of poetry in our fields, much less paying attention. Which may be a good thing, because it seems that SF poetry is thriving, thank you very much.

This current volume, in the reins of a new editor, Alessandro Manzetti, has an excellent selection of work by names you will be familiar with (prose authors can write poetry too, and vice versa) and some names which you'll no doubt be encountering soon enough.

And the cover art by Adrian Borda is gorgeous.

Copyright © 2021 by Richard Chwedyk.

Gregory Benford is a professor of physics at the University of California, Irvine and the author of Timescape, *among other novels.*

A SCIENTIST'S NOTEBOOK

by Gregory Benford

SELFNESS

[Editor's Note: This column was written in 1997, so the start of the article reflects Gregory Benford's experience as a twin, and the then political and societal opinion of cloning. But the rest of the article, with his insightful scientific extrapolation of where cloning can lead us on a physical, emotional and societal level, and how many permutations it could take, is still relevant today, and ahead of any scientific advancements undertaken in the 25 years since its original publication. It makes for a fascinating philosophical read.]

I am a clone.

Or rather, I am better than one. Or so any identical twin surely must see the matter.

The 1990s media feeding frenzy about a cloned sheep, Dolly, showed us journalism in its fullest modern form. Many of those writing about this genuine watershed moment in techno-culture followed current journalist practice: their foremost research instrument was the telephone. Of those who called me—an unlikely authority, since I am not a biologist—none realized that DNA does not solely determine the heritage a child gets from its parents.

My brother, Jim, and I shared a womb without a view for nine months. (Though not always restfully, our mother reports.) Genetically identical, we also enjoyed the same currents and chemicals of our mother. After a rather traumatic birth—both had our appendixes removed within days—we were brought up in the same house, with constant attentive parents, and even wore matching clothes until our late teens. (How much trauma this clothing ritual induced in our personalities I leave to others to decide; suffice to say that being seen as sugary-cute has left me with a decided prejudice against sweets in any form.)

True twins share womb chemistry and endure many fateful slings and arrows together. The fabled connection between twins is true, in my case. We are distantly dismissive of mere fraternal twins (different DNA, after all) and regard all others as "singletons," those condemned by birth to endure the isolation of never truly sharing the intuitive grasp that we enjoy without paying a price.

Or nearly so. There is mild statistical evidence that identicals have slightly lower IQ. This might be plausibly so; the comfort of ready communication may well lead to a certain mental laziness.

Jim and I felt the opposite. Reared in rural southern Alabama, we enjoyed an idyllic Huck Finn boyhood. But education there was casual at best. Our mother and father were high school teachers, and challenged the pervasive easy-going ignorance. We attended a one-room schoolhouse, with each row of seats a separate grade. Against this my brother and I united, reading widely and enjoying the clash of cultures parading by. After we were 9 our father became a career Army officer, whisking us to Japan for three years, Germany for another three, and further isolating the twins from a continuity that might have sucked us into the conventional.

So we are an odd pair, even among twins. Jim got his doctorate from the same institution as I, UC San Diego, in a similar area (plasma physics) and now lives a few kilometers from where I once lived, in northern California. Such correlations appear often among twins. We grow up in a culture of sameness, so have a sense of self always shared.

Twin intelligences are close to equal. Since we know—mostly from twin studies—that intelligence is about 50 percent genetic, this does not surprise. Jim and I have IQs separated by just 2 points, though our mother insured we don't know which is higher, though the average is 155.

Among singletons, interest in twins is enduring. Do we feel some mystical sense of connection? Of course; but whether it is mystical or not begs description. I am writing this at 35,000 feet over Greenland, on the way back to UC Irvine from Lapland. I know without thinking about it that my brother is probably body surfing on a beach near La Jolla, though

I have not spoken to him for ten days. I remember his itinerary and without conscious deliberation feel where he is likely to be. This is processing at the unconscious level, and as an experiment, when I see him in two days I shall check with him and let you know the outcome. [Later: my estimate was right to within the hour.]

But this is scarcely mystical. Instead, I attribute the innumerable similar incidents in our lives to a lot of automatic thinking, based on intuitions cooked up through more than five decades. To singletons this can look uncanny.

Speaking as a twin, clones seem a lesser form. They grow up in a later era than their genetic duplicates, with different upbringings. Would knowing that they were genetic duplicates trouble them? Surely such people would not be inherently more mentally fragile; Siamese twins are far more like each other than ordinary twins, yet suffer no higher incidence of mental illness than is usual, suggesting that even extreme parallels in nature and nurturer are not damaging.

The furor over Dolly puzzled me by the emotional level of debate. Reasonable people like political commentator George Will asked, "What if the great given—a human being is a product of the union of a man and a woman—is no longer a given?" This issue properly comes from a broader issue in biotechnology, the entire field of artificial birth in all forms, for there are no precise boundaries in this new territory.

Certainly I see no reason why society should prevent grieving parents from having a baby cloned from the cells of a dead child, if they wish. Beyond such emotionally wrenching cases, where should we erect walls? Oxford biologist Richard Dawkins asserted that he could see purely intellectual issues intriguing enough to justify cloning himself: "I think it would be mind-bogglingly fascinating to watch a younger edition of myself growing up in the twenty-first century instead of the 1940s."

Many no doubt find his position puzzling or even immoral or disgusting. Even so, why should Dawkins be prevented from having a cloned child? What is society's mandate?

The Dolly debate produced several claims that cloning violated the fundamental principle of individual dignity. Twins certainly belie that argument.

Fears of interchangeable people armies, usually marching robotically onward, come from a simple-minded genetic determinism. And the grounds for a principle of uniqueness seem vague at best.

After all, why treat clones differently? We twins and clones are all "monozygotes," as the biologists put it. In fact, clones necessarily separate in outside influences from their first moments in the womb, for the wombs are different. Another's DNA inserted into a host egg will acquire "maternal factors" from the proteins of that egg, affecting later development. The womb's complex chemical mix varies with each mother, so nine months of different "weather" will change the outcome in the fetus; the baby will not be a photocopy of its older original.

And clones will be full-fledged people with all rights attendant to that status. Nobody forces twins to serve as organ farms for their other twin; clones would have the same legal status.

The true first use of cloning will undoubtedly be in the "copying" of highly selected farm animals. These could first be excellent milk cows or racing horses. More futuristically, we shall see—and quite soon—the cloning of "pharm" animals which yield biotech products of use to us, such as insulin-rich milk from cows, and a whole array of therapeutic hormones, enzymes and proteins.

Plants have already been extensively engineered. More than three-quarters of the cotton grown in Alabama last year was genetically tuned to kill predatory insects. Already scientists are experimenting with cotton plants that contain polyester fibers, too, surely a boon for fans of leisure suits.

Still, cloning should indeed furrow the brow of long-perspective thinkers. We believe sexual reproduction holds sway over much of the kingdom of life because it provides ever-new gene mixes, allowing a species to build fresh defenses against the ever-mutating pathogens that infest the natural world. The perpetual arms race between prey and predator favors sex as a defense. Seen this way, we are men and women because the primary predator on humans have always been microbes, not tigers.

So "pharm" animals cloned over and over will face the very real threat of infectious diseases which wipe out a herd overnight. But surely nobody will clone huge numbers of humans, so such plagues will be quite unlikely. The breeds of influenza that regularly attack us genetically diverse humans will do far more damage.

As I write this, a presidential panel seems about to recommend a uniform federal ban on human cloning experiments. I believe this will be a mistake, generally, and an ineffective move anyway. The technology is fairly simple; others will pick it up. In Latin American countries or on offshore islands, clinics will offer the service at a hefty charge. Underground, without legal oversight, we will indeed see some tragedies and even horrors.

Bioethics is a field with many practitioners but few obviously qualified savants. Often the bans which spring from such federal committees prove ill-advised, their only long-term effects negative. This was the case with the two-year moratorium on recombinant DNA, which simply slowed the field without deciding anything. So did similar bans on selling organs or blood, and I predict, so shall the recent Clinton prohibition on using human embryos in federally backed medical research. The ultimate price for these momentary interruptions—and so far they have always been momentary—is lives lost because the resultant technology arrives too late for some patients.

Bioethicists tend to see problems everywhere, and saying no gives them visible power. Letting technology evolve willy-nilly, responding to what people want—maybe even people without advanced degrees!—gives bioethicists no perks or prominence; unsurprising, then, that they seldom go that route. They aren't the patients clinging to life, or infertile, or stunted in some potentially fixable way.

They also tend to think collectively, omitting the inconvenient needs of real people. Bioethics professor George Annas of Boston University flatly demands, "I want to put the burden of proof on scientists to show us why society needs this before society permits them to go ahead and [do] it." Note that he does not require this rule in his own work, including testing the above sentence by its own standards. Instead, Virginia Postrel has noted of Annas and many others, "We will hear the natural equated with the good, and fatalism lauded as maturity. That is a sentiment about which both green romantics and pious conservatives agree."

Indeed. We would save ourselves much trouble if we could agree that the proper place for most bioethical thought lies in counseling those affected, not in dictating the spectrum of possibilities.

✿

Cloning arouses anxieties stemming from a general uncertainty with the very concept of the self. Legally, even the mind-body unity seems shaky. In 1991 the California Supreme Court decided that a cancer patient did not have a right to share in the profits from UCLA's use of his diseased cells to produce new drugs. This meant that a patient does not even own his own body, and so his integral self is not simply bodily.

Consciousness seems to us to be slippery and yet intuitively obvious. We feel ourselves to be the same person all along our life trajectory, unique and self-contained. Just as an ant colony or a baseball game has an integrity even as its insects or players change, we have an irreducible selfness.

Of course, such assertions are hard to prove. (Indeed, proving who you are is done by showing a partial copy of yourself—fingerprints, or a drivers' license.) We all readily assent to knowing that we experience a continuous self.

Yet we fall asleep every day, a loss of conscious continuity. People who lapse into year-long comas can emerge again with the same personality. Still better, patients in brain operations who have their heads chilled down until they are legally brain dead, with no alpha and beta rhythms at all, are still themselves when they are warmed back up and revived. Their memories and mannerisms come through intact.

Over what spans of time and condition can we keep our sense of selfness unbroken?

The bedrock issue of preserving one's selfness then intersects the increasing interest in prolonging life—if necessary by either freezing oneself after death, or even "uploading" into computers.

Making yourself into a computer file and programs fits one present picture of our Self: the mind is software running on the hardware of the brain. The Self, then, is whatever program is running on your customized operating system, one developed by the rubs and rituals of your upbringing.

Of course, such an analogy is suspect, for our brains self-program themselves, laying down memories in chemical pathways that are not simply erased, and aren't under our conscious control.

But the uploader's central point is that one can copy a mind much as a tape copies a piece of music, without knowing how music is made. The brain, they say, is the same.

Minds are self-organizing, evolving systems, however, unlike fixed musical works; but the image is striking, still. Where does it lead us?

The first novel about uploading, Charles Platt's 1991 *The Silicon Man*, does not directly confront a basic problem of copying, Levinthal's paradox: to the degree that a copy approaches perfection, it defeats itself. In being an absolutely perfect copy—so that no one can tell it from the original—it transforms the original into a duplicate. This means the perfect copy is no longer a perfect copy, because it has obliterated, rather than preserved, the uniqueness of the original—and thus failed to copy a central aspect of the original.

A perfect, artificial human intelligence would inevitably have this effect on its natural original. Sf author Paul Levinson pointed out this feature, hinting that it portended even deeper problems, in the 1980s. While the paradox may seem a mere logical quibble, it underlines how little we know of how much fidelity to the original truly implies that the self has been preserved.

No mere technological improvement can remove this logical difficulty. Given enough memory maintenance, we could maintain numerical versions of ourselves, assuming that the recording process would not destroy our fleshy originals.

This raises great troubles, though. Termed variously Dittos, Duplicates or Copies, these digital entities lead a tenuous existence. Real, fleshy folk would decisively reject the Copy Fallacy: the belief that a digital Self was identical to the Original, and that an Original should feel that a Ditto itself somehow carried them forward into immortality. (As long as nobody pulls the plug, of course.)

Refuting this Copy Fallacy is straightforward. Imagine yourself promised that you will be resurrected digitally, immediately after your death. Assign a price tag you will pay for that, insurance of a sort. Then imagine the guy who sells you on this notion saying that, uh, well, maybe it would not be started right away, but sometime in future…we promise. As that date recedes, people's enthusiasm for paying for Self Copies dims—demonstrating that it is the hope of continuity they unconsciously relish.

As an identical twin, I have never bought the Copy Fallacy in any form. Though my brother and I have diverged in personality and appearance, due to differing environments and histories, for the first twenty years of our lives few could tell us apart. He and I could, though, and that's the nub of the argument: the Self is defined internally, not externally.

In the end, Copies benefit themselves, not the dead; machine immortality is more like having your twin live on, not yourself.

Some thinkers about computer identities, in the years since publication of *The Silicon Man*, have begun to push an agenda of Copy rights—the expansion of classical liberty into the digital wilderness. Dittos still will be people, the argument goes, with different skills and drawbacks, rather like the "differently abled."

The freedom to change your own clock speed, morph into anything, or even remake your own mind, goes along with the admitted liability of not being physically real. Unable to literally walk the streets, they will be like amputated souls.

Platt envisioned tele-presencing and some digital prosthetics that might reach in limited fashion into the concrete universe, but these would be re-creations; if a Ditto feared for its life, why lurk fully in the dangerous real world?

Also, "rights" for Dittos also get tied up with our own deep-seated fears—of digital immortals who amass wealth and like fungus reach into every avenue of natural, real lives; parasites, nothing less. Platt plainly foresees issues looming over the horizon, as soon as the digital world amasses financial power. Tycoon Dittos!

Running a Ditto of your Self, then giving it autonomy, means it could get rich and also change itself. Your Ditto could shape its own motivations, goals, habits, edit away memories and tastes. It then stops mimicking your own evolution. Your Ditto could erase any liking for Impressionist Opera and overlay instead a passion for rap, enjoying rhythms that would have bored the true Self into a coma.

The easy access of a Ditto to his entire underpinning—unlike ourselves, with much of our personality lying in our subconscious and not consciously fixable—implies constant change, personality tinkering, perhaps worse.

Is consciousness just a property of special algorithms, sliding sheets of information, digital packets jumping through conceptual hoops? How we envision our selfness depends on this huge question, now a hot topic.

Does a model simulating watching a sunset have to feel the same way its Original did? Why doubt simulated consciousness, when nobody asked the same question of programs that balance checkbooks? Such issues perplex many philosophers today, but I think feeling one's way through them in fiction is a rather more revealing path than abstract argument.

Consider that a Ditto is forcefully reminded that he is not the Original, but a mere fog of digits. All that gives him a sense of Self as continuity is the endless stepping forward of pattern. In people, the "real algorithm" computes itself by firing synapses, ringing nerves, getting the feel of continuity from the dance of cause and effect.

Dittos on the other hand are simply time-stepped forward, in processes that could just as easily run backward without the Ditto even noticing. Even time is fragile, a convention, in a digital universe.

Dittos surely would stand on shaky metaphysical ground here. Would we find that a Ditto fidgeted out of pure self-anxiety? His digital stress chem shoots up, metabolics lurch, heart-sims hammer, lungs flutter in intense uneasiness? Would typical Dittos talk incessantly, acutely uncomfortable, and make odd demands of their keepers?—that they be edited, truncated, improved, perhaps finally killed?

The dream of bodiless existence does not imply the end of the human condition, if we are still truly simulating humans.

Consider how well one would have to describe what our everyday life is like. Making a Ditto's body seem right to its critical intelligence demands sets of overlapping rules. After all, the Ditto remembers what a pleasure eating, say, used to be, back there in the gritty, real world.

As he (or she) chews, teeth have to thunk down on food, saliva squirt to greet the munched mass, enzymes started to work to extract the right nutrient ratios. The program can bypass the involved stomach and colon processes, simplifying into a satisfying concentration of blood sugars, giving him a carbohydrate lift, a pleasant electrolyte balance, hormones and stabilizers all calculated with patchwork templates for the appropriate emotional levels.

The body becomes a set of recipes for seeming like oneself. No underlying physics or biology at work, just a good-enough fake, put in by hand—the unseen hand of some Programmer God. So emerges an existential angst as profound as anything Camus felt, surely.

All other detail can be discarded, once the subroutines got the right effect, simulating the tingling of nerve endings. All this is to ground a visceral sense of Self, seemingly rock-solid, though it's really just a patched-in slug of digits, orchestrated by a mosaic of ten thousand ad hoc rules, running together.

So much effort, just to approximate what we get for free every day!

But of course, digital selves need not age or die, as long as somebody pays the power bill and doesn't pull the plug on us. Ordinary fear of mortal death will become a fear of being cut off, your Self never run again. Each interruption in running the Self will come to a Ditto as a possible final end, for he cannot act in the world while not running.

Indeed, when booted up again, he might not be able to tell he had suffered a hesitation-death, or whether it was a mere second or a hundred years of real time. This is a kind of heavenly eternity, to some. To me it seems like a hell of existential anxiety. If to us twins, singletons have to go through life with rather rickety mental identities, think of a Ditto's lot!

"But the possibilities!" proclaim some of the uploading Digiterati.

With enough computing space and speed, one could be King Me the Magnanimous, endowing many proto-Michelangelos with creative time…or perhaps becoming Michelangelo oneself, with time.

What if genius is just a matter of accumulating greater computing capacity?

Rebuilding yourself from the ground up then emerges as at least a hope. That which is buried in the digits might be harvested, changed. Learn to freezeframe your own emotional states, like painting a self portrait for study later. Perhaps that could help understand oneself, like a botanist putting himself on a slide and under a microscope. Could slices of the Self, multiplied, be the Self? With even emotions as programs?

Such ideas run through Platt's seminal book. They provoked later writers like Greg Egan, who in *Permutation City* sees a special SelfHood Suite menu, eerie in its temptations. With it one could present interior-configurations as separate subroutines, elements in the modeled brain. Here, grouped under headings—Qualms, Anxieties, Aversions, Likes, Habits, Unconscious Appeals—could rest items he could edit, improve, erase entirely. Not knowing what the Self is, which irreducible kernel of menu items define oneself, for oneself, suggests that Dittos will be tempted into rapt navel gazing.

Given the chance, which would you choose in pursuit of "immortality"—uploading or cryonics? Forget about the probabilities of success—each seems fraught with peril. (In an earlier column I estimated that the probability of being successfully frozen and later revived by future technology was at best one percent. A small chance, but infinitely larger than plain, flat zero…)

Uploading gives a pure Copy; cryonics yields your own brain, no doubt altered by much chemistry and microengineering necessary to pull your consciousness back out of the ice.

Which is truer? As far as I know, sf has yet to confront this question.

My intuitive choice is cryonics. At least in its perfect form, you recover the true you, the original synapses and holistic organization of the hopelessly complex brain. With uploading, you at best get a model of yourself, a rendering in 0s and 1s which reproduces for an outside audience—though not including you, the true best critic—your basic personality and memories.

Of course, having your brain frozen leaves out much: your physiology, your body instincts, will have to come from some body grown from your own cells (the reproductive ones, probably) to accompany the revival of your brain.

Here the cloning of humans is essential. Current cryonics organizations (I know of four) routinely preserve not just the head of their patients, but the reproductive organs and other body samples.

The idea is to send forward in time as much information as possible. While some patients elect to have their entire bodies frozen in liquid nitrogen, a far more expensive proposition, most take the head-only route.

They anticipate that a body can be cloned for them at some far future date when it will not only be technically possible, but even fairly inexpensive. Even more, they trust that no medical prohibitions will have halted cloning research. Further, cryonicists hope that cloning technology will have avoided the clear dangers.

But if a body is grown for a defrosted and repaired head, what becomes of the body's head? Was it deliberately stunted from "birth" so that it never developed as a conscious human? It seems unlikely that anyone could grow a body in some chemical vat, no matter how sophisticated, without using the many complex functions that the brain provides for that body.

So even to envision cryonics proceeding, one must require that future society has solved both scientific and moral questions about selfness and its implications. This is not an easy future to foresee, not at all.

But remember that the future is infinite, or at least very long indeed. Note how primitive medicine was a mere century ago. A few more centuries of steady growth could yield a social and philosophical landscape beyond our present comprehension.

Suppose cryonics could work. You would have grabbed back from time's maw the pure raw stuff of Self. Cybernetics gives a digital model, one always suspect because it has to choose how to configure the myriad data points of any brain-readout.

Choice begets the particular, and to have the whole Self, you must have the true, full general Self, in whatever deep labyrinths it lies.

Copyright © 1997 by Gregory Benford.

L. Penelope is the award-winning author of the Earthsinger Chronicles. The first book in the series, Song of Blood & Stone, *was chosen as one of* Time *magazine's 100 Best Fantasy Books of All Time. Equally left and right-brained, she studied filmmaking and computer science in college and sometimes dreams in HTML. She lives in Maryland with her husband and furry dependents. Visit her at: http://www.lpenelope.com.*

LONGHAND

by L. Penelope

WORLDBUILDING BLOCKS: CREATING CULTURE

Over recent years, there has been an increased awareness in the need for diversity in publishing. As an African-American author, I'm often called on to discuss topics of diversity and inclusion as well as writing across cultures. Topics like cultural appropriation have been hot buttons, causing discussion and debate and often dividing people along ideological lines. As our world shrinks, technology connects us, and more of us interface with people from a variety of races, religions, ethnicities, and backgrounds, these issues come to the forefront giving us an opportunity to confront our assumptions and look at things from a different point of view.

I was recently interviewed again about how I write cultures that are different from mine. As primarily a fantasy writer, creating worlds and cultures is always of interest to me; however, I think similar rules come into play whether you're creating a culture from scratch or writing about our world.

How to build a culture?

I try to start as close to the beginning as possible, if not with creation itself then with beliefs about creation. Where are these people from? What was the geography and climate of their place of origination and how did it impact the stories they told about themselves and the world? The influences on a culture are both from within and without, but I like to begin with the internals motivations.

What types of food—crops and wildlife—were readily available to them? Were they forced to be nomads following herds of livestock in order to survive? Were they a desert people who had to search for water or follow the migration patterns of their food source? Or did they live in a fertile land and became farmers, able to put down roots both literally and figuratively and grow in the same place for generations? If this was the case, did their society develop with less access to others who were not like them?

Worldbuilding involves answering a lot of questions and grounding those answers in a reality from which you can grow the people who populate your world. How did these circumstances—the land, seasons, climate, and resources—affect the stories the people told themselves? How do they show up in their myths and folklore, their deities and ideas about humanity? (I say humans because that's primarily what I write about, but insert whatever species you like here.)

How did the stories that these people told themselves evolve into religions? Who do they worship and what rituals does this include? What benefits did these people get from their veneration—were they making sacrifices to a deity for rain, clear skies, wind, or sun? How was their belief in their god or gods stoked and reinforced and who had the power over these beliefs: priests, kings, shamans, sorcerers?

Out of their beliefs about the world grow their beliefs about family structures. Did these beliefs create a matriarchy or patriarchy, and how does family design come into play? What are the gender roles and ideas about gender and identity? How are courtships handled? Did they foster arranged marriages, were women or men given away to form alliances or did they value love matches? What jobs can women hold and does their position as mothers, or potential mothers, earn them respect or marginalize them? What is the role of children in the society? Are they seen and not heard, pampered, put to work early and expect-ed to earn their keep? If the land is harsh and the people are just barely eking out a living then maybe children are needed to work. However, if resources are plentiful and fewer laborers are required, then perhaps childhood is extended. Does this create a class of spoiled and entitled youth with an excess of leisure time?

Can you switch up what might be expected? Create a reason that children in a harsh environment are pampered—perhaps fertility is an issue so each child is a blessing and held as cherished. And in a more hospitable environment maybe there are natural predators that hunt the children so they have to grow up fast and learn to protect themselves instead of lounging about idly.

What jobs do people have and what educational opportunities exist? Are there apprenticeships, schools, universities, and teachers? Do they value education and does this society have the available manpower for their daily existence so they can afford to have people devoted exclusively to educational goals?

What sort of government or leadership has arisen from this climate and resource allocation? Do they have a chief, king, senate, or oligarchy? Considering the history, who is allowed membership into the elite and why? Who is discriminated against in this culture and why? How do they treat their elders or the people with disabilities—are they cared for or cast out?

Languages are also a great way to learn about culture. The interest in conlangs—constructed languages such as Elvish, Klingon, or Dothraki—has sharply risen in visibility and popularity. There are many communities both online and in real life dedicated to the craft of creating new languages. Whether or not you take on this task in your own writing, considering your group's language, is key.

What does it sound like, is it fluid and melodious or harsh and guttural, and does this say anything about the land or the people? Do they even have spoken languages or do they use hand signals or sign language? Did they develop a system of writing and when? If so, how many can read and who is responsible for passing on the knowledge? How does this affect society, class, and interpersonal relationships? Are there various dialects of the spoken language and are they determined by class, caste, education level, occupation, ethnic background, or something else?

Is there media and how did it develop? Is there a version of a printing press, a messenger or postal system, the internet, or pneumatic tubes that send scrolls across the city? Technology is also another way to define culture. This, of course, will depend on the time period of the story: past, present, future, or some amalgam of them. For science fiction, perhaps the starting place for thinking about culture isn't so much with geography and climate as with technological developments—who discovered what first? Resources still come into play and can be excellent building blocks for story conflict—fuel, weapons, food, water—all of these are still vital for living creatures across the universe.

Which of course brings us to interpersonal conflict. Power and war. How does the culture view outsiders? Who do they hate and why? Who do they look down on, who is denigrated? What makes these people different? How does the marginalized group react to their societal position? What communities and systems have they created as a result of this treatment? You can learn a lot about a society by how they view their poorest or most downtrodden members. Don't forget them or forget to walk a mile in their shoes. That is often the germinating seed for entire stories, how the little guy beats back the oppressor to achieve justice or equality.

Creating a brand-new culture requires approaching your world with empathy. Writers must put themselves into the mindset of many characters who may be despots or heroes. But building a new culture can help us look at real-life ones differently, and the same questions can be asked when writing about existing cultures that you do not belong to. Consider how this group came to be in the position they occupy. What are the logical and non-logical reasons? How are they viewed by a variety of other groups both now and historically? Explore how different members of that group might respond to the same stimuli and place yourself in their position. Empathize with them. That is always the job of the writer no matter who they're writing about.

OVER THE WINE-DARK SEA

HARRY TURTLEDOVE
ORIGINALLY WRITING AS H. N. TURTELTAUB

Harry Turtledove writes alternate history, science fiction, fantasy and historical fiction and has won a Hugo Award, two Sidewise Awards for alternate history, and the Hal Clement Award for YA science fiction. With more than a hundred books, a couple of hundred pieces of short fiction, as well as a translation of a Byzantine chronicle and four academic articles published throughout his career, Turtledove also ended up with a doctorate in Byzantine history from UCLA. He wrote his dissertation alongside the first novel he sold. Along with teaching at UCLA, Cal State Fullerton, and Cal State Los Angeles, he worked as a technical writer for the Los Angeles County Office of Education before resigning from that job to freelance in 1991. He is married to Laura Frankos, herself a writer. They have three daughters (one also a published author) and two granddaughters. Two cats, Boris and Hotspur, run the household with iron, clawed fists.

OVER THE WINE-DARK SEA

by Harry Turtledove

V

O n the fourth afternoon after the brush with the pirates, the lookout at the bow called, "Land! Land dead ahead!" and Menedemos knew it had to be Cape Tainaron, the most southerly point on the mainland of Hellas. The *Aphrodite* had sailed through the narrow channel with Cape Maleai and Cape Onougnathos on the right hand and the little island of Kythera on the left not long before, so he'd been expecting the call, but it still sent a jolt of mixed excitement and alarm through him.

We'll pick up some mercenaries here, he thought. *We'll take them to Taras—maybe even to Syracuse, depending on what kind of news we hear when we get to Italy— and we'll rake in the silver doing it.* He did his best to keep that thought uppermost, but another one kept intruding. *We'll rake in the silver, provided we get away from Tainaron in one piece.*

Diokles said, "Even if the lookout hadn't seen land, all these other ships bound for the tip of Tainaron would tell us we were heading towards a fair-sized town."

"A fair-sized town at the tip of the cape has to be supplied by sea," Menedemos answered. "You can't get much in the way of grain down there by road. You can't get much of anything down there by road— which is why the mercenaries have their camp there."

"True enough." Diokles pointed to the rocky peninsula leading down to the sea. "A handful of men could hold off an army coming south just about forever."

"That's why this place is where it is," Menedemos agreed. "And, since Kassandros and Polyperhkon haven't got much in the way of ships, the mercenaries can do what they want—and hire out to whomever they want." He started to say more, but Sostratos came running back toward him, excitement on his face. Menedemos wasn't sure what sort of excitement it was. He tried to forestall his cousin, asking, "All right, who spilled the perfume into the soup?"

"No, no." Sostratos tossed his head so emphatically, a couple of locks of his hair flew loose. As he brushed them back from his eyes, he explained, "I was going to let the peahen called Helen out for a run when I found she'd laid an egg!"

"Ahh." Visions of drakhmai danced in front of Menedemos' face. "That is good news. And if Helen has started laying eggs, the others won't be far behind her. We can sell eggs for a nice price once we get across the Ionian Sea." He scratched his chin. Bristles rasped under his fingernails. "Have we got any straw, so the birds can make nests?"

Sostratos tossed his head again. "No, but I can get some light twigs from the dunnage without having amphorae knock together or anything like that. Those would probably be better than nothing."

"Good. Do it," Menedemos said. Sostratos turned to go. Menedemos pointed at him. "Wait. I didn't mean you personally go and do it right this instant. It's important, but it's not *that* important. Tell off a couple of sailors and have them take care of it."

"Oh. All right." Plainly, that hadn't occurred to Sostratos. He pointed ahead. "They've got themselves a real polis here, haven't they?—and not the smallest one in Hellas, either."

"No. Nor the worst-governed city in Hellas, probably," Menedemos said. As he'd thought it would, that made his cousin squirm. In musing tones, Menedemos went on, "This really *is* a polis, or something close to one. It's not just the mercenaries, not even close. They've got their wives here, and their concubines, and their brats, and their slaves—"

"And the people who sell things to them, like us," Sostratos put in.

"And the people who sell things to them," Menedemos agreed. "But you won't find too many merchants' shops right there in the mercenaries' encampment. Most of the traders come here by sea, too, and anchor out of bowshot from the shore."

Diokles said, "I hope you're going to do the same thing, skipper."

"I hope I am, too," Menedemos said, which made the keleustes laugh and Sostratos smile. Dipping his head, Menedemos went on, "I want to get away from Tainaron in one piece myself, you know."

"That would be good," Sostratos said. "The generals and the Italiote cities aren't the only ones recruiting here." He pointed toward a couple of low, lean craft painted blue-green. "If those aren't pirates, I'd sooner eat the peahen's egg than sell it."

"Even without that paint job, they'd be pirates," Menedemos said. "Not much else hemioliai are good for." The galley had two banks of oars, but the upper, or thranite, bank stopped short just after the mast, to give the crew plenty of space to stow mast and yard and sail when they took them down for a ramming attack. No other variety of galley was so fast and so perfectly suited to predation.

"I hope they aren't watching us the way we're watching them," Sostratos said.

"They aren't," Menedemos assured him. "The fox doesn't look at the hare the way the hare looks at the fox."

"You so relieve my mind," Sostratos murmured. Menedemos grinned.

"We're not your ordinary hare, though," Diokles said. "We showed that triakonter we're an armored hare." He chuckled. "*Aphrodite*'s a good name, mind, but I wouldn't mind sailing in a ship called *Hoplolagos*, just for the sake of surprising people."

"No one gives ships names like that," Menedemos said. "You name them for gods, or after the sea or the waves or the foam or something like that, or you call them swift or fierce or bold—or lucky, like that five of Ptolemaios' we met. I've never heard of a ship with a silly name."

"Does that mean there should never be one?" Sostratos asked, a certain glint in his eye. "Is the new bad merely for being new?"

With most men, that glint would have been lust. With Sostratos, Menedemos judged it likelier to be philosophy. He tossed his head. "Save that one for the Academy, cousin. I'm not going to thrash my way through it now. We've got more important things to worry about, like coming away from Tainaron without getting our throats cut."

He wondered if Sostratos would argue about that. When his cousin was feeling abstract, the real world often had a hard time making an impression on him. But Sostratos said, "That's true enough. It's so true, maybe you should have thought about it sooner, thought about it more. I tried to get you to, if you'll recall."

"I did think about it. You know that," Menedemos said. "I decided the chance for profit picking up men to go to Italy outweighs the risk. That doesn't mean I think there's no risk."

Diokles pointed. "There's the temple to Poseidon. It looks like the one building hereabouts that's made to last, set alongside all these huts and shacks and tents and things."

"That's the temple with the bronze of the man on the dolphin, isn't it?" Sostratos said. "I'd like to see it if I get the chance: it's the one Arion the minstrel offered after the dolphin took him to shore when he jumped into the sea to save himself from the crew of the ship he was on."

The keleustes gave him a quizzical look. "How do you know about that bronze? You've never been here before, have you?"

"No, he hasn't." Menedemos spoke before his cousin could. He pointed a finger at Sostratos. "All right, own up. Whose writing talks about it?"

"Herodotos'," Sostratos said sheepishly.

"Ha!" Menedemos wagged that finger. "I thought as much." He turned back to Diokles. "Let them bring us a couple of plethra closer to land, but no more than that. Then we'll go ashore and see if we can hunt up some passengers. Pick some proper bruisers to man the boat, too—I don't want to come back to the beach and find it's been stolen from under our noses."

"Right you are," the oarmaster said. "Matter of fact, if you don't think you've got to have me here aboard, I wouldn't mind taking boat duty myself."

Menedemos looked Diokles up and down. He dipped his head. "As far as I can see, any mercenary who's stupid enough to get frisky with you deserves whatever happens to him."

"I'm a peaceable man, captain," Diokles said. A slow smile spread over his face. "But I might—I just might, mind you—remember what to do in case somebody else didn't happen to feel peaceable."

"Good," Menedemos said.

"*Oöp!*" Diokles called. The other rowers in the *Aphrodite*'s boat rested at their oars. The boat grated on the sand. Sostratos wore only a tunic and a knife belt. As he stepped onto the beach, he wished he had on a bronze corselet and crested helm, greaves and shield, and long spear and shortsword. Armor and weapons might have made him feel safe. On the other hand, they might not have been enough.

"This is a place with no law," he murmured to Menedemos. "If anyone takes it into his mind to try to kill us, what's to stop him?"

"We are," Menedemos replied. Sostratos found that unsatisfactory. But his cousin was grinning from ear to ear and strutting a jaunty strut. Just as some men were wild for women or wine or fancy opson, so Menedemos was wild for trouble. He sometimes seemed to get into it deliberately so he could have the fun of getting himself out.

A couple of mercenaries dressed like Sostratos and Menedemos except for wearing sandals and having swords on their belts instead of knives came up to them. "'Ail," one of them said in Ionian dialect. "What are you selling, sailors?"

"Passage to Italy," Menedemos answered. "We're bound for Taras. Always something lively going on in Great Hellas." He used the common name for the colonies the Hellenes had planted in southern Italy and Sicily.

"That's so." The second mercenary dipped his head. "How much for the trip?" He sounded like an Athenian—his dialect wasn't far removed from Ionian, but preserved rough breathings.

Menedemos turned to Sostratos. As toikharkhos, he set fares. "Twelve drakhmai," he said.

Both mercenaries winced. "You won't find many who'll pay you that much," said the one who spoke Attic.

"We can't take many," Sostratos answered. "We've got a full crew and not a lot of room for passengers. But you'll get where you're going if you travel with us. We don't have to stay in the harbor for half a month if the winds are against us, and we won't get blown to Carthage if a storm comes up at sea."

"Even if all that's true, it's still robbery," the mercenary said.

He looked as if he knew plenty about robbery. *How many men have you murdered?* Sostratos wondered. *How many women and boys have you forced?* He didn't let any of what he was thinking show on his face. If he had, the mercenary probably would have yanked out that sword on his belt and gone after him with it. Instead, he just shrugged. "No one says you have to pay it if you don't want to."

Grumbling, both mercenaries walked on. Menedemos said, "Don't take such a hard line that you turn away business."

"I won't," Sostratos answered. "I think we can get five or six passengers at twelve drakhmai, and we don't want any more than that. If it turns out I'm wrong, I'll come down a little. But I don't want to do that too soon."

"No, I suppose not," Menedemos said. "You'd get a reputation like a girl who's easy with her virtue."

"That's right." The comparison was apt. Several others might have been, too, but Sostratos wasn't surprised that that one had occurred to his cousin.

Along with huts and tents, the mercenaries' encampment at Tainaron did boast taverns and cookshops and armorers' shops and swordsellers' establishments. Sostratos and Menedemos stopped at several of them, letting the proprietors know the *Aphrodite* lay offshore and where she was bound. Word would spread fast.

When one of the taverners heard they were coming from Khios, he surprised Sostratos by asking if they carried wine, and surprised him more by paying twenty-five drakhmai an amphora for some of the Ariousian without so much as a whimper. "I'll get it back," he said. "You bet I will. Some of these fellows won't take anything but the best, and they don't care what they have to pay to get it, either."

To celebrate the bargain, he poured cups of wine a long way from the best for Sostratos and Menedemos. Sostratos had taken one sip from his own when the ground jerked beneath his stool. The flimsy walls of the tavern rattled for a moment, then were still. "Earthquake!" he exclaimed as a nearby dog barked. "Just a little one, though."

"Gods be praised," the tavernkeeper said, and everybody else in the place, Sostratos and Menedemos included, dipped his head in agreement. Even though the quake had been small, Sostratos' heart still thudded in his chest. When the earth started to shudder, you couldn't tell ahead of time whether it would stop again right away—as it had here, as it did most of the time—or go on and get worse, sometimes bad enough to level a city. Everyone living around the Inner Sea knew that too well.

Menedemos said, "Let me have another cup of wine." When the taverner gave it to him, he poured a small libation onto the dirt floor. "That's for the Earthshaker, for not shaking too hard this time." Then he drained the cup. "And *that's* for me."

"It's the Spartan's curse, that's what it is," the tavernkeeper said.

"The what?" Menedemos asked.

Sostratos spoke before the taverner could: "A long time ago, back before the Peloponnesian War, some helots took refuge in Poseidon's temple here. The Spartans hauled them out and killed them. Not long afterwards, a big earthquake almost knocked Sparta flat. Plenty of people claimed it was Poseidon's vengeance."

"How did you know that?" The tavernkeeper stared at him. "You said you were a Rhodian."

"I am," Sostratos said.

"He must have read it in a book," Menedemos said. "He reads all sorts of things in books." Sostratos had trouble gauging his cousin's smile: was it proud or mocking? Some of each, he thought. Menedemos asked, "Is that your pal Herodotos again?"

"No, it's in Thoukydides' history," Sostratos replied.

"A book," the tavernkeeper said. "A *book*. Well, ain't that something? Don't have my letters myself, nor much want 'em, neither, but ain't that something?"

"Ain't that something?" Menedemos echoed wickedly as Sostratos and he headed for a cookshop not far away.

"Oh, shut up," Sostratos said, which made his cousin laugh out loud. Irked, he went on, "Natural philosophers say that earthquakes aren't Poseidon's fault at all, that they're as much a natural phenomenon as waves stirred up by wind."

"I don't know that I can believe that," Menedemos said. "What could cause them, if they're natural?"

"No one knows for sure," Sostratos replied, "but I've heard people suggest it's the motion of gas through subterranean caverns pushing the ground now this way, now that."

He'd always thought that seemed not only probable but sober and logical to boot. Menedemos, however, took it another way. His whoop of delight made several passing mercenaries whirl to gape at him. "Earthfarts!" he said. "Instead of Poseidon Earthshaker, we've got Kyamos Earthfarter. Bow down!" He stuck out his backside.

"No one ever made a bean into a god until you did just now," Sostratos said severely, resisting the urge to kick the proffered part. "You complain about the way I think sometimes, but you're more

blasphemous than I'd ever be. If you ask me, all that Aristophanes has curdled your wits."

His cousin tossed his head. "No, and I'll tell you why not. Aristophanes has fun mocking the gods, and so do I. When you say you don't believe, you mean it."

Sostratos grunted. That held more truth than he cared to admit. Instead of admitting it, he said, "Come on, let's tell this fellow we're looking for passengers."

"All right." Menedemos made a very rude noise. "Earthfarts!" He giggled. Sostratos wished he'd never started talking about the natural causes of earthquakes.

To get a measure of revenge—and perhaps expiation as well—he all but dragged Menedemos to Poseidon's temple. Sure enough, there among the offerings stood the statue of Arion astride the dolphin. Sostratos clicked his tongue between his teeth. "It's not so fine a piece of work as I thought it would be. See how stiff and old-fashioned it looks?"

"Arion jumped into the sea a long time ago," Menedemos said reasonably. "You can't expect the statue to look as if the sculptor set it there yesterday."

"I suppose not," Sostratos said, "but even so—"

"No. But me no buts," Menedemos said. "If you laid Aphrodite, you'd complain she wasn't as good in bed as you expected."

If I laid Aphrodite, she'd complain I wasn't as good in bed as she expected, Sostratos thought, and then, *Or would she? She being a goddess, wouldn't she know ahead of time what I was like in bed?* He scratched his head. After pondering that for a little while, he said, "The problem of how much the gods can see of the future is a complicated one, don't you think?"

"What I think is, I haven't got the faintest idea of what you're talking about," Menedemos answered, and Sostratos realized he'd assumed his cousin could follow along in a conversation he'd had with himself. While he was still feeling foolish, Menedemos went on, "Let's get back to the boat and see if we've got any passengers looking to go west."

"All right," Sostratos said. When they left the temple precinct, he let out a sigh. "Except for this shrine, Tainaron's about as *un*holy a place as I've ever seen."

"It's not Delphi," Menedemos agreed, "but we wouldn't pick up mercenaries bound for Italy at Delphi, now would we?" Sostratos could hardly argue with that. What he could do—and what he did—was keep a wary eye out for thieves and cutpurses all the way down to the beach. He credited his eagle eye for their getting to the boat unmolested.

A couple of brawny, sun-browned men with scars on their arms and legs and cheeks were talking with Diokles when Sostratos and Menedemos came up. The oarmaster looked very much at home with them: but for the scars, he might have been one of their number himself. "Here's the skipper and the toikharkhos," he said. "They'll tell you everything you need to know."

"Twelve drakhmai to Syracuse, we heard," one of the mercenaries said. "That right?"

Sostratos tossed his head. "Twelve drakhmai to Taras," he answered. "I don't know if we'll be putting in at Syracuse at all. There's no way to tell, not till we hear how the war with Carthage is going."

"Twelve drakhmai to Italy is a lot of money," the other mercenary grumbled, "especially when I've got to pay for my own food, too."

"That's the way things work," Menedemos said. "That's the way they've always worked. You don't expect me to change them, do you?"

To Sostratos, expecting things to work a certain way because they always had was nothing but foolishness. He started to say so, then shut up with a snap; as far as a dicker with mercenaries went, his cousin had come up with an excellent argument. "All right, all right," the second hired soldier said. "When do you figure you'll sail?"

"We have room for five or six passengers," Menedemos replied. "We'll stay till we've got 'em all, or till we decide we're not going to."

"Well, you've got one, even if you are a thief," the second mercenary said. "I'm Philippos."

"Two," the other Hellene said. "My name's Kallikrates son of Eumakhos."

"I'm the son of Megakles myself," Philippos added. He pointed out to the *Aphrodite*. "You're not sailing today, though?"

"Not unless we get three or four more passengers in a tearing hurry," Sostratos assured him. "We have some cargo to unload, too. Come down to the beach every morning for the next few days, and we won't leave without you."

"Fair enough," Philippos said. Kallikrates dipped his head in agreement. They both ambled off the beach and back up toward the town that had sprung into being at Tainaron.

"Well, there's two," Menedemos said to Sostratos. "Not so bad, the first day we anchor offshore."

"No, not so bad, provided we get away with coming here in the first place," Sostratos replied. "If this were a proper harbor, a harbor where honest men came, we wouldn't have to anchor offshore."

"This *is* a harbor where honest men come," Menedemos said with a grin he no doubt intended as disarming. "We're here, aren't we?"

"Yes, and I still wish we weren't," Sostratos said. His cousin's grin turned sour. That didn't keep Menedemos from getting into the boat with him and returning to the *Aphrodite*. Sostratos raised an eyebrow as they climbed up into the akatos. "I don't see you spending the night ashore, honest man."

This time, Menedemos was the one who said, "Oh, shut up," from which Sostratos concluded he'd made his point.

They got another passenger the next day, a Cretan slinger named Rhoikos. "I'm right glad to get out of here," he said, his Doric drawl far thicker than that of the Rhodians. "Everything's dear as can be in these here parts, and I was eating up my silver waiting around for somebody to hire me. Don't reckon I'll have much trouble getting 'em to take me on over across the sea. Always a war somewheres in them parts."

He tried to haggle Sostratos down from his price. Sostratos declined to haggle; Rhoikos had made it clear he didn't want to stay in Tainaron. The slinger complained, but he said he'd come down to the beach every morning, too.

For the next three days, though, nobody showed any interest in going to Italy. Menedemos grumbled and fumed up on the foredeck. Sostratos tried to console him: "The peahens are laying more eggs."

"You were the one who wanted to get out of here," Menedemos snapped. "D'you think you're the only one?"

Sostratos stared at him. "I thought you were as happy as a pig in acorns."

"Do I look that stupid?" his cousin said in a low voice. "I put up a bold front for the men. So I took you in, too, eh? Good. We'll make money here, and that's why we came, but I'll thank all the gods when the cape slides under the horizon."

Plucking at his beard, Sostratos murmured, "There's more to you than meets the eye."

"You don't need to sound so accusing," Menedemos said with a laugh.

When the sailors rowed them to the beach the next morning, Philippos, Kallikrates, and Rhoikos were all waiting for them. As Sostratos had for the past several days, he said, "Not today, not unless we get lucky." The mercenaries growled things that didn't sound complimentary under their breaths.

And then Menedemos pointed in the direction of the huts and tents and said, "Hello! Somebody wants to see us."

Sure enough, a man was trotting down toward the beach. He wore a tunic and sandals, and carried a soldier's panoply in a canvas sack. "You there!" he called. "Do I hear rightly that you're sailing for Italy?"

"Yes, that's so," Sostratos answered.

"I'll give you a quarter of a mina to take me there," the fellow said, "as long as you sail today."

Sostratos and Menedemos looked at each other. Here was somebody who didn't just want to go to Italy; here was someone who *needed* to go there. "You'd be our fourth passenger," Sostratos said. "We were hoping for six."

"What are you charging for each?" the newcomer asked.

"Twelve drakhmai," Sostratos answered. He and Menedemos exchanged another look, this one not altogether happy. If the other three mercenaries hadn't been standing right there, he could have named a higher figure.

"All right, then. I'll give you"—the newcomer paused to count on his fingers—"thirty-six drakhmai to leave today." He rummaged through the sack and pulled out a smaller leather bag that clinked.

Philippos and Rhoikos muttered under their breath. Rhoikos stared at the fellow with the fat moneybag, or perhaps at the moneybag itself. Along with the silver, they saw the same thing Sostratos had: anybody willing to spend so freely was bound to have an urgent reason to be so willing. "Hold on," Sostratos said. "Tell me who you are and why you're in such a hurry to leave Tainaron."

Menedemos looked sour. Sostratos pretended not to see him. No matter how sour Menedemos looked, no matter how anxious he was to come off with a profit, Sostratos didn't want to carry a murderer, say, away from justice—assuming any justice was to be found at this southernmost tip of the mainland of Hellas.

"I'm Alexidamos son of Alexion," the mercenary answered. "I'm a Rhodian—like you, if what I heard is right." Sostratos dipped his head. Alexidamos' accent wasn't far removed from his own. The fellow continued, "I, ah, got into a disagreement with a captain named Diotimos, and all his men are looking for me, or will be soon."

Kallikrates pointed. "So you're the fellow who buggered Diotimos' boy! I'd get out of Tainaron, too, if I were you."

That told Sostratos what he needed to know. It told Menedemos the same thing. "Pay my toikharkhos now," he said dryly. "Something tells me you won't be so grateful once we've put Tainaron under the horizon."

Alexidamos glared, from which Sostratos concluded his cousin was right. But the mercenary started counting out Athenian drakhmai with their familiar staring owls. Sostratos accepted the coins without a word and with his face carefully blank. Attic drakhmai were heavier than those of Rhodes, so he was getting more silver from Alexidamos than he'd expected. If Alexidamos didn't worry about that, Sostratos didn't feel obligated to bring it to his notice.

Having paid, Alexidamos said, "Now can we leave?" He looked anxiously over his shoulder.

"What about us?" the other three mercenaries chorused. Still in unison, they went on, "We haven't got our gear here."

Menedemos took charge. "Go fetch it," he said briskly. He turned to Diokles. "Take this fellow to the *Aphrodite*. Come to think of it, take Sostratos and me, too. Things are liable to get lively here."

"Thank you," Alexidamos said as he stowed his sack in the bottom of the boat.

"Don't thank me yet," Menedemos said. "If there's a commotion and those other fellows can't come aboard, you'll pay their fares, too. I'm telling you now, so you can't say it's a surprise."

"That's robbery," Alexidamos yelped.

"Call it what you want," Menedemos said coolly. "The way I see things, you might be hurting my business. If you don't see them that way, you can always talk them over with Diotimos, or whatever his name was. Now—have we got a bargain, or haven't we?"

"A bargain," the mercenary choked out.

"I thought you'd be sensible," Menedemos said. He climbed into the boat. So did Sostratos. The sailors pushed the boat into the sea, scrambled in themselves, and rowed back to the *Aphrodite*.

Once they'd come aboard, Diokles pointed back toward the beach. "I think maybe we got out of there right in the nick of time, skipper," he said.

Along with the oarmaster and Menedemos, Sostratos looked over to the shore. Several men stood there, looking across the water toward the *Aphrodite*. The sun glittered from swords and spearheads. One of the men shouted something, but the akatos stood too far out to sea for his words to carry. Even if Sostratos couldn't hear them, he didn't think the shouter was paying Alexidamos any compliments.

"Pity about those other chaps," Sostratos said to Menedemos. "How are we going to get them off the beach if these soldiers keep hanging around?"

Menedemos shrugged. "We end up with the same fare either way."

"I think you ought to try to get them, too," Alexidamos said, which surprised Sostratos not at all: he wouldn't have wanted to pay an extra thirty-six drakhmai, either. In its cage on the foredeck, the peacock screeched. Alexidamos jumped. "By the dog of Egypt, what's that?"

"A peacock," Sostratos answered. "Leave it alone."

"A peacock?" Alexidamos echoed. "Really?"

"Really." Sostratos looked in the direction of the beach again. He couldn't be sure, but he thought he saw Philippos, Kallikrates, and Rhoikos returning: three newcomers, at least, were staring out toward the merchant galley. Plucking at his beard, he beckoned to Menedemos. They put their heads together and talked in low voices for a little while.

Not much later, four rowers and Alexidamos got into the ship's boat. The boat made for one of the blue-green-painted pirate ships anchored a few plethra away. Diotimos and his bully boys hurried along the beach after the boat. It pulled up behind the pirate ship. When it came back to the *Aphrodite*, only the rowers were to be seen. They climbed back up into the akatos.

The angry mercenaries on the beach shouted at the pirate ship through cupped hands. A pirate shouted back. Neither side seemed to have much luck understanding the other.

Sostratos had counted on that. Quietly, he told the rowers, "I think you can try picking up the others now. Tell them to move fast. If they don't, or if Diotimos' men make trouble, turn around and come back."

"That's right," Menedemos said. "That's just right."

As Diokles had before, he headed this expedition to the beach. He didn't let the boat go aground. Instead, the three mercenaries who wanted to go to Italy waded out into the sea; the rowers helped them into the boat. They were on the way back to the *Aphrodite* before Diotimos and his pals came trotting back along the sand toward them.

Up came the rowers, into the merchant galley. Up came Rhoikos and Kallikrates and Philippos. And up came Alexidamos, who'd lain in the bottom of the boat since it used the pirate ship to screen it from Diotimos' men for a moment. He clasped Sostratos' hand. "Very neat. Very clever. You should be an admiral."

Sostratos tossed his head. "I leave that sort of thing to my cousin." He glanced toward Menedemos, about to suggest that sailing on the instant would be a good idea. But Menedemos had already gone to the bow. He was urging the men at the anchor lines to haul the anchors up to the catheads. He was plenty savvy enough to see what wanted doing here without any suggestions from Sostratos. And that suited Sostratos fine.

✿

Three days after leaving Cape Tainaron, the *Aphrodite* sailed northwest out of Zakynthos. "I could be Odysseus, coming home at last," Menedemos said, pointing out over the akatos' bow. "There's Kephallenia ahead, with Ithake just to the northeast of it."

"But you're not going to stop either place, or go up to Korkyra, either," Sostratos said. "You're going to strike straight across the Ionian Sea for Italy." He sighed. "And you the man who loves Homer so well."

Menedemos laughed and pointed a finger at him. "You can't fool me. You don't care a fig for trade. You just want to see the islands. I had to drag you away from Zakynthos."

"It's an interesting place," his cousin answered. "It's still a woody island, as the poet says. And the people speak an interesting dialect of Greek."

"Interesting?" Menedemos tossed his head. "I couldn't understand what they were saying half the time. It's almost as bad as Macedonian."

"I didn't have too much trouble with it," Sostratos said. "It's just old-fashioned. But are you sure you don't want to go up the coast and cross the sea where it's narrowest? We'd only spend one night—two at the outside—on the water that way, and sailing straight across we'll be out of sight of land for five or six days."

"I know. I have my reasons." That should have been all Menedemos needed to say; he was captain of the *Aphrodite*, after all. And Sostratos didn't argue, at least not with words. But he did raise an eyebrow, and Menedemos found himself explaining: "For one thing, most merchantmen sail from Korkyra across to Italy just because it's the shortest way."

"Exactly," Sostratos said. "Why are you doing something different, then?"

"Because all the pirates around—Hellenes, Epeirotes, Illyrians, Tyrrhenians—know what the merchantmen do, and they hover around the passage where the Adriatic opens out into the Ionian Sea the way vultures hover over a dead ox. Even if this trip across the open sea is longer, it should be safer."

"Ah." Sostratos spread his hands. "That does make good sense. You said it was one reason. You have more?"

"You've got no business grilling me," Menedemos said.

"No doubt you're right, O best one." Sostratos could be most annoying when he was most ironically polite. And then he struck a shrewder blow yet: "If anything goes wrong, though, our fathers will grill you, and it will be their business. Wouldn't you sooner practice your answers on me."

The thought of having to explain things to his father made Menedemos spit into the bosom of his tunic. He said, "I'm sure you want me to tell you for my own good, not for yours." Sostratos looked innocent. He looked so innocent, Menedemos burst out laugh-

ing. "The other reason I don't want to stop at Korkyra is, it's about the most dismal place in the world."

"Not surprising, after all the wars it's lost," Sostratos said. "And it was the place where the Peloponnesian War began, and that ruined all of Hellas. But Korkyra's free and independent nowadays." He raised that eyebrow again—more irony.

"Yes, Korkyra is free and independent, all right." Menedemos raised an eyebrow, too, and quoted a proverbial verse: "'Korkyra is free—shit wherever you want.'"

His cousin snorted. "Well, all right. Maybe it's just as well you didn't go up the coast. You would have recited that in a tavern after you'd had some wine, and got yourself knifed."

Since he was probably right, Menedemos didn't argue with him. Instead, he said, "I just wish the wind weren't right in our teeth. We'll have to row all the way. But it always comes out of the northwest hereabouts during sailing season."

With the passengers aboard, and with the peafowl cages taking up much of the foredeck, the poop deck was more crowded than usual. Philippos said, "You'll put right into the harbor at Taras, won't you?"

Menedemos didn't laugh out loud. Neither did Sostratos. But Diokles did, and so did Alexidamos and Rhoikos. They knew what an inexact art navigation was. Turning to his fellow mercenary, Rhoikos spoke in his broad Doric drawl: "Don't sail a whole lot, you tell me?"

"What's that got to do with anything?" Philippos asked.

At that, Menedemos did laugh. He couldn't help himself. He wasn't the only one, either. He said, "Best one, I'm sailing northwest. I'm keeping my course as true as I know how. And if the weather holds, we'll make the Italian coast within a couple of hundred stadia of Taras either way, and then sail along it to the city. If the weather doesn't hold..." He shrugged. He didn't want to talk about that, or even to think about it.

Philippos looked as astonished as a young boy might on first learning where babies come from. In tones that said he had trouble believing what he'd just heard, he asked, "But why can't you get right where you're going?"

Patiently, biting down on new laughter, Menedemos answered, "We'll be out of sight of land pretty soon. Once we are, what have we got to go on? The sun—the stars at night—the wind and the waves. That's all. I haven't got a magic pointer to tell me which way north is. I wish I did, but Hephaistos has never shown anybody how to make such a thing."

"If I'd known that, I'd've stayed at Tainaron till I found a general who'd march me off to his army," the unhappy mercenary said.

"You're welcome to go back," Menedemos said. Philippos brightened, but only till he added, "Provided you can swim that far."

"Perhaps the dolphins would carry him, as they did Arion," Sostratos said helpfully.

"You're making fun of me," Philippos said, which was true. He pushed by Menedemos to the *Aphrodite*'s stern. There he stood, staring out past the sternpost toward Zakynthos, which steadily dwindled in the southeast and finally vanished below the horizon. Philippos kept staring anyhow.

Menedemos fancied himself Prometheus rather than Epimetheus: he looked ahead, not behind. Fluffy white clouds drifted across the sky from north to south. The sea was low; the *Aphrodite* pitched a little because she headed straight into the swells, but the motion wasn't enough to make even a lubber like Philippos lean out over the rail.

In a low voice, Menedemos asked Diokles, "Do you think the weather will hold for the crossing?"

The oarmaster shrugged. "You'd do better asking the gods than me. We've got a pretty fair chance, I think—couldn't hardly ask for anything better than we've got right now. But it's still early in the sailing season, too."

"Would you head up to Korkyra?" Menedemos asked. "We could still swing back in that direction."

Diokles shrugged again. "If a blow comes, odds are we'd be at sea either which way. And we're a lot less likely to run into pirates cutting across—you're dead right about that, skipper. Six oboloi one way, a drakhma the other. You don't go to sea unless you're ready to take a chance now and then."

"That's true enough." Menedemos was about to say more when a yelp from the foredeck distracted him. Alexidamos stood there with a finger in his mouth. Menedemos raised his voice so it would carry: "Leave the peafowl alone, or you'll be sorry."

"I'm sorry already." Alexidamos inspected his wounded digit. "I didn't realize the polluted things could peck like that. I'm bleeding."

"Bandage yourself up, or get a sailor to do it for you." Menedemos showed no sympathy. No matter how much Alexidamos had paid, each peafowl was worth more. "You're lucky you won't have to face your foes nine-fingered from here on out."

"I'd have gone to law with you in that case," Alexidamos said.

"Go right ahead," Menedemos said cheerfully. "You're meddling with my cargo, and I've got the whole crew as witnesses." Alexidamos sent him a sour stare. Menedemos stared back. If the mercenary thought he could intimidate him on his own ship, he was daft. *Maybe I should have let that Diotimos have him, in spite of getting three fares out of him*, Menedemos thought. *He's nothing but trouble.*

But then Menedemos shrugged. Any passenger who made too much trouble aboard ship might unfortunately fail to reach his destination.

Diokles was thinking along with him. "Be a real pity if that fellow fell overboard, wouldn't it?" he murmured. "My heart would just break."

"Can't do that unless he really earns it," Menedemos answered. "Otherwise, the rowers start blabbing in taverns, and after a while nobody wants to go to sea with you."

"I suppose so," the oarmaster said. "If I had to guess, though, I'd say nobody would miss that chap much."

"Don't tempt me, Diokles, because I wouldn't miss him at all," Menedemos said. The keleustes laughed and dipped his head.

Menedemos kept twenty men on the oars, changing shifts every couple of hours to keep all the rowers fairly fresh. By the time the sun set ahead of them, they might have been alone on the sea. The bow anchors went into the water with twin splashes. The rowers ate bread and olives and cheese and drank wine. So did the mercenaries. "Are we really going to be several days at sea?" Alexidamos asked. "I fear I didn't bring enough in the way of victuals. Shall I hang a fishing line over the side?"

Yes, or else starve, Menedemos thought. But Sostratos said, "We'll sell you rations from the crew's supplies, at four oboloi a day."

"Still charging me triple, are you?" Alexidamos said with a nasty smile.

"Passengers are supposed to bring their own victuals—everyone knows that. If you don't…" Sostratos shrugged. "Whose fault is it?"

"I had to leave Tainaron in rather a hurry," Alexidamos pointed out.

Sostratos shrugged again. "And whose fault is *that*?" he answered, perfectly polite, perfectly deadpan. Alexidamos took a moment to realize he'd been skewered. When he did, he snarled a curse and let a hand fall to the hilt of his sword.

"Remember where you are, friend," Menedemos said. He wondered if he would have to say something more than that, if the mercenary from Rhodes was too dense to take a hint. But Alexidamos looked around and saw not a single friendly face anywhere. He also saw not a speck of land anywhere on the horizon. His hand jerked away from the sword as if the hilt were hot.

Menedemos sent Kallikrates and Philippos up to sleep on the foredeck; they'd shown no signs of causing trouble. With the other two mercenaries sharing the poop with him and Sostratos and Diokles, it was crowded. Even so, they all had room to stretch out. The rowers at their benches had to lean up against the ship's planking to steady themselves as they slept.

When Menedemos woke the next morning, the swells were bigger than they had been. The breeze had freshened, and brought more clouds out of the north with it. The sunrise was redder than he would have liked to see, too.

"We may be heading into a blow," he said to Diokles, hoping the oarmaster would tell him he was wrong.

But Diokles dipped his head. "Looks that way to me, too, skipper. One thing: no lee shore to be washed up on. We've got a good many stadia between us and the nearest land. If we ride it out, we're fine."

"Let's batten things down," Menedemos said. "We'd better do it, and then hope we don't need to." Rather to his dismay, Diokles dipped his head again.

When he gave the order, the sailors who weren't rowing hurried to obey. He drew the obvious conclusion from that: they thought a storm was coming, too. "Make sure the peafowl cages are well lashed down," Sostratos called. "We can't afford to lose any of the birds over the side." By the time the men were done with them, a spiderweb of lines secured them to the ship.

Philippos came up to Menedemos. "Is it…going to blow?" the mercenary asked nervously.

"Only cloud-gathering Zeus knows for certain," Menedemos answered, watching large, dark clouds gather in the north and spread across the sky. "We don't want to take any chances, though." Philippos dipped his head and went away. Menedemos didn't know how reassuring he'd been, but he didn't have a lot of reassurance to offer. The other mercenaries asked him no questions. They could see for themselves what was likely to happen.

"This is what's wrong with sailing in the Ionian Sea," Diokles said. "A storm will start building at the top of the Adriatic and just blow all the way down."

"How bad do you think it will be?" Menedemos asked: the oarmaster had been going to sea about as long as he'd been alive, and he valued Diokles' experience. Only after the question passed the barrier of his teeth did he wonder if he wasn't looking for some reassurance himself.

Diokles shrugged. "We'll find out. I've seen skies I liked less, but you can't always tell ahead of time, either."

The wind kept freshening, and shifted till it came straight out of the north. It was a chilly wind, as if, wherever it had started from, winter hadn't yet decided to give way to spring. The waves built, and struck with greater force now that they weren't quite head-on. The akatos yawed a little at each impact. Kallikrates clapped a hand to his mouth and dashed for the rail. Menedemos' smile wasn't pleasant. It would get worse before it got better. He could see that.

Rain began falling about an hour later. By then, all the sky save a blue strip in the south was the dirty gray of a sheep's back. That last reminder of good weather vanished a moment later. The rain, blowing into Menedemos' face, was cold and nasty. He did his best to keep the *Aphrodite* headed northwest, but without the sun to steer by he had much less idea how good his best was.

Thinking along with him once more, Diokles said, "Navigation's gone to Tartaros, hasn't it?"

"You might say so." But Menedemos did his best to sound cheerful: "Italy's a big place. We probably won't miss it."

The keleustes rewarded him with a chuckle. "That's good, captain. I'll tell you what I wouldn't miss right now: I wouldn't miss being in port."

"If sailing were easy all the time, any fool could do it." Menedemos relished the tossing timbers under his feet, the resistance the sea gave the steering oars. He particularly relished those steering oars. Once again, he discovered what fine work Khremes and the other carpenters had done. He was able to keep the *Aphrodite* on the course he wanted—the course he thought he wanted, judged by shifting wind and wave—with far less effort than he would have needed before the repair.

Off in the distance, a purple spear of lightning stabbed from sky to sea. Diokles rubbed the ring with the image of Herakles Alexikakos as thunder rumbled through the hiss and splash of the rain. Menedemos wished he had a ring, too. Lightning could so easily wreck a ship, and ships seemed to draw it.

Another flash, this one brighter. Another peal of thunder, this one louder. Menedemos did his best to put them out of his mind. He couldn't do anything about them. The waves slapped the akatos' flank harder and harder. After a while, seawater started splashing over the gunwale.

"I wish we had more freeboard," Menedemos said. "That five of Ptolemaios' can ride out seas that'd swamp us."

"That five of Ptolemaios' is back in the Aegean," Diokles answered. "The sun's probably shining on him."

"To the crows with him," Menedemos said. Diokles raised an eyebrow. Menedemos said it again, louder this time. Diokles dipped his head to show he understood. The wind was starting to howl, and to make the rigging thrum. Menedemos cocked his head to one side, gauging the notes from the forestay and backstay. They didn't sound as if they were in danger of giving way…yet.

Sostratos made his way up onto the poop deck. Like everyone else aboard the *Aphrodite*—*including me, no doubt*, Menedemos realized—he looked like a drowned pup. Water dripped from his nose and the end of his beard. He said something, or at least

his lips moved, but Menedemos couldn't make out a word of it. Seeing as much, Sostratos bawled in his ear: "How do we fare?"

"We're floating," Menedemos shouted back. It wasn't any enormous consolation, but, as with Philippos, it was what he had to give. He shouted again: "How are the peafowl?"

"Wet," his cousin answered. "Too much moisture can affect a man's humors and give him a flux of the lungs. We have to hope that doesn't happen to the birds."

Menedemos grimaced, not because Sostratos was wrong but because he was right. When it came to the peafowl, hope was all he could do. He hated that. He wanted to be able to make things happen. As the captain of a ship at sea, he was usually able to do just that. But how could he do anything about derangement of the humors, or whatever caused sickness? He couldn't, and he knew it. The best physicians could do precious little. And so…he would hope.

"Are the cages lashed down well enough?" he asked. He could do something about that if he had to.

But Sostratos dipped his head. "The ship will sink before they come loose."

"Don't say such things!" Menedemos exclaimed. He thanked the gods he was the only one who could have heard it. With any luck, the wind would blow it away so even the gods couldn't hear it.

"*Will* we sink?" Sostratos didn't sound afraid. As he usually did, he sounded interested, curious. It might have been a philosophical discussion, not one whose answer would decide whether he lived or died.

"I don't think so," Menedemos answered. "Not if the storm doesn't get any worse than this, anyhow." But it was getting worse, the wind blowing ever harder, the lines howling ever more shrilly. He had no idea how long the storm had been going on; he couldn't gauge time without the sun's motion across the sky, and the sun had long since vanished.

He turned the *Aphrodite* straight into the wind. That made the pitching worse; he felt as if the ship were climbing hills and sliding down into valleys every few heartbeats. But the yawing eased, and the ram and the cutwater meant that the akatos didn't ship quite so much water.

And so the merchant galley fought her way north. A couple of big waves did crash over the stempost, but only a couple. Sostratos made his way forward. His waving hand told Menedemos the peafowl still survived. Menedemos wanted to wave back, but didn't dare take a hand off the steering oar for even an instant.

The sky grew blacker yet. At first, Menedemos feared the storm was growing worse. Then he realized it was only night coming. "Do you want me to spell you, skipper?" Diokles asked. "You've been at it a goodish while."

Until the keleustes spoke, Menedemos didn't realize how worn he was. But he'd been standing on one spot for a long time. His legs ached. So did his arms and shoulders; the steering-oar tillers sent every shock from the sea straight through him. When he started to answer, he found himself yawning instead. "Will *you* be all right?" he asked.

"I think so," Diokles answered. "If I feel myself wearing down, I'll get one of the rowers to handle her for a bit. We've got a double handful of men, likely more, who've spent enough time aboard ship to have put their hands to a set of steering oars now and again. All you'll want to do is keep her straight into the wind, right?"

"I don't want those waves smacking us broadside-to," Menedemos said. "We're liable to end up on our beam-ends."

Diokles rubbed his ring again. "Right you are. Get some rest then, if you can."

Menedemos doubted he'd be able to, not with the *Aphrodite* pitching as much as she was and the rain pouring down in sheets. He lay down on the poop deck even so. He didn't bother with a wrapping. What point, in such weather? He closed his eyes....

When he opened them, it was still dark. He didn't think he'd slept till he noticed how the galley's motion had eased. It was still raining, but not so hard. "What's the hour?" he asked the man at the steering oars.

"Middle of the night sometime, captain—about the sixth hour, I'd say," the man replied: not Diokles, but a burly sailor named Hagesippos.

"How long has the oarmaster been off?" Menedemos asked.

"I've had the steering oars about an hour," Hagesippos answered. "He gave 'em to me not long after the weather started easing off a bit."

"That sounds like him." Menedemos yawned and stretched. He still felt abused, but he could return to duty. The *Aphrodite* was his ship. "I'll take them now, Hagesippos. Get some sleep yourself. Stretch out where I was, if you care to."

The sailor tossed his head. "All the same to you, I'll go back to my bench. That's how I'm used to sleeping when we're at sea."

"Suit yourself." Menedemos slapped the sailor's bare shoulder as Hagesippos went down into the waist of the akatos. The slap rang louder than he'd expected: his hand was wet, and so was Hagesippos' flesh.

As the rain diminished, men's snores came through it. The rowers who weren't at their oars grabbed rest as they could. Menedemos wondered how the peafowl had come through the storm. He peered up toward the bow, hoping to spot Sostratos' long, angular form silhouetted against the sky. When he didn't see his cousin, he felt miffed. He knew that was foolish—Sostratos had the right to rest, too—but he couldn't help it.

Because he was miffed, he took longer than he should have to realize he could see stars, there in the north. The rain died to spatters, and then stopped. The clouds blew past the *Aphrodite*. By the time rosy-fingered dawn began streaking the eastern sky, the storm might never have happened.

Diokles opened his eyes, saw Menedemos at the steering oars, and said, "Well, I might have known you'd be there. When did you take 'em back from Hagesippos?"

"Middle of the night sometime," Menedemos answered with a shrug. "That's what he told me, and how can I guess any closer?"

"You can't," the keleustes agreed. He got up, stretched as Menedemos had, and looked around. "Good weather after the storm."

"I'd sooner it were *instead of*, not *after*," Menedemos said. Diokles laughed. Easy to laugh under blue skies, on a calm sea. Menedemos laughed, too.

A few at a time, the sailors woke up. So did Sostratos, who'd slept between the rows of peafowl cages. "They all seem sound," he called to Menedemos. Then he stripped off his chiton to let it dry and went around as naked as most of the sailors. That struck Menedemos as a good idea, so he did the same. Bare skin proved a lot more comfortable than soaked wool.

When the whole crew had awakened, Menedemos ordered the men not rowing to break out the several wooden buckets the *Aphrodite* carried and start bailing the water she'd taken on during the storm. Getting the water out a bucketful at a time was slow, hard work, but he knew no better way to do it, nor did anyone else.

Philippos the mercenary said, "Where are we at, captain? I'm all topsy-turvy on account of that horrible storm."

"We're somewhere in the Ionian Sea," Menedemos answered. Philippos looked as if he wanted a more precise answer. Menedemos wanted one, too; again, he didn't know where to get one. "I couldn't have told you any more than that if the weather'd stayed perfect. If we sail northwest, we'll raise the Italian mainland. Once we do that, I promise we'll find Taras. Fair enough?"

"I suppose so." The mercenary didn't seem convinced. With a shudder, he went on, "Wasn't that the worst blow you ever went through in all your born days?"

"Not even close." Menedemos tossed his head. "We didn't have to lower the yard"—he pointed up to the long spar at the head of the sail—"let alone start throwing cargo overboard to make sure we stayed afloat. This wasn't a little storm, but there are plenty worse."

"Zeus strike me dead if I ever set foot on another boat as long as I live," Philippos said, and descended from the poop deck into the akatos' waist before Menedemos could dress him down for calling the ship a boat.

♢

Sostratos hadn't spent quite so much time asea as Menedemos. He was also a more thoughtful man, more in the habit of imagining things that could go wrong than was his cousin. Both those factors had made the storm seem worse to him than it had to Menedemos.

For once, he almost welcomed the attention he had to give the peafowl. As long as he was busy, he didn't have to think so much. He couldn't let the birds exercise while the sailors were bailing. They wouldn't have had much room to run around, and they would have made nuisances of themselves. He didn't need to give them water, not for a while; they'd had plenty during the storm. But he could pour barley into bowls for their breakfasts, and he did. His spirits lifted when the birds ate well. That was the surest sign the storm had done them no harm.

And he could check on the eggs in the peahens' cages. Being the meticulous man he was, he knew exactly how many each peahen had laid. One, to his annoyance, had broken the day it was laid, falling from the nest to the planks of the foredeck. He imagined drakhmai broken with it. How much would a rich man who couldn't get his hands on one of the peafowl pay for an egg? He didn't know, not to the last obolos, but he'd looked forward to finding out.

Checking the nests was easiest when the peahens came off them to feed. Helen had five eggs in her clutch. That made sense to Sostratos. The peacock had mated with her more than with any of the others, which was how she'd got her name.

"One, two, three, four…" Sostratos frowned. He leaned closer to the cage, risking a peck from Helen. He saw only four eggs. He didn't see any bits of shell that would have shown one had fallen out of the nest during the storm. The slats were too close together to have let an egg escape the cage altogether. His frown deepened as he went on to the next cage.

After finishing with the peafowl, he hurried back to the poop deck, pushing past anyone who got in his way. His face must have spoken before he did, for Menedemos asked, "What's wrong?"

"We're missing three eggs," Sostratos answered. "One from Helen's cage, one from the peahen with the scar on her leg, and one from the smallest bird."

"Are you sure?" Menedemos asked. Again, Sostratos' expression must have spoken for him, for his cousin said, "Never mind. You're sure. I can see it. They didn't fall out and break during the storm?"

"No. I thought of that." Sostratos explained why he didn't think it had happened. Menedemos dipped his head to show he agreed. Sostratos went on, "No, somebody's gone and stolen them. How much would a peacock egg be worth? Never mind—we don't know exactly, but more than a little. We can be sure of that. And it's money that belongs to us, not to some thief. We've earned it." As much as his sense of justice, his sense of order was outraged. That anyone else should try to take advantage of all the hard work Menedemos and he had done infuriated him.

"We'll get them back," Menedemos said, and then, less happily, "I hope we'll get them back. When was the last time you counted them?"

"Yesterday morning," Sostratos answered.

"Before the storm." Menedemos still didn't sound happy. "A lot of people have been up on the foredeck since, either securing the cages or just looking at the peafowl. The passengers have all been interested in them." He rubbed his chin. "I wonder if one of them got *too* interested."

In a low voice, Sostratos said, "I know which one I'd bet on."

"So do I," Menedemos said, also quietly. "Anybody who needed to come aboard in such a tearing hurry isn't to be trusted, not even a little. And Alexidamos is a Rhodian. He's liable to have a better notion of what those eggs are worth than the other fellows. Well, we'll find out." He turned to Diokles, who'd been listening. "Tell off the ten men you trust most. If they're on the oars, set others in their places. Belaying pins and knives should be plenty for this job, but nobody's going to raise a fuss when we search his gear."

"What do we do if we catch the thief?" Sostratos asked.

"If it's one of the rowers, we'll give him a set of lumps and he'll forfeit his pay and we'll put him ashore at Taras—and good riddance to bad rubbish," Menedemos answered. "If it's one of the passengers…well, we'll come up with something." Seeing the look on his cousin's face, Sostratos would not have wanted to be the thief.

Diokles gathered his sailors near the stern. He dipped his head to Sostratos and Menedemos to show they were ready. Sostratos raised his voice. He couldn't make it carry the way Menedemos did, but he managed: "Three peafowl eggs have been stolen. We are going to search for them. We *will* find them, and we *will* punish the thief. Each man will turn out his gear, starting with the passengers."

He eyed the four mercenaries. Philippos and Kallikrates looked astonished. Alexidamos and Rhoikos showed no expression. Rhoikos was Sostratos'

second suspect. He hadn't done anything illicit Sostratos knew about, but to Rhodians Cretans were thieves and pirates till proved otherwise.

Rhoikos also stood closest to Diokles and his search party. "Let's see your duffel," the oarmaster told him.

"I'll watch to make sure you don't take anything," Rhoikos said, and handed Diokles the leather sack. The keleustes and a couple of sailors started going through it.

Sostratos, meanwhile, kept his eye on the other mercenaries. "Let that be," he called to Kallikrates when the latter made a move toward his sack. "Your turn will come." Alexidamos stood calmly, watching everything going on as if it had nothing to do with him. *Isn't that interesting?* Sostratos thought. *Maybe I was wrong. Maybe Menedemos was, too.* Seeing his cousin wrong might almost be worth the blow to his own pride at making a mistake.

Diokles looked up from Rhoikos' weapons and tunic and mantle and kilt and his little sack of coins. "No eggs here."

"Kallikrates next," Sostratos said.

Reluctantly, the mercenary handed the keleustes the sack with his worldly goods: cuirass, greaves, helmet, wool headcover to fit inside the helm, sword, a wooden game board with ivory pieces and a pair of bone dice, and a leather sack. Diokles blinked when he picked it up. "Got to be three, four minai in there," he said.

"It's mine, every obolos of it," Kallikrates growled, warning in his voice.

"Nobody said it wasn't," the oarmaster replied, and set it down. "No eggs here, either." Kallikrates visibly relaxed.

"Now Alexidamos," Menedemos called from the steering oars.

The mercenary who'd paid a triple fare to come aboard the *Aphrodite* pointed to his sack. One of the sailors brought it back to Diokles. He took out Alexidamos' sword and his greaves and his helmet, in which the protective headcloth was bundled. Sostratos stooped and pulled up a corner of the cloth. Under it lay three large, off-white eggs, one of them speckled. "Oh, you bastard," Alexidamos said mildly, as if Sostratos had thrown a double six with Kallikrates' dice. "I thought I'd get away with it."

"You must have, or you wouldn't have done it," Sostratos answered. "Of course, you must have thought you'd get away with it when you took up with that captain's boy, too."

"Of course I did," the mercenary said. "And I would have, too, if the wide-arsed little fool had kept his mouth shut."

Sostratos looked back toward Menedemos. "It's your ship, cousin. What do we do with him?"

"If I threw him over the side, nobody would miss him," Menedemos said. That was true and more than true. No one but the *Aphrodite*'s crew and the other three passengers would even know what had happened to Alexidamos, and none of them seemed likely to care. Menedemos scratched his head. "How much silver has he got there, Diokles?"

"Let's have a look." The keleustes went through the canvas sack till he found Alexidamos' money bag. He hefted it. "Not as much as Kallikrates, but a couple minai, easy."

"I wonder how much is his by right, and how much he's stolen," Sostratos said.

"By the gods, it's mine," Alexidamos said.

"You're not in the best position to be believed," Sostratos pointed out.

"No, you're not," his cousin agreed. "Here's what I'll do. For stealing from the cargo, I fine you a mina of silver. Diokles, count out a hundred drakhmai. Take Athenian owls like he paid us before or turtles from Aigina: we'll make it a nice, heavy mina. And we'll keep him in bonds except when he eats or eases himself till we sight land. Then we'll put him ashore by himself wherever it happens to be, and many goodbyes to him, too."

"You might as well kill me now," Alexidamos muttered.

"If that's what you want, you'll have it." Menedemos' voice held no hesitation. If anything, it held eagerness. Alexidamos quickly tossed his head. "No?" Menedemos said. "Too bad." He took a hand off one steering oar to gesture to the sailors. "Tie him up."

They did, ignoring the mercenary's yelps of pain and protest. Diokles counted coins. They clinked musically as he stacked them in piles of ten. Sostratos took the eggs back to the peafowl cages on the foredeck. He got pecked twice replacing them. As far as he was concerned, Diokles was welcome to make a few drakhmai, or more than a few, disappear on his own behalf, too. Maybe the oarmaster

would. Diokles was a practical man in every sense of the word.

Alexidamos kept whining and complaining till Menedemos said, "If you don't shut up, we'll put a gag on you. You did this to yourself, and you've got no cause to moan." The mercenary did quiet down after that, but the look on his face was eloquent.

Flying fish jumped from the water and glided through the air. One unlucky fish, instead of falling back into the sea, landed in a rower's lap. "Isn't that nice?" the fellow said, grabbing it. "First time I ever had my opson come to me."

Dolphins leaped from the water, too. Sostratos recalled that Arion had set out from Taras on the journey where the dolphins carried him to shore at Cape Tainaron. When he said as much to Menedemos, his cousin answered, "Well, of course. That's why the Tarentines put a man riding a dolphin on their coins."

Sostratos made an irritated noise. He'd forgotten that, and he shouldn't have. He said, "Now that we've bailed out the ship, may I start exercising the peafowl again? We'll want them at their best when we get in to Taras."

"Yes, go ahead," Menedemos said. "It does look to do them good."

Sure enough, the birds seemed eager to run up and down the length of the *Aphrodite*. After a while, Sostratos wasn't so eager to run after them. But he and the sailors he detailed to help him stayed with the peafowl. Each one got its exercise and went back into its cage. Sostratos hoped being away from the peahens hadn't hurt the eggs Alexidamos had purloined.

As he hurried past Alexidamos after the peacock, the mercenary growled, "Who would've thought anybody'd keep track of how many eggs each miserable bird laid?"

"I keep track of all sorts of things," Sostratos answered. Alexidamos suggested something rude he could keep track of. He contrived to step on the thief's foot. Alexidamos cursed. Sostratos said, "I told you I keep track of all sorts of things," and went on by to keep track of the peacock.

So things went until, on the afternoon of the sixth day out from Zakynthos, the lookout at the bow—it wasn't Aristeidas, but Teleutas, one of the men Sostratos had taken on at the last moment when they set out from Rhodes—sang out: "Land ho! Land ho dead ahead!"

From his station at the steering oars, Menedemos said, "That's not bad. That's not bad at all. The storm hardly slowed us at all." He raised his voice to call to Teleutas: "Can you make out what land it is? It's got to be Italy, but whereabouts along the coast are we?"

"I'm sorry, captain, but I'm not the one to tell you," the sailor answered. "This is my first time in these waters."

Sostratos peered northwest, too, along with everyone else aboard the *Aphrodite* except the men at the oars, who naturally faced the other way. He couldn't see land yet. He stood in the waist of the ship, beside a peahen that had hopped up onto a rower's bench. The peahen looked toward the bow, too, but only for a couple of heartbeats. Then, taking advantage of Sostratos' momentary distraction, it leaped into the air and, wings whirring, struck out as if for that distant shore.

The motion drew Sostratos' eye—just too late. "*Oimoi!*" he cried in horror, and grabbed for the bird. One tail feather—one drab, worthless tail feather—was all he had to show for the desperate lunge. "*Oimoi!*" he cried again as the peafowl went into the sea perhaps ten cubits from the *Aphrodite*.

"Back oars!" Diokles shouted. "Bring her to a stop!" Sostratos yanked his tunic off over his head and jumped onto the rower's bench himself, ready to dive in after the peahen—unlike most of the sailors, he knew how to swim. But, before he could go into the water, the peahen, which had been swimming with surprising strength, let out a squawk and vanished. He never knew what took it—a tunny? a shark? one of the playful dolphins?—but it was gone. A few bubbles rose. That was all.

"Go on," Menedemos told the rowers, his voice frozen with shock. "You might as well go on." As they resumed their usual stroke, Menedemos added one word more—"Sostratos"—and gestured for him to come back to the poop.

Alexidamos laughed when Sostratos hurried past him. Not even pausing, Sostratos backhanded the mercenary across the face. He mounted the stairs to the poop deck as if about to be put to the sword. Diokles silently stepped out of his way. When he

came up to Menedemos, he said, "Say what you want to say. Do what you want to do. Whatever it is, I deserve it."

"It's over," Menedemos said. "It's done. I've thought all along that we'd be lucky to get to Italy with all the peafowl. We came close. Gods be praised, we didn't lose the peacock." He slapped Sostratos on the back. "We'll sell the birds we've still got for a little more, that's all. Forget it."

"Thank you," Sostratos whispered. Then, to his own astonished dismay, he burst into tears.

continued in issue 52…

A NEW NOVEL BY

BEN BOVA
WINNER OF SIX HUGO AWARDS

POWER
CHALLENGES

www.ingramcontent.com/pod-product-compliance
Lightning Source LLC
Chambersburg PA
CBHW082227140626
46556CB00020B/3373